KING'S
PLEASURE

KING'S
PLEASURE

KING'S PLEASURE

ESSENCE BESTSELLING AUTHOR
ADRIANNE
BYRD

ARABESQUE®

Recycling programs
for this product may
not exist in your area.

KING'S PLEASURE

ISBN-13: 978-0-373-53449-4

Copyright © 2011 by Adrianne Byrd

www.kimanipress.com

Printed in U.S.A.

To Alice: Forever my inspiration

ACKNOWLEDGMENT

To my family and friends, thanks for all the support
and love that you've given me.
To my editor, Evette Porter, for helping me
through one crazy year. To my wonderful fans
and readers, thank you for allowing me to do
what I do. It's always a pleasure to entertain you.
I wish you all the best of love.

The House of Kings series

Many of you have followed the Unforgettable series, which morphed into the Hinton Brothers series. Now I'm introducing you to the Hintons' playboy bachelor cousins—the Kings.

Eamon, Xavier and Jeremy, along with their infamous cousin Quentin Hinton, are business partners in a gentlemen's club franchise called The Dollhouse. One of their most popular and lucrative specialties is their bachelor party services. With clubs in Atlanta, Las Vegas and Los Angeles, the brothers are determined to make sure their clients' last night of bachelorhood is one they'll never forget. But it's not as easy as it sounds dealing with hotel managers, outrageous clients and, of course, *the entertainment.* The brothers are prepared for anything…except when love comes knocking on *their* door.

In *King's Pleasure,* Jeremy King meets beautiful Malibu party-crasher Leigh Matthews. Within minutes, he knows that she's a woman who is used to getting whatever she wants. And for one wild night, she wants *him.* After their torrid, one-night affair, his bikini-clad goddess disappears only to return weeks later to hire him to plan *her* bachelorette bash. Stunned, he refuses to host her party, but quickly reconsiders. After all, the wedding is six weeks away, and there's not a sexual trick in the books that he won't use to try and change her mind.

If you missed the first two books in the House of Kings trilogy—*King's Passion* and *King's Promise*—both are still available. Better yet, buy all three and enjoy this sizzling summer series.

Remember, in love, never bet against a King.…

Adrianne

Prologue

Quentin Dewayne Hinton was getting desperate. It began slowly, but now it was picking up steam. A part of him longed for the days when he was reckless and carefree—drinking by day, screwing by night. Why, oh why, did it have to end? Deep down, he knew the answer. His carefree life had ended when he became the very thing he detested: a successful businessman.

In the beginning, of course, it had been fun. But that was only because he had joined forces with his cousins, the Kings. And just like the three Musketeers—there were four of them. But as the late, great Biggie Smalls said: "More money, more problems." And Quentin's biggest problem seemed to follow him around wherever he went.

"Let me get this straight," said Father Dickerson, braiding his fingers together. "You want me to perform an exorcism on you?"

Quentin coughed to clear his throat. "Well, me and my house…and my car. And if it's not too much to ask, at this club that I work at."

"You mean the strip club?"

Q coughed a little harder this time and straightened upright in his chair. "I guess for a lack of a better term… Uh, yes. I, uh, own a chain of strip clubs called The Dollhouse. Actually, there used to be four of us. Well, three, really. *They* were supposed to operate the clubs and I was just the money man—the silent partner. Then they started settling down and selling their shares in the business. The next thing you know—pow! I own the whole kit and caboodle." He flashed the cleric an awkward smile.

Father Dickerson's eyebrows crashed together in the center of his forehead. "Son, please forgive me if this next question offends you. But, uh, are you well?"

Quentin actually gave the question serious thought. "To tell you the truth, Father, I'm not sure I'm qualified to answer that just yet. I mean, honestly. I can be frank with you, can't I?"

"Sure. Absolutely."

"Good." Another smile crept across Q's face as he tried to clear his throat again with a deep cough. "To be honest, I feel fine—better than fine on most days. I mean, how could you own the hottest strip clubs in three cities and not feel upbeat about life, right?"

Father Dickerson just stared at him:

"Well, maybe you don't know. But trust me. A man like me, still in his prime and surrounded by beautiful, firm, heavily oiled bodies is its own blessing."

"I'll take your word for it," the priest said.

"Yeah, uh, right. Anyway, there has been some *un-*

usual— Well, not quite paranormal activity happening from time to time."

"Paranormal? Like ghosts?" the priest asked, trying to quickly get to the crux of the problem.

"Well, that's the 'not quite' part of it," Quentin said, squirming.

"Son, if you've come to me for an exorcism, that leads me to believe that you're seeing or hearing some sort of, shall we say, disturbing spirits?"

Quentin looped the phrase through his head a couple of times, but he was still uncomfortable with it. "Now, does your definition of spirits mean that the person or persons are…"

"…Dead," Father Dickerson supplied as more lines creased his forehead.

"Well, see, that's still my gray issue."

"Come again?"

"Well, the entity that I'm dealing with hasn't exactly died."

Father Dickerson continued to stare at Quentin.

"She—"

"It's a woman?"

"Yes. Actually, she's my sister-in-law, Alyssa."

"Your *living* sister-in-law?"

"As far as I know." Quentin shrugged. "I mean, I haven't talked to her in a few months, but I'm sure someone in the family would've contacted me if something had happened to her. Then again, who knows? I'm not exactly on the best of terms with my family."

Father Dickerson snatched off his black-rimmed glasses and proceeded to rub his eyelids. "Let me try this again," he said. "You want an exorcist to get rid of a spirit that isn't really a spirit but a recurring vision of a woman who is very much alive? Do I have that right?" he said in disbelief.

"Well, it's more than just a vision. She talks to me and tries to give me advice—most of the time when I'm not asking for it. She's made me look crazy in front of some of my dates. Her specialty is popping up right after I— Well just because you wear that collar doesn't mean you don't know what goes on between a man and a woman. Am I right?"

When the joke fell flat, Quentin couldn't cough long or hard enough to clear whatever the hell it was that was stuck in his throat.

"Son, this is probably the first time in my thirty-one years at this parish that I've ever said this to someone who has come to me for guidance. I would love to help you, but what you need—neither I nor the church can really help you with. I think that you need to see someone in the mental-health field—maybe someone in a white coat, with the authority to prescribe medication or who can admit you to someplace safe."

"I'm not crazy," Quentin declared defensively. "At least my shrink doesn't think I'm crazy."

Relief flooded Father Dickerson's face. "Ah, so you *are* seeing someone." He reached over and picked up the phone. "Is there a number or...?"

"What about the exorcism?"

"Son, I can't exorcise a spirit that doesn't exist. It is metaphysically impossible for someone who is alive to haunt you. Clearly you are seeing and hearing things that just aren't there. I'm sorry. I'm sure that's not the answer you wanted to hear, but that's the cold, hard truth."

Quentin shook his head. "Well, can't you just sprinkle some holy water around? I mean, what's it going to hurt?"

"Mr. Hinton, are you even Catholic?"

"Is that a prerequisite?"

With a deep sigh, Father Dickerson pushed his glasses back onto his face. "Good day, Mr. Hinton."

"But—"

"I said, 'good day.'"

"Unbelievable." Quentin rose to his feet, barely managing to refrain from giving him a piece of his mind, which is what he really wanted to dish to the insensitive priest. "I guess I'll just see myself out."

He turned toward the door and stopped short when he spotted a bored Alyssa, still beautiful in the wedding gown she wore when she'd married his brother, Sterling, utterly breaking his heart. She was leaning against the wall with her arms folded and a smug look plastered on her face.

"I told you this was a waste of time," she said.

"Oh, shut up," he snapped as he resumed his charge toward the door.

"Excuse me?" Father Dickerson said.

"I wasn't talking to you." Quentin snatched open the door, but decided to leave the priest with just one bit of parting advice. "If I were you, I'd sprinkle some holy water up this office, because whatever you've been doing is clearly not working." He stormed out, with his fake apparition following close behind him.

"Does this mean that we're going back to Dr. Turner now?" Alyssa asked.

"It's either that or the loony bin."

"Good. Because I think you're on the verge of a breakthrough."

"God, I hope so."

"Aah, Quentin. You're back," said Dr. Turner, greeting him in her downtown Atlanta office with a smile. "I wondered whether I'd ever see you again. It's been a couple of months."

"Yeah, I've been a little busy…."

"It's okay," she said. "It's not that unusual for patients to disappear from time to time, especially when they're anxious for results."

Alyssa laughed. "She really does have you pegged."

"Would you like to come in and sit down?" She stepped back and moved away from the door so that the next move was his.

Quentin's gaze shifted to the black leather chaise in the center of the room, and unbelievably he felt a strange sensation, like he was finally home. "Just like old times," he said, strolling into the office.

Dr. Julianne Turner's thick, luscious coral-tinted lips spread into a breathtaking smile as she closed the door behind him.

Being a connoisseur of women, as he'd proudly proclaimed, Quentin immediately noticed that the good doctor's perfume had changed. It was no longer soft and floral, but more fruity and woodsy. That wasn't all he noticed in his short jaunt across the room to the chaise. Her clothes were different. Gone were the knee-length skirts that let her legs play peek-a-boo when she sat down. Now they were proudly showcased in a black number that hit her thigh a good five inches above her knees. Not only that, the tailored cut of the shorter dress led his eyes to her rounded hips and ass.

"What's going on?" he suddenly asked.

"Sorry?" She leaned back so that she could look up to his tall frame.

That's when he noticed the extra burst of color in her redbone complexion and that unmistakable twinkle in her eyes that let him know what time it was. "What's his name?"

"What's whose name?" She blinked, but the smile never left her face.

Quentin flashed his secret weapon—his dimples. "The name of the brother that put that huge, Kool-Aid grin on your face," he said. When she opened her mouth to respond, Q held up a finger to cut her off. "And please, don't insult my intelligence and tell me there isn't a guy. You have that *glow* that women have when they're with child or after a night of unbridled—"

"Quentin!" Alyssa snapped.

Dr. Turner finally blanched. "Mr. Hinton!"

"Quentin," he corrected as his smile wrapped around his face like a rubber band.

"It's been a while since you've been to my office, so maybe I need to remind you that these visits are for your benefit. I'm not the topic of conversation here. I would appreciate it if you would keep your sly comments and wolfish gaze to yourself. Do I make myself clear?"

"Wolfish?"

"I guess she told you." Alyssa laughed.

"Now would you like to have a seat?" She gestured to the chaise and when she did so, Quentin caught the flash of a three-carat diamond ring.

He quickly grabbed her hand and pulled it toward him for closer inspection. "Silly me, how did I forget the third reason?" His gaze returned to her face as hurt and betrayal dueled for top billing.

Dr. Turner pulled her hand out of his grasp. "Now that you've satisfied your curiosity, can we get down to the reason you're here?"

"Sure. But I'm still waiting for the name of this lucky bastard, and where I can find him so that I can wring his neck."

"Mr. Hinton—"

"It's still Quentin."

"Is this going to be problem?"

"What, you bailing on me too, so that you can participate in this ridiculous institution?"

"Who said anything about my bailing on you? You're the one who stopped coming to your therapy sessions. I could look at that as you bailing on me."

"All right. I'm back. Now you can give this clown back his ring."

"Reginald is not a clown."

"Reginald?" He laughed. "You're marrying someone named Reginald?"

Her brows arched above her eyes. "There's nothing wrong with the name *Reginald.* He's a very respectable and distinguished doctor in his field."

"Oh, respectable *and* distinguished." Quentin rolled his eyes. "That's another way of saying comfortable and reliable." He moved toward her and crowded her space. "Tell me, how is old Reggie in the sack?"

Dr. Turner gasped and stepped back. "Careful, Mr. Hinton! You're in dangerous territory."

He smirked and erased the space she'd put between

them. "Does that mean I'll get a spanking if I don't behave?"

"No, it means I'll have to terminate this and any future sessions. And I won't hesitate to do so."

After his therapist's declaration, Quentin stood his ground, engaging in a staring contest to see whether she was serious or not.

She was.

He exhaled a long breath and then slowly gave her a lazy smile. "Well, I had to give it the old college try. Congratulations are in order."

Dr. Turner drew in a deep sigh of relief as if she'd narrowly escaped a predator. "Thank you. Now would you like to take a seat?"

Q weighed the question in his head as his gaze bounced from the chaise to the door—and then to a frowning Alyssa. "Well, since I'm here." He walked toward the chaise and then stretched out.

Dr. Turner took her usual chair and picked up her ever-ready notepad. "So what would you like to discuss today?"

"You mean, other than my abandonment issues? My war against love? Or these crazy dreams I keep having?"

"Dreams? What sort of dreams?"

"What else—wedding dreams."

"You've been dreaming about weddings?"

"Hell, that shouldn't be much of a surprise, considering how everyone keeps dropping to their knees and popping the big question. I swear, love has become a global epidemic that, quite frankly, some scientists need to hurry up and make a pill to eradicate."

"That's a bit extreme, isn't it?"

"Humph. Not from where I'm standing. My once-devout bachelors-for-life are dropping like flies at the slightest whiff of a woman's perfume. All my dogs have traded in their Milk-Bones for collars and short leashes. And, get this, they're happy to stay and play in their own backyard. What kind of madness is this?"

"All right. So, no love. No marriage. It's just you and your cousin Jeremy living the bachelor lifestyle from here till eternity?"

"Ha!" Quentin rolled his eyes.

"Problem?"

"Yeah. My family is nothing but a bunch of Judases."

"Oh. So you lost the last member of your boys' club?"

Quentin grumbled.

Dr. Turner laughed.

"Maybe I need to just change doctors," Quentin mumbled under his breath.

"No. No. Please. I *have* to hear this story."

Quentin rolled his eyes.

"You might as well tell her," Alyssa said, shrugging. "Who knows? It might help."

"Fine." Quentin shrugged. "After my so-called best friend, Xavier, decided to jump the broom, Atlanta sort of…lost its luster. So I figured I'd just hop a plane and go find me a California girl."

The Playful King

Chapter 1

"Welcome to The Dollhouse, Los Angeles," Jeremy shouted above the pulsing music as he directed the Strozier bachelor party through the doors of the chateau-style building. Upon entering, the group of two dozen thirty-something men focused their attention on the main stage where the beautiful and incredibly talented Chocolate Dolls captivated and titillated the crowd.

"Pick up your bottom lips off the floor, boys." Jeremy laughed, taking in their awestruck expressions. "I can't afford too many workers-compensation claims when my girls start tripping over them."

"I've died and have gone to heaven," one man declared as his gaze locked on to an ebony Barbie doll, rolling her hips and sliding her tongue across her glossy lips.

Jeremy's smile doubled in size as he grabbed a cocktail napkin off one of the passing trays and handed it

over to the young man to help mop up the saliva drooling from his mouth. "Please let me know if you need
a bib," he said, laughing. Jeremy wrapped his arm
around the brother's head and then led him and his
boys toward the VIP room, where even more heavenly
delights awaited them.

Literally.

Heaven was tonight's theme. The Dollhouse Dolls
wore costumes with glittering wings and halos. Everywhere their eyes roamed, the men at the bachelor party
were welcomed by the sight of beautiful, well-oiled,
well-toned bodies, dancing, twirling and gyrating on
gold stripper poles. It didn't matter what their preference was, The Dollhouse showcased women in every
flavor of the rainbow, and they were all willing and ca-
pable of fulfilling their clientele's every fantasy.

With a state-of-the-art sound system bumping, a dazzling light show swirling around, The Dollhouse fea-
tured the most beautiful women Los Angeles had to
offer. Jeremy knew that the club had the potential to set
another record-profit night. It was part of a little wager
that he and his cousin Quentin had going since Jeremy
had taken over the Atlanta club from his brother Xavier.

It had only been a few months, but Jeremy already
missed having his brothers, Eamon and Xavier, involved the business. Hell, he still couldn't wrap his
brain around Eamon being married and Xavier *acting*
like a married man. He even had a bet going with his
cousin Quentin as to whether Xavier was going to
throw in the towel and pop the big question to his cur-
rent girlfriend, Cheryl Grier.

Jeremy had ten grand riding on Xavier not losing
his right mind completely. But Quentin made a very

persuasive argument about all the signs that pointed to matrimony. Like selling his shares in the club, and bringing Cheryl's name up in *every* conversation. Hell, they were talking about a buddy of theirs who recently suffered a herniated disc, and Xavier somehow managed to find a way to weave Cheryl into the conversation.

The ten grand was going to be like taking candy from a baby, Quentin kept saying.

Married? *Xavier?* Jeremy just couldn't see it—and hoped that he never would—especially since Quentin would undoubtedly make him pay the ten grand in one-dollar bills, and he would make him sit down in front of him and count it all out. He could be an ass like that sometimes.

Sure he was happy for his brothers, but there was also a part of him that was more than a little irritated. They'd had a good thing going. Three bachelors—and their supposedly silent partner, Quentin—were running the hottest gentlemen's clubs in three different cities. Damn, talk about recession-proof! They had everything that any man could possibly want to wake up to every day with a smile on his face.

Hell, Jeremy usually bounced out of bed—sometimes even his own—because he couldn't wait to get to the club where he was surrounded by gravity-defying breasts and booty-popping goddesses. They were lucky sons of bitches to call what they did a job. As far as he was concerned, he was never going to understand his brothers' deciding to just punk out of the business.

Sure, he liked Victoria and Cheryl okay. They were nice considering Victoria initially tried to sue them for fifty million dollars and Cheryl had been working undercover in a drug-trafficking sting operation at the Atlanta club. He just didn't understand how you could fall in love with women who were either trying to put you in the poorhouse or behind bars.

But whatever.

It was going to be a cold day in hell before he turned his leash over to someone. And yes, he knew perfectly well that he met the definition of "a dog" for at least half the women in the world. But that was not the half that he was concerned with. It was the other half that labeled him "a hell of a good time under the sheet" that he focused on.

Unlike his brothers, he was never going to leave this life. God willing, he was going to ride this bachelor-hood thang until he was a hundred years old, getting a sponge bath from the hottest nurses he could find. Of course, if he had his way, he wanted to go out getting a lap dance in the club's VIP room with a smile on his face and a hard-on in his pants.

That wasn't asking too much, was it?

Besides the personal benefits, there was something quite noble in being a man who brought so much joy and happiness to guys who otherwise led dreadfully dull lives. Surely such an unselfish deed would guarantee him easy passage through the pearly gates when the time came. Of course, that all depended on if the good man upstairs was indeed *a man*. If not, then he would just have to soothe his conscience with the knowledge that while he was here on earth, he'd led one hell of a life.

Schlepping through life doing a regular nine-to-five terrified Jeremy. Always had. Dull and ordinary was not the kind of life he'd envisioned for himself. And thanks to his older brothers, Eamon and Xavier, that wasn't something he ever had to worry about.

Hopping up onto the VIP stage, Jeremy scanned the crowd with a huge smile on his face. "All right. It's that time—time to bring the man of the hour up on stage!"

The crowd roared with excitement, as a steady chant of "Cal-vin! Cal-vin" filled the VIP room.

"Come on up, big man!"

The shouts and cheers went up another decibel as Calvin "Hoopstar" Strozier shouldered his way through the cheering homeys.

Hoopstar, who was the NBA's Los Angeles Razors' third-highest-paid player, finally hopped up on stage, tossed two deuces to the crowd and just let his fifty-foot ego drink in the applause.

Jeremy laughed, and then when he was ready, shared a fist-bump with the baller.

"All right!" Jeremy laughed, grabbing a microphone. "It sounds like y'all are ready to par-tay!"

The volume cranked up a few more decibels as Jeremy slapped his favorite pro basketball player on his back and waited for the cheering to die down. "Well, my man. You know how this works…since it's our *third* time hosting a bachelor party for you at The Dollhouse in two years."

His friends laughed.

Hoopstar let the jab roll off him like water. "Hey. What can I say? I'm determined to get this marriage thang right."

"Well, you know what they say, 'If at first you don't succeed…'" Jeremy cheesed and shook his head. It seemed to him that the brother could cut down on the alimony payments if his boy didn't try to put a ring on every hot groupie he met. "With that in mind," Jeremy continued, "we at The Dollhouse will be happy to keep throwing you the best bachelor parties until you *do* get this love thang right."

"Bet!" The men exchanged fist-bumps before Hoopstar gave the crowd the thumbs-up signal for another round of cheers.

"All right, my man. You know I believe in bringing nothing but the best to the stage. I want you to know I found just the right flavor for all of you to enjoy tonight."

The room roared with excitement.

"A'ight, man. A'ight." Hoopstar clapped his hands and rubbed them together. "I know you ain't gonna let a brotha down."

"You know *this,* maaaaan." Jeremy slapped his boy hard on the back. "Y'all brothers ready for this?"

"Hell yeah!"

Joking, Jeremy stuck a finger in his ear and wiggled it around. "Then without further ado, you boys get ready to make it rain for the lovely—and the incredibly *sexy*—Caramel Swirl!"

The thunderous applause that followed as the Brazilian goddess took the stage penetrated the club's walls and probably echoed through the streets of downtown Los Angeles. Meanwhile, inside the VIP room, gigantic ballplayers grabbed their money clips as Jeremy exited the stage and Caramel Swirl gyrated her oil-slicked body onto the stage.

Forget what you heard, absolutely everybody in the business knew that nobody made it rain harder than overpaid pro athletes. They were like grown children with impulse-control issues and more testosterone and money than they knew what to do with.

All in all, they were Jeremy's favorite customers.

In less than a minute, Caramel Swirl shook her money-maker in a green globe of Benjamins while the club's hostesses strutted in with their angelic wings and buckets of chilled Cristal.

Money, money, money, mon-nay! Jeremy grinned while the sound of cash registers filled his head.

"Looks like the boys love her," Delilah grudgingly admitted.

Jeremy whipped his head around and saw his head hostess. "Disappointed?"

Delilah brushed off his smug I-told-you-so tone with an eye roll. "I never said the girl didn't have talent. I just said that she carries a lot of baggage."

"Name one dancer up in here that doesn't have baggage. Scratch that—name me one *woman* who doesn't have baggage—and that includes Emilio behind the fourth-station bar," Jeremy said as he laughed. "Frankly, I'll be happy when he's off those hormone pills. His mood swings are driving me crazy." He turned and started to leave the VIP bar.

"That's a very sexist thing to say," Delilah said, trailing behind him.

"But true."

"Jeremy Jorell King, you take that B.S. back."

His smile exploded across his face. "Not until you prove me wrong."

"Like you don't have baggage."

"Actually, I don't," he said with a lazy shrug as they headed down the stairs and through the main room of the club. The regulars immediately started competing to get his attention. Most of them knew that if Jeremy stopped by their table, it meant a round of free drinks and maybe a free lap dance with one of the club's hottest girls.

"Yo, Jeremy!"

"Jeremy, my man!"

"Dr. J!"

He ignored them all because he didn't have time to play the game tonight. The Dollhouse's side business, Bachelor Adventures, was pulling double duty. If he timed this right, he had only forty minutes to get from the club to Malibu for the second bachelor party.

His staff pretty much had the parties down to a science, so that everything ran like a well-oiled machine. His main role was to show up as the face of The Dollhouse, make a speech and introduce the first performer of the night. After that, it was usually time for him to get his party on.

Jeremy checked his watch and then picked up his pace. Undoubtedly he and Delilah would resume their pointless conversation about who had the most baggage another time. It just wasn't in Delilah to let something go.

Weaving through the crowd then out the front door, he hopped into his bright red Porsche Boxster S. He loved his car. It was his baby girl—his heart. Every time he slid behind the leather seat, it was like sliding in behind a good woman. It coasted and cornered like a dream. And when he got her on an open stretch of road, the power under the hood gave him a natural high that was second only to sex.

No surprise, he made it to the ten-million-dollar Malibu beach house with twelve minutes to spare. The music was already bumping and the house looked like it was nearing capacity. Malibu parties were always the best because there were always neighbors who crashed along with just about anyone who happened to be hanging out at the time—usually women in teeny-weeny bikinis.

Jeremy checked himself in the rearview mirror, and then smiled at his flawless reflection. "I got a feeling that this is going to be a good night." He winked and then hopped out of the car. As he strolled toward the modern glass-front beach house, he mentally raced through his nightly checklist.

Condoms? He touched his back pocket. *Check.*

Breath? He cupped his mouth, puffed out a pocket of air and sniffed. *Check.*

Swagger? Definitely check.

By the time he breezed into the house, Jeremy was seriously ready to get his party on. In his initial survey of the room, he saw that the women outnumbered the men by a ratio of three-to-one. *Perfect.* Most *ménages à trois* happened at bachelor parties—usually involving the groom. But you needed to have the right ratio for that fantasy to be fulfilled.

"Heeey, Jeremy," his first fan of the evening cooed, sashaying her way up to him and looping her arm around his neck. "Long time no see," she said, poking out her bottom lip, and walking her fingers up the center of his chest.

"Hey, Keya." He lowered his gaze and caressed her petite figure. "I've been meaning to call you."

"Yeah, right." She playfully rolled her eyes at the lie, but continued to smile at him. "Tell you what, since we're both here, you can save yourself the hassle of trying to find my number and we can just hook up to-night."

"Tonight?" Jeremy glanced around, uncomfortable making plans before he had the chance to check out all the goodies this party had to offer. "Well, you know I'm working tonight."

"After work," she insisted, pressing her body against his.

He smiled. "After work, I may be tired."

"In that case," Keya said as she reached down and grabbed his crotch, "I have just the remedy to help you get your second wind."

Jeremy's white smile stretched around his face. "In that case, I'll keep an eye out for you at the end of the night." He tossed her a wink, carefully extracted his balls from her firm grip and then strolled into the party.

"There's my boy," Dylan Freedman shouted, strolling over to Jeremy with his hand held up for a high-five.

"Aw. The man of the hour," Jeremy proclaimed before slapping palms and engaging in a one-arm shoul-der-hug.

"Can you believe this—*me* tying the knot?"

"Hell nah," Jeremy answered honestly. "But a lot of brothers are dropping like flies into that matrimony trap. I'm starting to think that it's something in the water."

"Oh, that's right. Your brother Eamon just walked the plank, didn't he?"

"That he did," Jeremy said, shaking his head. "I don't know what the hell came over him. But it is what it is, I guess."

Dylan bobbed his head. "Yeah, yeah. I think I read about it in the paper. He locked down some billionaire heiress or something. She's quite the dime-piece, too, if I recall." He laughed. "Talk about a brother upgrading."

"C'mon, you know Eamon. Money is the last thing that turns his head."

"True that. True that. Still, your brother won the wife sweepstakes, especially if she's a dime and got a mint in the bank. A man can't lock that down every day."

"Says the man who's about to marry the daughter of one of the most powerful men in Hollywood," Jeremy responded. "Something tells me you finally got the financing for your next picture."

Dylan tapped the side of his temple while his slick grin looked like it was about ready to slide right off his face. "Turns out I got lady luck on my side, too."

Jeremy frowned. "So are you doing it for love or power?"

Dylan's shoulders bobbed up and down. "I'm going to plead the fifth on that in case your ass is wearing a wire."

"Oh, it's like that."

His shoulders bounced again.

"A'ight then, bro. You do you," Jeremy said while his gut twisted in disgust. It wasn't his place to lecture his friend and—more importantly—his client about how to enter into the sanctity of marriage. If it was one thing he knew, it was how to fall back and play his position, and that position in this drama was on the sidelines.

"Ooooh, Big Daaaaddy." Twins, Brandi and Candi, flanked his sides and hit him with identical smiles.

"Laaadies," he drawled, as a memory instantly re-wound in his head. He certainly would be up for some two-on-one action tonight. "I didn't know that you two knew my man Dylan."

"Who?" They blinked.

Jeremy laughed. "The groom to-be—Dylan Freedman. This is his bachelor party."

The girls giggled.

"Actually, we didn't know whose party this was," Brandi said. Her beauty mole was on the right, Jeremy remembered. "We were just hanging out on the beach when someone shouted that there was a party going on."

Candi cut in. "You know us. We *love* crashing a good party."

"Actually, I did know that." He tossed them a playful wink before his gaze dived to check out the girls' heavy silicone investments. As far as he was concerned, they were living up to be *damn* good investments.

"So what do you say about hooking up later?" Brandi inquired.

Jeremy hesitated. The girls were fun, but the sibling rivalry tended to get a little out of control. "I'm open. We can all hang loose and whatever happens, happens."

He got two winks as they slapped him on the ass.

"We'll be looking for you at the end of the night," Brandi promised before taking her sister by the hand and leading her away.

Jeremy watched their booties jiggle away in matching sky-blue bikinis. *Good thing I'm up on my B vitamins.*

"I don't know how you do it, man," Dylan said. "Please tell me that when you die your family is donating your body to science. Your stamina should be bottled and sold on the stock market."

"Get on with that, man." Jeremy laughed, even though his ego inflated a few more inches.

The friends moved farther into the expansive house where the entire glass wall at the back of the house showcased an incredible view of the sun setting over the ocean. With summer's longer days, dusk usually hit late in the evening.

Jeremy stopped for a second to take it all in. "I love this house."

"You want to buy it?"

"You're selling it?" he asked, surprised.

"Yeah. Turns out that wives don't like their husbands keeping bachelor pads." Dylan shook his head. "Who knew?"

"You don't say?" Jeremy chuckled, but he was seriously considering the offer. He loved L.A., and he loved Malibu even more. "Let me think on it and I'll get back at you."

"A'ight, but don't leave me hanging too long. Malibu is still a hot market. It's one of the main reasons why I wanted to have the party here. It's a bachelor-and-farewell party all rolled up into one." Dylan's eyes grew misty. "I need a drink. Damn, I'm getting *married!*"

"Aah," said Dave Killion, Dylan's best man, who popped up like a jack-in-the-box with a tray of tequila shots. "You said the forbidden word. *Drink!*"

Dylan rolled his eyes as he reached for one of the shot glasses.

"What's the forbidden word?" Jeremy asked.

"Married," Dave answered. "Consider that your only warning."

"Got it." Jeremy gave him the thumbs-up and then watched as Dylan tossed back his shot.

"I still can't believe that I'm losing this place," Dylan moaned.

Jeremy struggled not to laugh. It was usually during the last twenty-four hours of bachelorhood that all the things brothers were truly giving up finally hit them. Losing the crib was one thing. Their only private space was about to be reduced to just a "man cave" in the basement—if they were lucky. He knew plenty of dudes who were still begging or negotiating to have even that. Their wardrobe would decrease to a quarter of the closet where they could own no more than three pairs of shoes—usually, two pairs for work and one pair of sneakers. God forbid if there wasn't enough space for the entire department-store-size shoe collection that the missus was bringing to the table. Not to mention the guest pass to the feminized bathroom issued by the wife, where a stick of deodorant and one bottle of cologne that she's selected resides in the medicine cabinet.

"Actually, I'm going to need some more liquor," Dylan announced after Dave strolled off.

Jeremy followed him. "How's it going, Robbie?" Jeremy shouted above the music.

The bartender glanced up and smiled. "Never better, Boss Man."

Jeremy glanced over at the tip jar and saw that it was already full. "Looks like it's going to be a good night."

"It's always a good night at Bachelor Adventures's parties." He winked after spouting the company line.

"Heeeeey, now, that's what I'm talking about." Jeremy gave Robbie the thumbs-up. "Hit me with a Heineken."

"You got it." Robbie turned toward the portable chiller and grabbed one of the green bottles. "Here you go," he said, popping the top and setting it down on the bar.

"Thanks." Jeremy stuffed a couple bills into the tip jar and then turned around to take another survey of the growing party. It was just an hour into the bash and already a few of the ladies had done away with their bikini tops, and more than a few of them were tossing smiles and winks his way.

He turned up the bottle to swallow, and began his mental checklist of possibilities for the evening. *What am I in the mood for this evening?*

Malibu being Malibu, the selection had more vanilla than his preferred chocolate, but there was enough of an assortment to keep his libido in the game.

When the sun disappeared, the bamboo and seashell Tiki Torches were lit, along with several campfires, to give the partygoers outside on the beach enough light. With beer in hand, Jeremy moved around the crowd, primarily checking on his employees and the groom-to-be.

On deck, his two nude models lay still on buffet tables with an assortment of sushi and sashimi placed strategically over their bodies. Some of the men made their selections by carefully using chopsticks, while others got their jollies off by using their mouths. As a precaution, Jeremy had two security guards posted near the girls to make sure that guests didn't get too carried away.

As minutes ticked into hours, the drunken games changed from Pin the Condom on the Model to Booby Dodgeball (throwing a ball in the shape of a boob and hitting another player). Jeremy joined in on that one and won.

By the time The Dollhouse Dolls's glistening bodies did what they did best, working the portable stripper poles, the party was classified as being off the hook. One of his popular dancers, Dime Piece, had one brother fiendin' so hard that he let her walk him around the room on his hands and knees with a gold leash around his neck.

Still clamoring for more, Dime ordered two of the bouncers to tie him to a coffee table where she then proceeded to climb on top of him in the classic sixty-nine position and simulate a sexual act. The look on dude's face let everyone know that he was in hog heaven.

By midnight, the Dolls had finished their acts, but the party was far from over. Dylan eventually showed up at the bar, shirtless and with his fly open, demanding another drink—which was the last thing it looked like he needed.

Jeremy greeted him with two potential honeys tucked under each arm, and his own smile stretched across his face. "How you holding up, Dylan?"

His buddy turned toward him, smelling like Mary Jane and looking higher than the satellites orbiting the earth.

"Dr. J, man. You throw the best damn parties," he slurred.

Another satisfied customer. "Thanks, bro. I'm glad to see that you're having a good time."

Dylan looked at the two ebony beauties next to Jeremy and struggled to straighten up. "You don't look like you're having too bad a time yourself."

Jeremy laughed. "You know me. I get in where I fit in—most of the time."

"Awww...that's my dawg!" Dylan held up his fist for

a bump, while Robbie set the next drink down for the groom-to-be.

When Dylan's gaze lingered on the ladies, Jeremy leaned down and whispered, "Why don't you two be nice to my friend here?"

They shared a brief disappointed look, but then slid over to either side of the man of the evening and poured on the charm.

"Damn," Dylan said. "Nobody can say you're not a generous man."

"My momma always taught me to share." Jeremy laughed, but while he was laughing, he caught sight of the most unbelievable hourglass figure out of the corner of his eye.

"Whoo, girl. Shake it!"

Jeremy's head twisted all the way around as his gaze zoomed toward a stunningly beautiful cinnamon-brown beauty in a white bikini top and matching wraparound sarong. "Who is that?"

Despite being a man who was accustomed to seeing beautiful bodies, Jeremy was positive that he had never seen curves that lush and dangerous in his entire adult life. Baby Girl was so fine that he personally wanted to call and thank her momma for doing one *hell* of a job.

And man, could this chick move. Rock, rock, dip and back it on up. *Baby Girl.* He shook his head. She had just the right bounce and jiggle to set it off.

It was hard to look at her without a brother twisting up his face because she was putting a hurting on everyone watching her. Before he knew it he was rocking his own hips as if he was already partnered up with her on the dance floor.

She's the one, he decided as his erection stretched down one side of his leg.

Jeremy didn't immediately bounce up out of his chair. Instead, he spent a good deal of time itemizing a mental list of all the things he wanted to do to her—some were illegal in twelve states.

His gaze finally inched upward, but she was moving and grooving so much that it actually took a moment before she finally turned so that he could see her face. When she turned, Jeremy's heart stopped.

At least, that's what it felt like—because there was suddenly an unbelievable pain in his chest. Baby Girl had the face of an angel, with round, doll-like eyes, big-apple cheeks and a pair of incredibly shapely, full lips that reminded him of the singer Angie Stone. He loved a nice set of lips.

Suddenly, a brother pulled up all onto her bumper, and jealousy stabbed him so hard that it was a good thing he didn't pack heat or CSI would have been all up in there tonight. With an inner strength that he didn't know he had, he forced himself to hang back and watch Baby Girl's reaction. Hell, for all he knew, the brother could be her man. No sense in looking crazy until he had a few more facts.

His mysterious angel-slash-sex kitten turned and smiled over her shoulder at her new dance partner. Though she dipped and rolled her hips, he quickly con-cluded that the two-step-challenged brother wasn't her man. And when it became clear that dude couldn't keep up with what she was working with, Baby Girl gave homey the cold shoulder.

"Damn, he went down in flames," Dylan said, watching the same scene.

Hell, Jeremy had forgotten all about Dylan and the two honeys still holding up the bar. Jeremy's singular focus was on the woman that could clearly give his dancers a good run for their money.

Jeremy watched brother after brother step up. But one by one, she shot them down with either a roll of her eyes or a sudden twist of her back. Baby Girl wasn't playing on the dance floor.

"Cold," he mumbled, but what still impressed him was Baby Girl's skills.

"Why don't you get up there?" Dylan said, elbowing him. "Show us how it's done, dawg."

Tempting. However, something else coursed down the center of Jeremy's back. *Nervousness.* The emotion was so new to him that for a couple of minutes, he didn't know what to do. Rejection was never something he'd even considered before.

"A body like that," Dylan slurred, "was made for one thing, and one thing only—sin."

Jeremy bobbed his head in agreement. It had been a minute since he'd been up in somebody's church and he certainly wasn't interested in being saved tonight. He glanced around, and with a quick eyeball check he was pretty sure that the laughing beauty was drawing nearly every man's attention. Playing the odds, he knew that if he didn't bust a move soon, a worthwhile competitor would surely knock him out of the game before he even got up to bat.

"Don't tell me you ain't gonna make a move." Dylan laughed. "I've never known you to turn down a challenge."

Jeremy cut an annoyed look over his way. "Then you know that I'm not going to start tonight." He twisted his head back toward the floor. "A hunter needs to study his prey before he makes a move." However, it only took a few seconds for some major action to start happening along the seams of his pants.

His gaze performed another slow drag down her long neck, graceful shoulders and incredibly perky and very real breasts. Every inch of this woman's body was a work of art. Flat stomach, small waist and an ass he wouldn't mind spending time bouncing quarters off—or just bouncing off it himself.

That brought a smile to his face.

"She's got to be an actress. Please say she's an actress. I'll make her a star," Dylan promised.

"Calm down, Lassie," Jeremy said. "Your bone is showing."

Dylan glanced down and finally zipped up his pants, but not before peeking into Jeremy's lap. "Looks like mine isn't the only one. You might want to hit that with a hammer before you think about standing up."

Jeremy chuckled, tossed back his drink and then stood up. "Stop hating on the pipes, man, and carry your ass on back to the minor leagues. I got this."

Chapter 2

"Promiscuous" bumped from the DJ's speakers and put Leigh Matthews's body into a trance. A good beat always had that effect on her. And tonight she needed the music to mentally take her to another place.

The men that stepped up to her trying to impress her failed to do just that—mainly because men were the last thing she wanted to deal with. In all honesty, she was sick of the games and the lies. Sure, she got a kick out of it when men approached her and tried to get their bump and grind on. But it never took them long to realize that she wasn't interested in taking it any further than that. As quick as they rolled up on her, they got dismissed.

Still, there was a certain satisfaction watching them lose their cool when she got her hips dipping and rolling and her ass popping and backing up. She didn't mind them fantasizing and spitting weak game in her ear. It was good to know that she still had it like that. Lord knew DeShawn had stopped appreciating her and started taking her for granted.

How much longer was she going to put up with it? How much longer was just being his *good* girl—the one he always relied on to welcome him back with open arms—going to last?

Hell, did she even love him anymore?

Eyes closed, Leigh allowed herself to become one with the music. Her limbs flowed with the melody, while her hips rocked to the hard-driving bass. It wasn't long before she was turning herself on. She rolled her hands across the top of her chest, then let them flow over her breasts, glide down her hard-earned abs, and then rolled over her hips.

Soon, she forgot about the number of men crowding her space, trying to rock a two-step or the whack-ass "lean back" that didn't require them to even move their feet. Seriously, if you can't keep up, then step the hell aside. Not until she could feel the first beads of sweat rolling down her face did she flutter her long lashes open. When she did the sexiest pair of eyes she'd ever seen watched her from across the room.

Dark.

Chocolate.

Hypnotic.

Everything from her toes to her nipples tingled, especially when her gaze expanded to take in the magnificent specimen those eyes belonged to. *Good Lord. Am I dreaming?* The man was as solid as an African warrior ready to wrestle a lion with his bare hands. The thought of wrestling with him butt-naked with a bottle of baby oil crossed her mind, and then a heat wave flushed her entire body. Maybe tonight she didn't have to be such a good girl.

Judging by the look in his eyes, her mysterious stranger was thinking the same thing. The question now was what type of games were they going to play before they answered the call of their bodies?

Their gazes still locked from across the room, Leigh rocked her hips and touched her body in a way that one would have to be blind, crippled or crazy not to know what time it was. She tossed her thick hair back, giving him a sneak preview of what she looked like in the throes of passion.

Her smile slid wider as his gaze roamed over every inch of her body. It wasn't long before the rest of the crowd melted away while she concentrated on giving him his own private dance. It was a tall order, seeing as how she was in a house full of professional strippers and weekend party girls.

She turned, giving her mysterious gawker a backside view of what she was working with. While she worked her hips and jiggled her ass, she still felt her future lover's gaze caressing her frame. The image of them grinding together in a heated fury made her tits hard as rocks and her bikini bottoms as wet as if she'd just stepped out of the ocean.

Leigh turned to see his face again just as he said something to the dude next to him holding up the bar, before he finally stalked toward her.

He even walked like a man among boys. His gait, long, smooth and sexy as hell, made her knees knock. But it was those dark, penetrating eyes that hypnotized her.

She needed him—wanted him.

When he was just halfway through the crowd, her body caught fire. She was more than willing to bet that nibbling on all that chocolate could send a woman into a diabetic coma. Then again, if a girl's gotta go, she may as well go out with a smile on her face.

Five feet away— Damn, it didn't make any sense for a man to be that fine.

Four feet away— Wouldn't it be hot if he just ripped her clothes off right there in the middle of a crowded room?

Three feet away— Would anyone notice or care if they went at in the middle of the floor like it was the wild kingdom?

Two feet away— If he so much as touched her, she was sure her bikini bottoms were going to be hit with a tsunami of honey.

One foot— His large hand snaked out across her waist and just as expected, her clit exploded and her knees buckled. Luckily for her, she had his broad chest to fall back against while she tried to catch her breath. Damn—a one-touch orgasm. Who would've ever thought?

As an added surprise, her future lover was not a simple two-step brother with a bump-and-grind routine. He had skillz—yes, with a *Z*. He rocked, dipped and moved like he was born on the dance floor. Leigh had long subscribed to the notion that how a man danced was directly correlated with how he performed beneath the sheets.

It wasn't long before they were moving as one and definitely scorching up the designated dance floor. While a few beads of sweat rolled down her hairline, Mr. Sexy-As-Hell remained calm, cool and *dry*. It wasn't long before she wondered if she could keep up with *him*—on the dance floor *and* between the sheets.

One thing was for sure, she wouldn't mind finding out.

For three songs, their bodies moved and grooved against each other in ways that were more than just suggestive—they were scandalous. Leigh's breasts ached to the point that they were painful and her heart dropped so low that she was convinced that it was now pounding away inside her clit.

Another two songs later and they were still at it, with hardly an inch between them—at times exchanging the same breath whenever her breasts and his chest grazed each other.

A few times Leigh caught his gaze dropping to her nipples. A second later, his tongue would roll across his lips, making them glisten. Never in her life had she ever had to suppress the urge to kiss a complete stranger. But here she was, drawing on every ounce of willpower.

And losing.

Before she could question what she was doing, let alone why she was doing it, she slid her arms up his broad chest and then looped them around his neck. From there, gravity took its course, and her future lover lowered his head.

Please, Lord, let him know how to kiss. If Leigh had a dime for every good-looking brother she'd encountered since her training-bra days that thought kissing somehow involved licking her nose or chomping on her tongue, she'd be as rich as Oprah.

So with her toes and fingers crossed, she waited anxiously for his luscious-looking lips to touch down. *Please, please, Lord.*

Turns out God still answered prayers.

The instant their lips touched, something akin to a heat wave blazed through Leigh's entire body and melted every thought right out of her head. With something this hot, reflex should have interceded and made her jump back from the flames. Instead, the exact opposite happened. She pressed her body closer—like she wanted to be consumed by him. It was maddening.

Once she got used to the fire, she noticed other things about him. Not only were his lips pillowy soft, but his mouth was as wicked as his rhythmic hips. What his tongue was doing with hers was downright pornographic—and she was the star.

Thank you, Lord!

Leigh lost her sense of time and space while her body temperature skyrocketed. She didn't care that her lungs were on the brink of collapse because of lack of oxygen. As far as she was concerned, collapsing in his arms wasn't such a bad way to go. Even as she felt his lips pull away, it didn't stop her from conjuring up a vision of coasting through imaginary clouds. Quite simply, it was the best kiss she'd ever had.

Period.

After a few gulps of oxygen, she was finally able to reboot her system and open her eyes—but only to be sucked back into this man's hypnotic gaze. *Damn. Who in the hell is this guy?* Just as one voice asked the question, there was another part of her that wondered if half the thrill was in not knowing.

So when Mr. Tall-Dark-and-Handsome opened his mouth to speak, Leigh quickly pressed a finger against his lips. "Shhh. I don't want to know your name or your zodiac sign. I just want us to go someplace where you can just screw my brains out."

His handsome features barely registered surprise before he smiled and said, "I think I can handle that."

Chapter 3

Either it was Jeremy's birthday or he'd died and gone to heaven. Frankly, if this was a sample of heaven's delights, he hoped that no one would mourn his passing. As far as he was concerned, he was definitely about to be in a better place. His Coke-bottle-curved diva took him by the hand and led him through the bumping and grinding crowd without another word.

Bounce.

Jiggle.

Wiggle.

"Damn." He twisted his face at the woman's backside view and felt his erection stretch a few more inches down his leg. He was the luckiest son of a bitch walking and he knew it.

Bounce.

Jiggle.

Wiggle.

"Yo, Dr. J!"

Hypnotized, Jeremy didn't risk taking his eyes off the grand prize. He tossed up a couple of deuces and gave whoever was hollering at him the cold shoulder. He knew how most of the brothers on the West Coast operated. They weren't like the brothers in the South who knew how to fall back and let you play your position. L.A. playas see you heading out with the hottest chick in the room, and suddenly there's a cock-blocking army trying to intercept.

Not tonight.

He'd rather catch a case before he'd give this up.

From the sidelines, Dylan waved to get his attention. Glancing over, tomorrow's groom gave him the thumbs-up. Jeremy held up his hand and pretended to be smacking, flipping and rubbing his diva down—preferably with some honey or baby oil.

Baby Girl chose that moment to glance over her shoulder. He straightened up, and flashed her a devilish smile.

She laughed, released his hand—but only so that she could grab him by the waistband of his pants. "A'ight, handsome. Let's see what you can do."

"Please don't hurt me," he said.

"A little pain never hurt nobody." She winked.

Jeremy's brows jumped higher. *I like this chick.* Plus, he was more turned on than he'd ever been in his entire life. And that was saying something.

They stepped out of the sliding glass doors at the back of the house and onto the crowded deck where topless beach divas and drooling brothers danced and stumbled around.

Jeremy followed the night's dessert down the stairs

leading from the deck to the beach below. The cool night breeze whipped and flapped the sarong, hugging the woman's luscious hips. His smile stretched wider at the constant peek-a-boo snapshots of her firm, heart-shaped ass.

Lord have mercy. He touched his forehead to make sure that he wasn't running a fever. After a moment, he grew concerned. "Where are we going?"

"Where else? To get wet!" She released his hand and started racing toward the crashing waves.

At this late hour the Pacific Ocean was a dark blue-black abyss with strips of silvery moonlight dancing across the surface. But before he could object, the diva whipped off her sarong and flung it and her bikini top off. Next thing he knew they were smacking him in the face.

The intoxicating scent that lingered in the clothes buckled his knees. He stopped and clawed the clothes off his head. He had exactly two seconds to take in his cinnamon-brown beauty bathed in moonlight before she splashed into the water. For the second time that night, his heart stopped.

He grabbed his arm. *Am I having a heart attack?*

Any thought of yelling for help vanished when his gaze was drawn back to his moon-bathed angel splashing around.

"Aren't you coming in?" she asked with a teasing lilt.

Jeremy stripped, ignoring the voice in his head, trying to remind him that, unlike his brothers, he didn't know how to swim. Well, he could doggy-paddle, but he shouldn't risk that kiddie maneuver in any depth of water that was higher than his height and clearly the ocean tended to go deeper than six-three.

"C'mon. The water feels great!"

Damn. She even had a voice like an angel.

"Two seconds," he said, picking up the pace instead of confessing his handicap. He could do this. He just needed to make sure that he stayed close to shore. Once he was down to just his briefs, Jeremy gave himself one last pep talk and then rushed into the ocean with one last prayer: *Please, Lord, don't let me drown.*

However, he wasn't quite prepared for the water to be quite so cold. By the time he made it waist-deep, he was shivering and trying like hell not to scream like a damsel in distress. This was not the night to be losing manly points.

"There you are," his moonlit goddess said as she popped up next to him. "I thought that you were going to keep me waiting out here all night."

"Believe me. That's the last thing I want to do." He boldly wrapped an arm around the curve of her hip and then pressed her closer. She offered no resistance as her firm yet soft breasts pressed against his chest, so he took the next step, and tilted his head down and drew her full lips in for another kiss.

Sweeter than the richest chocolate and more potent than a shot of absinthe, Jeremy's mind started tripping and his body heated an extra twenty degrees. Still, he plundered her lips like a starving man. Within seconds they were swallowing each other's moans while dying to get even closer.

Suddenly she jumped up and wrapped her long legs around his trim waist. She also made sure that his iron-hard cock was jammed against the crotch of her bikini bottoms.

Pulling back, he caught her bright white smile beaming in the silvery light.

"Oooh. Impressive," she murmured.

"I aim to please." He nibbled on her bottom lip.

"Then you're off to a great start."

"You're not doing so bad yourself." Jeremy worked his hips and grinded against the thin material shielding her pussy.

"Is that right?" Her laugh blended beautifully with the night, which only added to her intoxicating allure.

"Mm-hmm." He worked his way to the left earlobe while his hands slid down her firm yet squeezable ass.

She followed his lead and started brushing kisses against the side of his neck.

He smiled and kept his feet planted on the ocean's rocky floor as waves crashed around them. Frankly he could nibble on her all night. When he caught a break in the surf, he reached down between their bodies and freed his cock from his tight briefs, and then slid her bikini bottoms to the corner of her right thigh.

Jeremy watched transfixed while his new lover sucked in a quick breath in preparation, but he knew that it wasn't going to be enough. With a slick Cheshire grin, he directed his near double-digit-size cock toward her pussy's entrance to give them a proper introduction.

But then a huge wave hit them. Jeremy held back a scream as the icy water swallowed him whole. The crashing wave provided him with the chance to experience the pleasure of his seductive nymph's erotic curves as she rolled on top of him, her luscious breasts brushing against his chest. Suddenly the ocean wasn't so cold after all.

Bobbing back up to the surface, his playmate's laughter filled his ears. But what made him awestruck was that she was perfectly positioned, so that at just the right angle the moonlight bouncing off her honey-brown skin convinced him that he really was dealing with some sort of water goddess.

"My God, you're beautiful," he whispered, unable to stop staring.

"Aw. I bet you say that to every half-naked woman you meet."

"I'm going to plead the Fifth on that one," he said to be safe. "Though it doesn't change the fact that you're very, *very* beautiful."

"Thank you. And if you don't mind my saying, so are you."

Jeremy's face twisted again. "Men aren't beautiful."

"They aren't?" She laughed.

"No. You're supposed to say that they are either handsome or good-looking." He reached up and grabbed her around the waist and pulled her closer. "Men are not beautiful."

She cocked her head. "Sounds like I've ruffled someone's manly feathers."

"Nah. I'm just saying." Her breasts brushed up against him again, making him lose his train of thought. In fact, his eyes focused on her full, luscious mouth.

"You were just saying what?"

He blinked. "Hell. I forgot."

She laughed as they bobbed up and down in the water. Her hardening nipples added more inches to his erection. After staring at her for so long and enjoying the rush of foreplay endorphins, he could no longer suppress the urge to just kiss her.

His moon-bathed goddess welcomed his lips with a soft moan, but he was completely unprepared for the Godiva's kiss that was as sweet as it was decadent. Immediately he was addicted. He found himself greedily deepening the kiss, barely mindful of keeping his body afloat as they drifted farther from the beach.

Not only was his temptress sweet, she was aggressive, as well.

She locked her hands around the back of his head and held him in place while her tongue practically molested his mouth, which was equal parts dirty and seductive. When she finally released him, he didn't know whether he needed to file a police report or sign over his life savings for her to do it again.

If I'm not careful, a girl like her...

Jeremy fiercely shook off the rogue thought, but his gaze zoomed back to her buxom breasts and started having their own conversation. "Who are you?"

She pulled one of her hands from behind his head and pressed a finger to his lips. "No names, remember?"

He cocked a half grin to cover his sudden wave of irritation. "I have to call you something."

"In that case, you can call me..." she teased, "...the best you'll ever have."

The silvery light picked up the wicked gleam in her eyes as she peeled her bikini bottoms off her hips, Never in all of Jeremy's life had he ever experienced such an intense and powerful tremor that seemed to originate in the center of his soul. Baby Girl climbed back up into his arms and locked her silky legs around his hips. This time, there were no bikini bottoms blocking their connection. He received another surprise when he tried to squeeze into her incredibly tight walls. They gasped and then watched their reactions mirrored as their bodies slowly fit together.

Ignoring the sharp rocks stabbing the pads of his feet, Jeremy's toes began to curl. But that was nothing compared to the way his thick arms trembled despite her slight weight. There was just something about the way the muscles in her velvety pussy tightened and rippled, causing his tear ducts to water and blur his vision.

She adjusted to his size and thickness faster than he could regain his bearings, as she started working her hips in perfect figure eights.

"Oh, damn, Baby Girl," he gasped, and then clenched his jaw. Soon, sucking air through his teeth was the only way he could breathe. This experience was all new to him. Her body was activating all kinds of switches that he didn't even know existed.

"Daddy, you feel good." Leigh flung her head back and set her hips with that extra room.

Jeremy had no doubts that he was dealing with a woman who was the queen of Kegel exercises. She was putting him through the wringer. Less than a minute in, he started tightening his abdominal muscles to try to stave off coming too soon. However, that trick wasn't working tonight. He was about the come whether he wanted to or not.

"What's the matter? Hmm?" She leaned in close and whispered into his ear. "You can't keep up, Big Daddy?"

Jeremy wanted to brag that he could handle anything she tossed his way, but that was shaping up to be a huge lie. Hell, he wanted to call a timeout, regroup and go at this again after a big bowl of Wheaties and some Gatorade. But that's not how a playa handled things.

After witnessing his struggle, Baby Girl leaned forward and sucked his left earlobe into her hot mouth. He gasped at the feel of his skin scraping against her teeth. She pulled back and chuckled.

"I told you a little pain never hurt nobody." Her smile widened. "What happened to all that swag you had earlier tonight?"

No, Baby Girl wasn't challenging his manhood. He had to pick this up a notch or forever be defined as a two-minute brother. And he wasn't having that.

The big guy upstairs was still answering prayers because suddenly they were hit with a huge wave, knocking them off balance and dipping them into the ocean. Seconds ticked by like minutes, while he splashed around and kicked. Just before panic settled in, the ocean spat him out—in nothing but his birthday suit.

The sound of Baby Girl's laughter filled his ears and when he scanned the moonlit beach, he caught sight of her brick-house frame jiggling away—with his clothes.

"'Ey, yo! Where are you going?"

She glanced over her shoulder and laughed.

"Oh. All right. So you want to play," he said to himself as he pushed himself up onto his feet and then gave chase.

She sped up, waving his underwear over her head and whooping it up.

Frankly, she looked adorable—footloose and carefree.

"Yo! Get back here!"

"You got to catch me!" the woman yelled as her long

legs carried her away from the bachelor party and from shore.

They raced across the beach like children, drawing attention from the bachelor party.

"Hey, baby," one woman hollered out. "You don't have to chase me!"

"Me, either, with your fine ass!"

And not to be out done, a few dudes hollered out propositions to Baby Girl.

Before Jeremy knew it, he had beach full of groupies heckling and tossing their bikini tops at him.

"Damn, do you see that one brother's pipe?" one girl shrieked.

With his ego expanding, Jeremy remained in hot pursuit of the curvy diva running off with his clothes. Three houses down, his clothes bandit disappeared. "Where in the hell did you go?"

Certain that she had ducked behind one of the smaller white houses, he raced around the entire building.

Nothing. He tried the front door, but it was locked. Next, the side door—locked. Maybe it was one of the other houses. Should he risk running to another house—naked? What if it was the wrong one and someone called the cops?

"All right," he called out. "Very funny. Where are you?" He glanced around again and strained his ears to hear even the slightest sound. *This would be the perfect time to at least have the girl's name.*

"I know you're around here somewhere." Jeremy smiled, still expecting her to jump out at any moment. All he could hear was the booming music from the party that he was supposed to be hosting. "All right. You've had your fun. C'mon out."

No answer.

"If you're trying to jack me, all you got is a wallet full of condoms," he warned as he crept toward the back of the house again.

No answer.

She was still nowhere to be seen. His playful smile dropped. *What the hell?* He stood there for a moment and put his hands on his hips.

I should have known that she was too good to be true.

Then, the sound of running water caught his attention. He paused and tried hard to listen more closely. It sounded like it was coming from below him. He looked around and discovered a plank of wooden steps that descended and curved below the house.

"Okay." He hitched up a smile and walked down. A few seconds later, he was able to make out that the running water was an outdoor shower. Sure enough, he found Baby Girl rinsing her lush body under the spray.

"Ahh. There you are."

She turned and hit him with a dazzling smile. "Here I am."

"I see you're a woman who loves to play games."

"I'm sure I don't know what you're talking about."

"Uh-huh."

"How do you feel about getting my back for me?"

"Oooh." He strolled toward her, grinning like a six-year-old on Christmas morning. "I think I can handle that, as well."

"You're a handy man indeed."

Her sexy smile did funny things to Jeremy's chest.

One second it felt as if his rib cage was squeezing the life out of him, and the next his heart was melting into a pool of goo. The way the full moon's glow shimmered made everything seem as if they were cast in a dream. It made sense; she had an ethereal Hollywood beauty and she was effortlessly seducing his mind as well as his body.

Jeremy reached for the liquid soap sitting on a wooden ledge, poured some of it into the palm of his hand. "Turn around," he ordered.

"Yes, sir." She followed his command, but then swept her hair over her shoulder so that she could watch him as he pressed his hands against her back and started working the soap into a lather.

"Mmm."

Jeremy laughed. "You're definitely a tease."

"I'm not teasing you. You'll get what you want in due time—especially after I had a sample out there in the water."

"You liked that, did you?" Slowly, Jeremy's hands moved in large circles. He couldn't help but wonder at the softness of her skin, plus the heat that was rushing up his hands. He was experienced enough to know that this was not normal.

"Mmm. Has anyone ever told you that you have magical hands?"

"Well…I don't want to brag."

She laughed, and then turned around.

At the sight of her full-frontal nude body, Jeremy experienced another tightening in his chest. It took everything he had not to grab his arm like Fred Sanford and call on Elizabeth about having "the big one."

Pleased by his reaction, Baby Girl's smile grew

as wide as the whole state of California. "What's the matter? Aren't you going to finish washing me?"

"I, uh…" His gaze kept sweeping up and down her body. "Uh…" Was his brain fried? How come he couldn't think of a damn thing to say? Abandoning his verbal skills, he extended his hands instead and started soaping her breasts first. He made large circles around her globes, gently pinching them. *Damn, it's hot out here.*

Never mind that they were both standing under the spray of cold, icy water, the two were as hot as if they were stranded on the Sahara Desert.

Baby Girl bit her lower lip while her eyes dropped.

"You like that?" he asked.

"Mmm-hmm."

They moved closer and Baby Girl's eyes sprung open when Jeremy's large cock nudged her open thighs. Their eyes locked together for a long, heated moment— each wondering and wanting to make the first move.

Just when Jeremy was beginning to conclude that his silvery beach goddess had finally lost her own swag, she boldly grabbed hold of his cock and started stroking him.

His moan rumbled through his chest before he had a chance to stop it.

"You like that?" she tossed back at him.

Hell, yeah. Were her hands made out of silk? Between the tightening in his chest and the tingling sensations rushing up and down his body, Jeremy was torn between plunging ahead or demanding that she call 9-1-1.

Then that beautiful laugh of hers filled the night as

she leaned up on her toes and nibbled on his ear again. "Yeah, you like that."

Jeremy turned his head and captured her lips in a kiss so powerful that he could've sworn the ground beneath them shook. From there, he was on a mindless roller-coaster ride that was as thrilling as it was frightening. When their lips finally pulled apart, the same question drifted through his mind: *who are you?*

Baby Girl wore the same dazed and confused look for a brief moment, and then that cocky, confident grin hooked the corner of her lips before her knees dipped.

His brows inched upward in surprise, but then his breath caught in his chest when she lifted his cock and eased it in the direction of her full lips. The caress of her warm breath made his toes curl. He stood transfixed while she maintained eye contact as she opened her mouth. And it was the most beautiful, glorious mouth he'd ever seen wrapped around his cock.

"Ooooh, gaaawd." He reached out and sank his fingers into her long hair.

She moaned as her lips painted his cock with coral lipstick.

"Shhhh. Oooooh." Jeremy was vaguely aware of the reduction in his vocabulary, but it didn't matter. Hell, nothing in the world mattered—nothing existed other than this woman—and her wonderful mouth. With her gaze still locked on him, Jeremy found it hard to remain cool while his face twisted into a thousand expressions. Pretty soon, even his one-syllable words were incomprehensible.

He needed to sit down—or fall down. Either way, it was going to happen and he had only seconds to choose. From the corner of his eye he noticed the stall had a small bench, and he quickly and gently eased his way over to it. However, the moment he lowered himself onto the bench, Baby Girl's head accelerated and the sound of her moans and slurps played bass to the shower's steady spray.

He couldn't believe what was happening. His vision blurred as the task of just keeping his mouth closed became impossible. He was putty in her hands, and she knew it. All he could hope for was that she would show mercy.

And thank God she did.

Popping her lips off his cock, she smiled as she smacked it against her closed mouth. "I'm not ready for you to come just yet, Big Daddy," she said.

Jeremy struggled to open his eyes. Honestly, he felt as if he'd been drugged.

"I have something else in mind," she said, winking. With that, she stood, reached over and shut off the cold water that had been pelting her back, and walked over to his clothes draped over the wall on the other side of the wooden shower stall. From there, she found his wallet and pulled out a sleeve of condoms.

"I like a man that's always prepared."

He smiled as he started to stroke himself. *This just has to be a dream.*

Less than five seconds later, he was wrapped and she was climbing up into his lap. When her knees touched either side of his hips, Jeremy held his cock straight up and then gave her the okay to slide her lush body down on him.

"Aaah," Baby Girl moaned as she slowly eased down his shaft. Her mouth had the same trouble closing as his did a few minutes ago.

He couldn't help but smile as the power ball zoomed back into his court. "That's right, Baby Girl. You can do it." He planted his hands onto her hips to help her out and when she seemed to stall three quarters of the way, Jeremy surged his hips upward and sealed the deal.

"Aaah."

"There you go, Baby Girl." He leaned forward and sucked one of her hard nipples into his mouth. From there, it seemed that the night was filled with the sounds of her sexy sighs and moans.

"You ready, Baby Girl?"

He waited a few seconds while she caught her breath, until she finally managed to open her eyes again, and gave a slight nod. Then it was on. Jeremy pumped his hips into her honeyed walls and watched as thousands of different expressions coursed through her face—all of them breathtakingly beautiful.

"Oh, gawd, you feel so good," she chanted and grabbed hold of his shoulders.

Hell, the way her walls caressed and massaged his cock, she was an armful of paradise herself. As their bodies slapped together, and her honey glazed everything between, the new lovers witnessed the most earthshattering fireworks exploding behind their closed lids.

The brief cooldown from the shower was forgotten as their body temperatures started heating up again. Wanting and needing more leverage, Jeremy grabbed Baby Girl around her ass cheeks and stood up.

She had just enough time to wrap her long legs around his waist to avoid falling. From there, Jeremy leaned her back against the stall and started hammering his hips as if the fate of the whole world depended on his making her come.

"Aah, aah, aah!"

"You want to come for me, Baby Girl?"

Stroke.

"Yes!"

Stroke.

"What? I can't hear you, Baby Girl."

"Yes! Yes! Oh, God, yes!"

Stroke. Stroke.

"Give Daddy all this good candy."

Stroke.

Stroke.

Panic started to set in when Jeremy's toes curled and his abdominal muscles clenched. The last thing he wanted to do was come before she did. But it seemed that he was on a ride that even he couldn't stop. Before long, their groans and moans competed for dominance, and before they knew it they hurdled toward the finish line together in one long, silent orgasmic scream.

Chapter 4

"Maybe we should take this inside," Baby Girl suggested.

Jeremy drew his head back from between her breasts and looked up into her beautiful face. At that moment, she could've suggested that they continued this wild night on top of the Empire State Building and he would've followed her.

"That is...if you're not too tired."

He blinked. "What? I know you're not insinuating that I can't hang."

Baby Girl shrugged her shoulders, and then climbed out of his lap. "I'm just saying, you can rest if you need to." She walked over to the other end of the stall and gathered up his clothes. "Tell you what. I'll be inside if you want me."

Amused, he watched her leave the wooden stall. *Oh, it's on now.* He jumped up and raced after her. When he reached the back door of the beach house, he could see her through the glass in all her naked glory—beautiful ass, a gorgeous pair of natural tits and nicely groomed pussy that was absolutely calling his name.

"Lord, have mercy."

"Are you going to run around outside the house all night or are you coming inside?"

"Aw. You really do like to play games, don't you?" Jeremy reached and slid open the glass door.

Baby Girl stepped back, her full lips teasing him in a seductive smile. "There's nothing wrong with making you work a little bit for what you want."

He walked toward her. "Oh, this brother isn't afraid to put in some work," Jeremy said.

Her brows rose. "Is that right?"

Jeremy's arms snaked out and grabbed her by the waist before she had another chance to dash off. "I'm not a man afraid of a little work."

"Mmm." Her arms looped back up around his neck as he pressed their bodies closer. "Good to know."

Their lips came together for another sweet, decadent kiss. Jeremy thought that he was more prepared this time, but turned out—to his moaning and groaning embarrassment—that simply was not true. He tried to play it cool for as long as he could, but this woman kept hitting that spot up against the side of his tongue that not only made his dick as hard as a brick, but it even made his nipples tingle.

What the hell?

Meanwhile, he couldn't seem to control his hands. They were already sliding away from her small waist to roam over her ass, which was smooth, soft and wonderfully squeezable. In fact, every time she hit that magic spot on the side of his tongue, he squeezed and parted her ass cheeks in a way that would make her moan as loud as he did. No sense in him being the only one sounding like he was on the verge of another orgasm.

At some point, she started moving, forcing him to walk backward. Hell, he didn't care where they were going as long as she was coming with him. But then he bumped into something hard and she delivered a hard shove against his chest that sent him reeling backward.

"Heeey...?" He landed on his back on a soft couch that had at least two-dozen pillows on it.

"Comfy?" she asked, standing above him with her hands nestled on her hips.

He smiled, loving how she towered over him like an Amazon warrior. Yet he still had the same recurring thought looping inside of his head: *please don't hurt me.*

"What's the matter? Cat got your tongue?" she inquired.

"Not yet. But why don't you turn some lights on in here? I want to be able to see every inch of you."

She walked over to the lamp behind the couch and clicked it on. "Better?"

"Much better." His gaze danced over her curves again.

Grinning like a Cheshire cat, Baby Girl crawled up and over the arm of the sofa, and then up his long, muscular body. "My God, you look like somebody chiseled you out of milk chocolate," she cooed. Then she dipped her head and ran her tongue over the ridges of his hard six-pack. "Mmm. Sweet."

The air oozed out of Jeremy's lungs in a long, soft hiss as he watched her wicked pink tongue as it rolled up the center of his body. He was so turned on that his cock jumped reflexively against his thigh.

"Now, since you've tasted me, you could give a brother a sample."

Her brow hitched. "Just a sample?"

"Well, if you're offering a brother all he can eat, then I can handle that, too." He reached down and gave her ass a hard squeeze.

"I think that I can handle that." But before she complied, Baby Girl slanted her mouth over his so that their tongues could dance and caress each other.

Hot, wet and sweet as hell, Jeremy didn't mind the sugar rush that shot straight to his head. But he absolutely loved the extraordinary sensations that twirled and swirled inside him. In all honesty, Jeremy had never felt anything like it—and it was definitely a feeling that he could get used to.

When their lips finally pulled away, Baby Girl smiled. "I hope that you're hungry."

"Starved." His lips hitched upward as he delivered a smack against the bottom of her ass. He watched as her eyes twinkled with excitement before she resumed her languid climb up his body. In no time, Baby Girl planted her knees on both sides of his head and he was face-to-face with her beautifully trimmed pussy. His chest tightened and if he didn't know any better, he would say that there were butterflies fluttering behind his iron-hard abs, to say nothing of his cock, which was standing as straight and hard as a flagpole.

He reached up and parted her brown lips and was rewarded with the husky-sweet scent of her pussy. He could honestly say that if he died there tonight, he would be a very happy man. Lifting his head just as she widened her knees, Jeremy glided his tongue down the side of her soft, honeyed clit.

Baby Girl threw her head back and released a whining moan toward the ceiling. His second stroke made her knees and thighs tremble. From there, Jeremy pressed his face even closer while his tongue went deep.

Jeremy was pretty sure the words flowing from Baby Girl's mouth were nothing but half-baked vowels and stuttering consonants. Encouraged by her reaction, he slid his hands around the corners of her thighs and took hold of her ample ass. Once he had a good grip on her, he feasted like a starved man.

Baby Girl dripped so much honey that it covered his fingers, so he used it as a lubricant and started stroking himself. Call him crazy, but one second he could've sworn that her body was a giant honeycomb and in the next, she was a field of strawberries.

Finally her free-flowing sound cohered long enough to call on God but soon dissolved into sigh and moans. Then she was as clear as a bell. "I—I—I'm coming."

Instead of speeding up or intensifying his strokes, Jeremy slowed down...waaaay down. Baby Girl pressed her bottom down in silent urging. When that didn't work, she started grinding her hips in an attempt to just use his tongue as a prop for her to find her own release.

Amused, Jeremy smiled, turned his head and absently peppered kisses along her inner thigh.

"No...no...please," she begged.

"Hmm?"

"Please...don't stop, baby."

He continued pressing kisses against her trembling thighs. "Don't stop what?"

"Please, don't tease me," she begged. "I need..."

"Hmm? What is it that you need, baby?" His lips moved a little closer to her open pussy.

"I need *it. Please.*"

It was the note of desperation in her voice that convinced Jeremy to end his torture and to give her what she truly needed. "All right, baby. Here you go." He pulled her lips open again and dove in—his relentless tongue showed no mercy as it tugged and licked her clit. Next he pulled out his cock and started delivering short, stinging slaps to the bottom of her ass. With each smack, she gasped.

In no time, the beach house was filled with the sounds of her moaning and his smacking. Soon after, she cried out in a pitch just an octave shy of shattering glass.

And still he feasted.

"Okay...okay...please."

Now she wanted—no, she needed—for him to stop. The aftershocks left her plump clit sensitive and she could hardly stand him blowing on it, much less his tongue's continued brutal assault.

A second scream ripped from her throat.

Jeremy almost felt sorry for her.

Almost.

Baby Girl's legs collapsed, causing her body to almost smother his head.

Almost.

After the third orgasm, Baby Girl was as limp as a wet noodle and Jeremy was the one grinning like a Cheshire as he cleaned her up. When he finally unlatched his mouth from her throbbing pussy, he had to physically lift her body up so that he could escape his erotic prison. Once he was sitting up, he looked over at her rosy bottom and gave it one more smack.

"I hope you don't think that I'm through with you," he chuckled as he reached in between his legs and started stroking his cock again.

"I—I need a minute," she said, chugging in huge gulps of air. "Please."

His laughter rumbled. "You got thirty seconds," he told her, standing. "After that, you need to pick a position—any position." He walked over to his pile of clothes that she had tossed onto the floor.

A few seconds later, he ripped open a condom and rolled it on. There was a small popping sound. He glanced down at the snug fit, but continued rolling the condom up his shaft.

"Are you ready?" he asked, walking back to the cushy couch.

Baby Girl glanced over her shoulder, looking sexy as hell with her flushed face and wet hair.

"Anything you like," he repeated, stroking himself. "Remember, I'm here to fulfill your request."

"Is that right?"

"You know it."

"Well, in that case…" Baby Girl pushed herself back up onto her knees.

Jeremy could still see his hand print on her lush bottom and it made him that much harder. He moved up behind her, and this time paddled her butt with his iron-hard cock. "Are you ready for another round, baby?"

"I'm more than ready, *Daddy.*"

Jeremy grinned. "You really are a trip. You know that?"

She laughed, and then pushed back on him so that

his dick was sausaged between her ass for a few strokes. But then she sucked in a long breath as he eased his shaft down to the entrance to her pussy.

Once again, he didn't just surge inside of her. He held back and waited.

Baby Girl moaned and wiggled her butt. When that still didn't get her what she wanted, she rocked back trying to impale herself.

Jeremy gave her a firm whack on the ass for her trouble.

She gasped and shuddered while more honey dripped onto the head of his cock. "Please," she begged.

"You sure you can handle this? Maybe you need another break?"

She did a half-moan and laugh. "You're sooo wrong."

He chuckled. "All right. If you think that you can handle it." He thrust up his hips, but his cockiness dissipated when her slippery walls tightened around him. Inch by glorious inch, he experienced something akin to a nuclear meltdown. Beads of sweat broke out along his hairline, his chest muscles constricted around his heart, his legs turned to rubber and his toes curled so tight that he was almost certain that they were digging into the hardwood floor.

"D-daaaamnn."

For Leigh, she was sure that she was losing her mind. There was just something exquisite about the way he felt inside of her. Earlier, she thought that maybe it was the adventure of being outside and the danger of them being caught or seen. But now she knew that the extraordinary pleasure was all him. He was the sole reason her body was behaving the way it did. He elicited the bad girl inside of her.

She absolutely loved it—even if it was only for one night.

Just when she thought that she was filled beyond capacity, her sex daddy started stroking—slow, but deep. Her mind spun like a pinwheel as every emotion rippled through her like a tidal wave. Her fingers dug into the throw pillows on the couch, and when that didn't help, she dropped her head and bit into one.

"Awww, damn. You're so tight," he gasped raggedly.

It was the first hint for her that she was having the same effect on him that he was on her. With her teeth ready to tear the pillow fabric, she mustered the strength to start thrusting back on him.

From his reaction, she knew it had thrown him—jacked up his rhythm and control. His hands gripped her hips, but if he thought that was going to stop her, then he had another thing coming. She rocked harder—faster. His gasping for air made him sound like a child's choo-choo train. She didn't care that the hard slaps against his pelvis and thighs was intensifying the burning pain in her bottom. She was just enjoying the power too much.

Finally, she pulled her teeth from the pillow and indeed a pile of cotton burst from the seams. She was far from caring. Leigh craned her neck over her shoulder and watched his twisted expressions. Before she could revel in her victory, three orgasms took her by surprise, detonating in quick succession.

She cried out and tears raced from the corners of her eyes. Her legs liquefied and threatened to collapse. Then suddenly, he stopped.

"Stand up."

Leigh blinked. She wasn't sure that she had heard him correctly.

"C'mon." He slapped her on the ass.

She backed up so that she could stretch her legs off the edge of the couch and plant them on the floor, all the while keeping their bodies connected. Once she'd completed that task, her lover barked out another order.

"Grab your ankles."

Leigh's belly fluttered as excitement coursed up her spine.

"C'mon. hurry up." *Smack.*

Leigh dipped her upper body all the way over and grabbed her ankles.

The stroking resumed and what Leigh got were deeper and whole lot more intense sensations ripping through her. If it weren't for the fact that his hands were locked around her hips to anchor her in place, she would have crashed against the hard floor just from the pleasure of it all.

Soon, every nerve ending exploded like Fourth-of-July fireworks and God only knew what the jumble of words that tumbled out of her mouth meant. As for the man behind her, his moans and groans had long stopped sounding human. She was nearing something like her sixth orgasm when he exploded and howled toward the ceiling. Slowly he stepped back and disconnected their bodies.

Leigh stood up, but then quickly dropped to the floor because all the blood had rushed to her head.

"Whoa," her Big Daddy chuckled and rushed over to help. "Are you all right?"

"I'm fine. I'm fine," she panted. In truth, her limbs had returned to their wet-noodle stage. "I just—just…"

"Need another break?" he suggested.

She smiled meekly. "Just a small one."

He laughed, but headed back over to his wallet for another condom. "Tell you what," he said, spotting the half-bath on the bottom floor. "You have one minute— and then you need to come and meet me in one of these bedrooms up here." He held up a finger. "One minute."

Leigh tried to nod, but all she could manage was just breathing. Through her lowered lashes, she watched him strut off with his well-defined muscles while his glazed cock swung like a pendulum between his thighs.

She picked one hell of a stallion to ride this night. And she was definitely satisfied. Leigh closed her eyes for a second, waiting to reboot.

"Time's up!"

Leigh smiled, jumped up and raced to the bedroom.

Chapter 5

Leigh awoke from her dreams with a smile on her face and a tingling ache between her legs. When she arrived in Malibu yesterday it was more so to throw a pity party for herself than to be on the prowl for a one-night stand. But after a few glasses of wine, she heard the laughter and the music just a couple of houses away and she thought, *why not*. Before she knew it, she'd given herself permission to just let her hair down and to do things that she never even dared to do without having pyschoanalyzed it to death.

After all, she was entitled, especially after dealing with a man most people thought she would marry. But he happened to be the same guy who habitually broke her heart.

Now, after five years, it was over. She was pretty sure this time, given their history of boomeranging. It had gotten to the point that she wondered whether she stuck it out just because of the time she'd already invested in the relationship—not because of love. At least, she didn't think it was love anymore.

It's over. The best way to ensure that was true was to stay the hell away from DeShawn Carter. He was too charming and persistent by half, especially when he wanted to be. He always had a way of convincing her that he was truly sorry and that somehow, his dick just happened to fall into the random chicks he met on the road. Hell, he might even pull out a stack of Bibles and swear on it.

Did she care anymore? Should she care?

Not right now. Right now she felt too good.

Leigh moaned as she stretched out of the spoon position. Her ass bumped into something hard. That was all it took for a night of memories to come flooding back to her, each one better than the next. She almost didn't even trust that the cinematic frames running through her head were real—until she gathered the courage to turn around and peek over her shoulder.

The moment she did her heart stopped. Big Daddy was as gorgeous in the morning light as he was in moonlight. *Can a man be described as* gorgeous?

Just looking at his creamy milk-chocolate skin was enough to give her hunger pangs, but his handsome features themselves gave her the impression that God took his time creating a specimen like him. There was strength emanating everywhere—from his nicely chiseled jawline, boulder-size shoulders, mountainous chest and, she lifted up the sheet and took a peek at the view below.

That was real, too.

Leigh sucked in a deep breath, but it did nothing

to reverse her accelerating heartbeat. "You were reee-aaally a bad girl." A wicked smile touched her lips as she slowly pulled her eyes away from his morning erection and returned to his sleeping face. As much as she was attracted to this man's strength, he had another quality that she couldn't quite put her finger on that had her heart tripping inside her chest—something that pulled at her.

Leigh slammed her eyes shut, and then shook her head. What the hell was wrong with her?

She'd just gotten out of a relationship—and there she was weighing the possibility of starting another one—and with a man she'd just met?

This was why women couldn't have no-strings-attached sex. They invariably open a sewing-kit and start stitching.

No. As nice a man as this guy seemed to be, what sort of relationship could they possibly have with this as their beginning? This was worse than sex on the first date. This was sex before knowing each other's names.

Leigh pulled in a deep breath and forced herself to climb out of bed. As quietly as she could, she searched for some clothes to put on. The thought that she should stick around, perhaps cook him breakfast and return him to wherever it was he came from crossed her mind. But she had never done that sort of thing before and she didn't know if she could deal with the awkwardness. Bottom line, she didn't want him to see *her* in the light of day. It would make things *too* complicated and he would ask too many questions.

In the top drawer of the nightstand she pulled out a pad and paper and jotted down, *'Thanks. I needed that.'*

She stared at the short note and struggled for something else to add, but other than leaving money on the dresser, what else was there to say? Leigh placed the note on top of his clothes, certain that he would see it there and then creep out of the bedroom and out of his life.

Jeremy stirred from the best sleep he'd ever had with a smile on his face. Sure, he was sore in a few places from twisting in ways he didn't have any business twisting. But he was sure that it was nothing a good massage couldn't work out. Moaning and stretching, he still didn't quite have enough strength to open his eyes. That is until the smell of bacon wafted under his nose and got his stomach growling like Cujo.

Food was the second best way to wake a man in the morning. *The first...* Jeremy finally peeled open his eyes to see his morning hard-on standing straight as a flagpole. He groaned, wishing that Baby Girl was lying next to him instead of in the kitchen, but he appreciated her trying to feed a brother after the grueling workout she put him through.

With one last groan, he finally sat up and noticed for the first time that the top mattress was actually on the floor. Assessing the room while he tried to rub the sleep out of his eyes, a smile traveled up the corner of his lips. The place was wrecked: overturned lamps and nightstands—and were those his drawers hanging on the doorknob?

He snickered as he propelled himself from off the floor. His first stop was to the adjoining bathroom where he opted for a quick shower. Though he was tempted to work the edge off his erection, he was more interested to see if he could get Baby Girl to do a few instant-replay moves like she put on him the night before. Hell, there were a few moves that even he had never tried before.

Stepping out of the shower, Jeremy smiled as the old-school Jacksons' hit "Blame it on the Boogie" filled the beach house. He bobbed his head and tucked his towel around his hips as he closed in on the kitchen. When he heard Baby Girl singing, he was a little surprised to hear that she was an alto. Given how high he had her crying out to the Almighty, her versatile range was impressive. *Now, if this girl is as bad in the kitchen as she is in the bedroom, I might have to keep her around a little longer.*

"Whatcha got cookin' up in here?" he asked, rounding the corner, but then quickly stopping in his tracks, when a blond-haired white woman jerked around, took one look at him and then proceeded to scream her head off.

"Whoa, whoa—what the hell!" His brain scrambled and he was unable to make sense of what was going on.

"George!"

"Wait! I can explain," he shouted. However, the woman's scream edged closer toward hysteria.

"Cathy? Are you all right?"

Behind him, Jeremy heard the mad rush of something—or someone—heavy heading toward him. "No. It's okay," he said, turning with his hands up in a defensive maneuver.

Unfortunately, his towel wasn't tucked too securely and the sucker picked the moment when this big sumo wrestler-looking brother, rounded the corner. All explanations flew right out of Jeremy's head about the same time his jaw had the misfortune to be in the direct line of this angry brother's fist.

After that, he blacked out.

"All right. Here you go," a bored Los Angeles police officer said, pushing Jeremy's wallet and car keys toward him. "Sign here and here." He pointed to the X's on a clipboard form. "And you're free to go."

"Thanks," Jeremy mumbled and then was punished by his swollen jaw. He quickly scrawled his name twice. Turning, he was then escorted out of the precinct by another officer. Once he was directed to the department's crowded lobby, his cousin Quentin climbed to his feet with a Cheshire-size grin from ear to ear.

"Damn," Q said, wincing at the sight of him. "What the hell happened to the side of your face?"

"Zip it, Q. I'm not in the mood," Jeremy groaned as he marched past his cousin and out of the precinct's glass doors.

"I wouldn't be in the mood either if I looked like I'd just been run over by a Mack truck." Quentin laughed as he struggled to keep up with his cousin. "Did you at least get the license-plate number?"

"Yeah. K-S-S-M-Y-A-Z-Z!"

Quentin threw his head back and laughed.

Jeremy reached the parking lot and then glanced around. "Where did you park?"

"This way, convict." Quentin pointed in the direction of a Mercedes rental. "Let me hurry up and get you off the streets before you break into someone else's house butt-naked and flash your junk."

"I didn't break in," Jeremy said, jerking open the

passenger door and throwing his body onto the leather interior. "I was invited."

"By the hysterical woman that's telling every news camera in a fifty-mile radius that she feared for her life when a strange naked black man just popped up behind her in the kitchen?"

Jeremy's head fell back against the headrest. "It's all over the news?"

"Local news—I haven't seen anything on the CNN ticker yet."

"Great. Juuusssst great." Jeremy closed his eyes and for at least the millionth time prayed that when he opened them back up this whole thing would've just been some horrible nightmare.

"Chill out. Don't get your panties in a wad, I've been in your position numerous times myself," Quentin continued his style of consoling. "You go to a party, toss back one or two too many drinks and then next thing you know someone has called the damn law. Trust me. You called the right man for the job on this one."

"I called you because Eamon is still on his extended honeymoon and Xavier didn't answer his phone."

"Well, at least I was third in line," Quentin said, with a wink. "I already got you lined up with some of the best lawyers money can buy. You were robbed."

"I had my wallet and clothes," he reminded him.

"You were disoriented—you have a medical condition," Quentin amended. "It doesn't matter. My lawyer, Ernest Files, got you covered like Allstate. This whole thing will get swept under the rug. No problem."

Jeremy continued to just shake his head. "Look, I'm telling you the truth, Baby Girl took me over to her crib during Dylan Freedman's bachelor party…and—"

"Say what? Dylan Freedman got hitched?"

Jeremy huffed at being interrupted. "Yeah. The Doll-house threw him this cool party. I met this one chick— I mean, damn!" He shook his head, remembering some of her moves both on the dance floor and then a few other ones that answered how that mattress ended up on the floor.

"That fine, huh?"

Despite the soreness, a smile crept onto Jeremy's face. "Baby Girl was a whole 'nother level," he said. Hell, there were still parts on his body that were aching that had absolutely nothing to do with the sucker punch that knocked his butt out.

"Damn, playa." Q laughed. "Are you daydreaming over there?"

"What?" Jeremy jerked. "Nah. Nah. I'm just trying to figure out what the hell happened."

"Well, first off, does this Baby Girl happen to have a *real* name?" At his cousin's silence, Quentin pulled his eyes from off the road to catch the embarrassed look ripple across Jeremy's face. "Ah, playa, please tell me you didn't just get played."

Jeremy turned defensive. "She said that she didn't want to exchange names."

"Why? Is she in the Secret Service or something? Is the Navy SEALs looking for her ass?"

"Nah. I mean, I don't think so." He struggled with the possibility of having been played. "Look. You had to have been there. The no names just added to the whole mystique. It was hot."

"Uh-huh," Q shook his head and then turned his attention back to the road. "Well, while you were burning up the sheets in somebody *else's* crib, did you at least remember to wrap it up?"

Jeremy blanched.

"Aww, nah. Playa, are you for real?"

"What are you, hood now?"

"Are you stupid now?" Q counterattacked. "You're out drilling in mysterious and nameless pussy and you didn't even bother to protect yourself? Cuz, just hand over your black book and playa card. You're out here making it dangerous for everybody." He suddenly swerved over three lanes to make the next exit.

"Hey, where are you going?"

"Taking you to the nearest clinic. You definitely need to get yourself checked out before I let you out back on the streets."

"Man, I used condoms. It's just that one of them broke near the end."

Quentin eyeballed him dubiously. "Broke? What the hell were you doing?"

"Uh, none of your damn business, cuz. I done told you that your old-school moves can't keep up."

"Junior, stop all that noise. All you toddlers out here think y'all invented sex. How in the hell do you think y'all got here? Plus, I'm not that much older than you."

Jeremy smirked because age jokes always got under Quentin's skin.

"Anyway, a real professional playa's condoms don't break."

"Look, just because you got all that *extra* room in your condoms, don't be hatin' on us snug-fit brothas. Hell, I hear some chicks think that nice things come in *small* packages."

"You're not funny."

Jeremy's laugh deepened and then rumbled the rest of the way to The Dollhouse.

"Get the hell up out of my car," Q barked, throwing the car into Park and then exiting the vehicle in almost the same fluid motion.

"C'mon, Quentin," Jeremy continued laughing as he climbed out of the car. "You know I got nothing but love for you, baby."

Quentin tossed up his middle finger while he strolled faster toward the back door, where he quickly produced a key and jetted inside.

Jeremy just barely caught the door before it slammed shut in his face. "Aww. Did I hurt somebody's *itty-bitty* feelings?"

"There you are, Jeremy," said Thomas, the club's head chef, glancing up from his inventory accounting. "We've been wondering where you've been." His expression twisted. "What the hell happened to your face?"

"Everybody, meet the Naked Malibu Burglar—fresh outta the joint!" Quentin barked bitterly.

Jeremy's jaw dropped open as he chased after his cousin. "Yo, man. You don't broadcast something like that in a place of business. Like I said, the whole thing is just a misunderstanding." He puffed up his chest

Q stopped in the middle of the main club. "Yeah. Let me make sure I got this straight. Your imaginary future baby momma broke you two into a house, sexed you up, scrammed and then left you in a trashed bedroom where you then got up and paraded around naked until Malibu Barbie started screaming her head off and a sumo wrestler raced in and knocked you unconscious before calling the police. Did I get all of that straight?"

Jeremy blinked. "Well…I admit that it sounds a bit far-fetched when you say it like that."

"Then how would you like for me to say it?" Quentin folded his arms and waited.

"Look, I don't know why the girl broke into the place, but I swear I thought she lived there."

"…Because she was *sooo* forthcoming with her name?"

Jeremy ground his teeth. "Fine. Maybe it was a little lapse in judgment—a little one—because I can't say that I'm at all sorry for hooking up with Baby Girl. I mean…" He shook his head as erotic memories scrolled through his head.

"Damn, are you going to start drooling now? You take thinking with the wrong head to a whole new level." Q rolled his eyes and resumed his march toward the offices on the other side of the club.

"Whatever," Jeremy said, rolling his eyes behind Q's back. "You need to climb off your high horse. It's not like you've never been led astray by a big butt and a smile."

Quentin held up a pointed finger and opened his mouth to rebut the charge, but then clearly thought better of whatever lie he was about to tell and admitted, "We're not talking about me. What's with you Kings always flipping the script?"

Jeremy smirked. "Stop preaching and there won't be a problem."

"The only problem we have right now is your mouth," Q said, charging into Jeremy's office. "We're going to put an end to this right now." He started jerking and slamming desk drawers.

"Mind if I ask what the hell you're doing?" Jeremy closed the door, and then folded his arms.

Q ignored him for about a full minute until he found what he was looking for. "Ah! I found it." He jerked out a ruler. "How about we put some money where your lying mouth is?" Before Jeremy could answer, Q started unbuttoning his pants.

"What the hell?"

"Hundred dollars says I'm bigger than you." He unzipped his pants.

Jeremy's laughter exploded in the room, but just as quickly, he had to clutch his throbbing jaw. "Man, don't make me laugh. I don't want to take your money. It'll be like taking candy from a baby."

"Scared?" Q's confident smile stretched wider. "Two hundred."

"Q, man—"

"Cluck, cluck, cluck."

"You're clucking?" His face twisted. "Man, you sound like a chicken on crack."

"C'mon, big boy. There's two hundred dollars on the table. Put up or shut up."

Jeremy caught the greedy gleam in his cousin's eyes. "You're serious?"

"As a heart attack."

"A'ight. Bet." Jeremy unbuttoned and unzipped his pants as he moved closer to the desk. "Time to shut you down."

"On the count of three," Quentin said. "One, two… three!"

The cousins whipped out their cocks at the same moment Delilah burst through the door. "Jeremy, I heard that— What the hell!" She turned her head away.

Jeremy and Quentin quickly crammed themselves back into their pants.

"Uh, sorry about that, Dee," Jeremy said sheepishly, as his face burned with embarrassment.

Delilah peeked back over her shoulder to make sure that the coast was clear. She turned around with her hands on her hips. "Let me guess—another bet?"

"Hell, while you're in here, maybe you can just be the judge," Quentin suggested, reaching for his zipper again.

"Uh-uh-uh. Don't you dare," Delilah warned before Q whipped it out again. "What the hell is wrong with you two? Does everything have to be a damn competition?"

"It'll just take a second," Quentin said, unmoved by her outrage.

"No!"

Jeremy laughed. "I guess it would be considered unprofessional."

"You think?" Delilah shook her head and then finally took a good look at her boss's face. "Ohmigod! What happened?" She rushed over to Jeremy and grabbed the sides of his face so that she could take a good look.

"Ssss." Jeremy winced. "Careful. I'm not sure my jaw isn't broken."

"Then why aren't you at the hospital or something?"

"Because Q thought it was much more important for us to measure his dick."

Quentin rolled his eyes. "Whatever, cuz. You owe me two hundred dollars—*plus* your bail money."

"Bail?" Delilah said, astonished.

"Are you crazy?" Jeremy's chest puffed out indigently. "You didn't win."

"I most certainly didn't lose."

"Oh, my God. You two are giving me a headache. Why is it every time you two get together you start acting like children?"

"Because he always starts it," Jeremy said, pointing.

"Nuh-uh. You started it," Quentin countered.

"Geez Louise." Delilah rolled her eyes. "Just shut up before I put you both in a time out."

They both clamped their mouths shut and exchanged heated glares.

"Now tell me what the hell happened to your face?" she instructed.

"Yeah, Jeremy." Quentin leaned a hip against the corner of the desk. "Tell good ol' Delilah how half your face caved in."

Jeremy knocked Q's hip off the desk and threw his head back in a hearty laugh when his cousin went tumbling to the floor.

Delilah counted to ten. "I swear you two need constant supervision."

Quentin pulled himself off the floor. "That's all right. Chuckle it up. Next time you need to be bailed out of jail, call one of your Boy Scout brothers so you can get the tongue lashing you deserve."

"I'm still waiting to hear the story," Delilah reminded Jeremy.

"There was just this misunderstanding yesterday morning." He shrugged, but saw that his mother-hen employee was going to need more than that if he wanted to get her off his back.

"What sort of misunderstanding?" Q prompted as he

settled his elbows on the desk, cupped his face in his hands and proceeded to give him the innocent puppy-dog look.

Jeremy was beginning to think that he would've been better off if he had just called someone else in the family—anyone else.

"There was this woman," Jeremy started.

"I figured that much," Delilah said. "The question is, did she or her man give you that shiner?"

"Oooh. Good question," Quentin leaned in closer—until Jeremy gave him a look that made it clear that he was in danger of receiving a matching black eye.

Jeremy quickly gave Delilah the abridged version of what happened at Dylan Freedman's bachelor party. However, every time he referred to Baby Girl, a smile kept spreading across his face. When he finished, Delilah was laughing and Quentin looked horror-struck.

"Why are you smiling like that?" Q asked, his brows dipped toward his nose.

"Smiling like what?"

Quentin jumped up onto his feet and started waving his finger. "Don't play stupid with me. I *know* that look. That look is trouble. Have you forgotten our deal? No more weddings."

"What? No. Who said anything about weddings? I'm just saying that I had a nice time with the girl."

"Wait a minute," Delilah interrupted. "You two have a deal about not getting married?"

Quentin bobbed his head. "Yep. And I even got it in writing." He reached into his jacket and pulled out a crumpled-up piece of paper.

Jeremy frowned. "You carry that thing around with you?"

"Are you kidding me? It's my American Express card. I never leave home without it."

"You have issues."

"Whatever." He slapped the paper down on the desk and pointed. "See? It's right here in black and white. I...you...'Jeremy Jorell King, do solemnly swear that I will not get married *or* sell my shares in The Dollhouse Enterprise.' That is your signature, isn't it?"

"Yes," Jeremy acknowledged, rolling his eyes. "Now will you please put that away? I'm *not* getting married."

Q's eyes narrowed as he carefully studied his cousin's face.

"I'm serious. It was just a wild fling. We met. We had fun. No big deal." He laughed. "Hell, chances are that I'll never see Baby Girl again."

Chapter 6

"I was a bad girl this weekend," Leigh confessed. She'd kept her secret from her best friend for two days. In her mind, that just had to be some kind of record.

Ariel snatched out one of her iPod earplugs without stumbling during their run through Torry Pine State Park. "Who was bad?"

"I was," Leigh repeated as a rush of heat coursed through her entire body.

"Bad how?" Ariel asked, dubious about her friend's confession.

The corners of Leigh's mouth felt as though they were just inches from touching each other in the back of her head her smile was so wide. "I had a one-night stand."

Ariel finally slowed down as doubt gave way to shock. "Get the hell out of here."

Leigh bobbed her head. "I know. I know. I can hardly

believe it myself. But I did it and I don't feel the slightest bit guilty about it. I don't." She shook her head and accelerated past her friend.

It took Ariel a few seconds to process that Leigh was serious. She rushed to catch up with her again. "But what about DeShawn?"

"What about him?"

"Uh, is he cool with your suddenly liberated take on your relationship?"

"Screw DeShawn. We are *soooo* through."

"Again?" Ariel laughed. "What did he do this time?"

"What does he always do? He cheated on me—again."

Ariel's amusement didn't falter. "What, with another groupie or some miscellaneous ho?" her friend continued. "C'mon, Leigh. You knew what the deal was when you hooked up with a pro basketball player. These trifling women out here are no joke. You're expecting a lot from a man—especially a man in his position—to resist that kind of temptation 24/7."

"Gee, thanks. Silly me, I thought that you were supposed to be on my side."

"I *am* on your side! DeShawn is a good man. And faults aside, he's crazy about you. A blind person can see that."

"Well if he loved me, he'd keep his damn pants zipped," Leigh shot back as she slowed her pace. "I can't believe you think I'm being unreasonable because I expect my man to be faithful to me."

Ariel shook her head. "Look, if he was Joe Schmo with a regular 9-to-5, then yeah. I feel you," Ariel said. "But any guy who's a celebrity has women conniving and scheming to get them into bed around the clock.

And most of these men are in the prime of their sex lives. Their testosterone is through the roof and they're on the road all the time. Sure they're going to slip up. It's the law of averages."

"Then he can just go and find him some other woman that's gonna give him a pass with these skanks. I'm not putting up with it anymore. I'm tired of every time I call and he doesn't pick up the phone I'm thinking that he's screwing some trick. I'm tired of seeing lipstick on his collar or smelling perfume on his skin. That's no way to live."

"What's different now than the past five years?"

"The difference is I'm tired of it—sick and tired of it, as a matter of fact," Leigh said, picking up the pace.

Ariel pulled up beside her. "Leigh—"

"Look, if you're going to defend DeShawn, then I don't want to hear it. I've already heard a million excuses from him. I didn't expect to hear them from my best friend."

Ariel kept quiet for about five seconds. "I just think that you're making a big mistake."

Leigh huffed and rolled her eyes.

After another five seconds, Ariel said, "Sooo…you don't love him anymore?"

"I didn't say that I don't love him." Leigh sighed. "I just don't know if I'm *in* love with him. There's a difference." From the corner of her eye, she could see her best friend shaking her head. "You just don't understand."

"You're damn right I don't understand," Ariel said. "Do you know how hard it is to find a good man out here? DeShawn is a nice guy. He's funny, charming, handsome and *rich*. Hell, I'd settle for one out of four on that list. The last date I had, the brother rolled my ass through the drive-thru at Taco Bell and caught a serious attitude because I wanted extra cheese on my taco."

Leigh snickered.

"Laugh if you want to. But if you jump out here, you're going to find out quick, fast and in a hurry that the difference between mangy dogs and dogs is that you can *potty train* dogs. Trust me. I've been out here longer than you have. When you finish picking off all the fleas and ticks, you're going to be pissed that DeShawn's next chick is rockin' a Maybach and VVS stones. And I'm going to be on the sidelines with a big-ass sign that reads I Told You So."

Leigh stopped running and bent over to catch her breath.

Ariel stopped and glanced back at her.

"Are you through?" Leigh said.

"Look, I'm just keeping it real—and trying to stop you from making the biggest mistake of your life."

"I was never with DeShawn for the money," Leigh countered. "Everything I floss, I bought and paid for myself."

"All right, Ms. Independent. There're still plenty of little boys out here looking for a good sugar momma, too. And when you get tired of letting them always borrow your car, eat your food and run up your credit card, you come holler at me."

"Damn, Ariel!"

"What? You can't handle the truth? Or are you one of these women who thinks *Sex and the City* represents what the single life is really like out here? It's rough. Just because you had *one* one-night stand with a brother that put a smile on your face doesn't mean that you've found the pot of gold at the end of the rainbow."

Leigh shook her head, still not wanting to buy what her friend was selling.

"Just promise me that you'll think about it some more before you go out and have too many one-night stands."

Leigh was on the verge of telling her that she was through thinking about it. She and DeShawn had been riding the same roller-coaster ride for five years. When do you just toss in the towel and say enough is enough?

"Leigh?"

"Fine," she said defensively. "I'll think about it."

Ariel smiled. "Good. That's all I ask."

Leigh straightened up and then forced herself to resume their five-mile run. Gone were her good mood *and* the instant replays in her head of her one steamy night with a handsome stranger that did more than just put a smile on her face.

An hour later, Leigh returned to her West Hollywood condo feeling more confused than ever. Was she throwing a good thing away? Were her expectations too high in this day and age of sexual liberation? It pained her to admit it, but Ariel was right. Women threw themselves at DeShawn nonstop—a lot of times right when she was hooked on his arm. *What was it Ariel said about the law of averages?*

After slamming her front door and kicking off her Nikes with her toes, the blinking red light on the answering machine drew Leigh's eyes. As she peeled out of her sweaty tank top, she walked over and hit Play.

"You have twenty messages." Beep!

"What?" She glanced down at her watch. She'd only been gone two hours.

"Hey, Leigh, it's DeShawn."

She rolled her eyes.

"I was just calling to see...you know, if you've calmed down a bit so we can actually talk about this situation. I know—I know that I screwed up. But, baby, I said I was sorry, and I meant it. Now, surely you're not about to just throw away these past five years. I mean, call me crazy, but I think this relationship is worth fighting for...."

"Then you should have fought a little harder to keep your pants zipped," Leigh argued aloud at the answering machine.

"You mean the world to me, Leigh. I love you. You gotta know this by now..."

Leigh closed her eyes and tried to untangle her raw emotions.

"All right. I guess you're not there. When you get back, please hit me on my cell. We need to talk about this."

Beep!

Before Leigh could draw a breath, her mother's booming voice rattled the answering machine's speakers.

"Leigh, are you there? Pick up!" After a long pause, she continued. "Chile, when you get home, give me a call and tell me why DeShawn is calling my house every ten minutes. What the hell happened between you two?"

Leigh groaned. It was a typical DeShawn Carter move. When he couldn't get Leigh to budge on something, he went through her mother.

"I mean it, Leigh. You better call and tell me why I

have this boy sounding like Keith Sweat on my phone. Whatever this chile done did, you two need to work it out. You know that you two belong together. Y'all need to stop with all this foolishness and go on ahead and get married. You don't want to be like all these other career women who wait until their forties and then start wondering why all their eggs done dried up. Your father and I have been wanting some grandbabies for a while now. You need to give us something to do before we kill each other up in here. You know, ever since he sold the company and retired, he's been rocking my last damn…" *Beep!*

Leigh chuckled at the way the answering machine had cut her mother off. Of course, the answering machine always cut her off because the one thing her mother was not blessed with was the gift of brevity.

"Hey, Leigh this is Cathy. I, um… I know this may sound crazy, but, um, did you happen to come by and use the beach house this past weekend? There was this sort of incident when George and I came up Saturday. You won't believe this, but there was a naked guy parading around the house—"

"Oh, shit." Leigh's eyes widened. Cathy hardly ever used the beach house and had always extended an open invitation to Leigh—which she hardly ever took advantage of, until this past weekend. She needed a place to go and just clear her head. She left the one-night stand guy a note—and hoped that he would just see his way out.

"I'm asking because George found this note and it sort of looks like your handwriting. Anyway, just give me a call. It would really clear up a lot of confusion." Cathy laughed. "And we probably should drop

the breaking-and-entering charge if this guy is in fact
a friend of yours."

"Ohmigod." Leigh slapped her hand against her forehead. "Stupid, stupid, stupid." She sighed, trying to
figure out how she was going to fix this one.

Beep!

To her complete shock the next message was from
her father.

"Leigh, honey. Are you home?" he asked, suspi-
cious that she was just screening her calls. "Well, this
is Douglas, your father...."

Leigh shook her head—like she wouldn't recognize
her father's voice.

"Anyway, sweetheart, I just wanted you to know that
I just got off the phone with DeShawn Carter."

"You've got to be kidding me." She blinked. "He's
going through my father now?"

"Now, Cupcake, I'm not trying to get up in y'all's
business, but I got to tell you whatever this boy has
done, I got a feeling that he's real sorry."

"Unbelievable," she mumbled under her breath,
as she stormed toward the adjoining bathroom in the
master bedroom. "First Ariel and now my own parents."

But as much as DeShawn's tactics disgusted Leigh,
they were beginning to work. Maybe she was being too
hard. Maybe she was asking for too much from a man
in his position. Groupies, gold diggers and just down-
and-out hos were always a problem for *any* woman
dating or married to a pro athlete. Ariel was right.
She'd been warned countless times by her family and
friends that this was just simply the life of being with

a celebrity. The only question was whether she could deal with it.

No.

She stepped into the shower and lowered her head so that she felt the full force of the hot-water spray. There was a time when DeShawn, at least, put up an effort to convince her that he wasn't like other pro athletes. That he *could* resist temptation. Was it ever true, or had she merely wanted to believe the lie?

While her troubling thoughts circled inside her head, another image began to penetrate the chaos: a tall, milk-chocolate brother who had taken away her troubles with a simple smile. Never mind all the other stuff he did. She closed her eyes while she soaped her body, which only brought more erotic memories to the forefront. He was the only other guy she had slept with in five years—and quite frankly she couldn't have made a better selection. She couldn't have dreamed up a more handsome, virile man if she tried.

Leigh didn't crash the party looking for a one-night stand, but when the chance presented itself, she threw caution to the wind—and even now she wasn't sorry about it. How could she be?

She remembered how strong and large her mystery lover's hands were when they roamed up and down her body. Plus, how could she ever forget how muscular his chest and arms were? The man must have been performing bench presses and ab crunches in his sleep. He was as hard as a brick wall—*everywhere*. And he personified the term "hung like a horse."

Leigh felt a flush of heat recalling vivid memories of her one-night stand. Where on earth had she found the courage to do the things she did with him? Lord knew she had never been so brazen and uninhibited with De-Shawn or the others before DeShawn—that she'd slept with.

That night was different.

She was different.

Her soapy fingers squeezed and pinched her breasts. Relishing the twinge of pain, Leigh's head dropped back while her jaw sagged. With barely any effort, her thin, delicate hands had transformed into the strong, masculine ones that had haunted her last night. Then, as now, her fingers slowly fell away from her breasts and descended over her flat belly before dipping through the soft curls shielding her sex. Parting her legs, she discovered her clit was swollen and pulsing. It was no surprise that it throbbed in time with her hammering heartbeat. When the pads of her wet fingers slid over the tip, it was lubricated from her body's dripping honey. But she knew just where to stroke.

"Mmm." Her head fell back even farther and her mouth formed a complete circle.

"You want to come for me, Baby Girl?" she remembered as she masturbated.

Stroke.

"Yes!"

Stroke.

"What? I can't hear you, Baby Girl."

"Yes! Yes!"

Stroke. Stroke.

"Give Daddy all this good candy."

Stroke.

"Oh—oh." Leigh's imploded as a silent scream dangled from her open mouth. Seconds later, every limb on her body started quivering. Her hands dropped away from her firm thighs in order for her to brace her weight against the tiled shower stall. It took another minute for her to realize that the water had turned ice-cold.

Shutting off the shower spray, Leigh quickly splashed on some baby oil and grabbed a towel. When she walked into her bedroom, she was stunned by the fact that there was a trail of rose petals. "What in the…?" She finished wrapping the towel around herself, and then followed the trail.

In the short time that she was in the shower, her living room had been transformed with what looked like hundreds of flickering candles. In the center of the room, on bended knee was DeShawn Carter in a three-piece suit.

"Hello, Leigh." He puffed out his chest and swallowed nervously.

She walked up to him, shaking her head. "DeShawn, what are you doing here?"

"I came to do what I should've done a long time ago." He reached into his jacket pocket and took out a Harry Winston jewelry box.

She gasped as her knees buckled.

DeShawn's smile grew more confident at her reaction. "Leigh, this past week has been hell for me. I don't like it when we fight…and I know that we usually fight because I've done something stupid. But, sweetheart, you have to know that you mean the world to me. I know beyond a shadow of a doubt that you are the woman that I want to share the rest of my life with. And I think, deep down, you feel the same way."

Leigh's heart started skipping beats as tears pooled in her eyes.

"So, I'm asking you, Leigh Imani Matthews, will you marry me?"

Chapter 7

Two weeks later...

"You're getting married?" Jeremy deadpanned as he stared across the dinner table at The Palm. It was his brother's favorite get-together in West Hollywood, mainly because the restaurant served the best steaks. But now that Xavier had cheerily dropped this bomb on them, Jeremy lost his appetite.

"Congratulations," Eamon said, and then reached over and pounded Xavier hard on the back. "Glad to see you taking the plunge."

"Plunge," Quentin scoffed. "How appropriate."

Xavier gave his cousin and best friend a warning look. "Don't start."

"What'd I do?" He tried to give his famous puppy-dog expression, but there was just too much anger stiffening his jaw. "I'm simply pointing out what an appropriate term 'taking the plunge' is for this momentous occasion. I don't see you trying to leap frog down Eamon's throat—or is that since you both have lost the good sense God gave you, you're trying to double-team the sane people at the table now?"

Jeremy tossed his hands up. "Please don't drag me into this."

"Hell, I'm not quite sure that I know what *this* is," Xavier said, as his facial expression twisted.

"That makes two of us," Eamon added, looking equally confused.

"There. I just proved my point," Q insisted. "You two are on the same crazy wavelength or something. You've always been competitive with each other. Admit it. Eamon married a woman that tried to put us in the poorhouse, and now you want to marry the chick who tried to put us all behind bars. Crazy. And you guys are always trying to tell me that I need a shrink."

"You *do* need a shrink," the King brothers said in unison.

"Then all of y'all can go to hell."

Xavier tried to squash the conflict. "All right. Calm down and take a deep breath."

Q ignored him. "Let me ask you, if Eamon jumped off a building, would you do it, too?"

Jeremy sighed. He knew better than to jump into this melee. Quentin and Xavier were best friends, but when they got into it, they could be at it for hours. For a moment, he turned his attention away from the table and thought he caught a glimpse of a face he recognized. *Baby Girl?*

He leaned over the table to try and get another look.

"Yo, dude," Quentin stopped arguing long enough

to bring it to Jeremy's attention that he was damn near leaning into his lap.

"Oh. I'm sorry. I thought I saw someone I recognized."

Q blinked. "Are you seeing people who aren't there?" He leaned in closer. "Do they talk to you, too?"

"What?" Jeremy's expression twisted as he stared at his cousin.

As if realizing his mistake, Quentin straightened, and then tried to brush aside the conversation. "N-nothing. Forget it."

Jeremy ignored his cousin's comment, and took one more sweeping glance around the restaurant. *She wasn't there.* He leaned back in his chair and tried to brush off his disappointment. That had been the second time today that he thought he'd seen his Baby Girl—and about the hundredth time in the last two weeks.

Plus, he didn't want to mention the times that he'd practiced in the mirror what he would say if in fact their paths did cross again. The first part was something like, "Hey, thanks for the police record." Never mind that Cathy and George Atwater had since dropped the charges without explanation, but it didn't change the fact that Los Angeles County now and forever had him photographed and fingerprinted.

The second part of his rehearsed conversation had something to do with asking for her name. One thing that might surprise a lot of women about him was that, despite his long list of naked activities with the opposite sex, he knew the name of every woman he'd ever slept with.

The irony was that the one woman whose name he didn't know was the one that he most wanted to see again. *Don't let it be said that God didn't have a sense of humor.*

Xavier pushed back from his steak and stared his cousin down. "Look, Q. I know that this may be hard for you, but just because I'm getting married it doesn't mean that anything is going to change between us. We're always going to be best buds."

"Yeah, yeah, yeah. You say that now, but wait until after the wedding vows. People always change after the 'I do's."

"You didn't change."

Quentin frowned. "You can hardly call my six-month trip down that crazy rabbit hole a marriage. I was crazy—she was definitely crazy—and the whole thing lasted a hundred and seventy-nine days longer than it should have."

"Well it's different when you do it for love instead of money."

Quentin set down his empty glass, leaned back and gave Xavier a small round of applause. "Wow. That must have set some type of record. What did that take—three minutes before you brought that little tidbit up again? Yes, I married to recoup my inheritance. Good thing too because that temporary lapse of judgment cost me the only woman I'll probably ever love. But I seem to recall that my first investment with that blood money provided capital for a few ungrateful cousins sitting around this table."

Jeremy held up a hand. "I'm grateful."

"Well, apparently not this jackass," he thundered at Xavier.

"Whoa. Whoa," Xavier said, getting testy himself. "Let's take this down a notch before your mouth writes a check your ass can't cash up in here." He stared pointedly at Q. "Now, I know that you're still working out whatever the hell you're working out, but your issue is with *Sterling*—not us. And, frankly, I think it's past time you handled that situation. Call him, write him or send him a damn smoke signal—but do something if we're going to continue being boys."

Xavier turned his attention to his baby brother. "I know that this may be coming as a total surprise to you but—"

"Not to me." Quentin laughed as he signaled their waiter to bring him another whiskey sour. "I saw this coming the first time you cock-blocked me at Cheryl's job interview."

"What?" Xavier twisted up his face. "I did no such thing."

"Oh, now you have amnesia?" Q challenged. "A'ight. Go ahead on. I remember what happened that day. What about you, Jeremy?"

"Sorry, bro, but I'm gonna have to go with cuz on this one. There was an awful lot of cock-blocking going on." He tossed up his hands. "Not that I blame you. I still have an image of Cheryl in those panted-on jeans emblazoned in my mind, as well."

"Hey, yo!" Xavier slammed his fist down on the white-linen table. "Cut it out. That's my future wife you're talking about. So get those painted-on jeans out of your heads."

Eamon cracked up. "Damn, bro. You're going to pop a blood vessel. Maybe you need to calm down and take a deep breath."

Xavier tried, but the devout bachelors at the table had officially ruined the mood. "Look, I don't ask much from either one of you, but I do know that I've been a faithful friend *and* brother. So it pisses me off that when I come here to share one of the most important decisions of my life, that I've found someone who truly makes me happy, you two selfish bastards can only think about how it affects you."

Jeremy and Quentin glanced at each other and then dropped their heads.

"Technically," Jeremy piped up, "I never said that I wasn't happy for you. Look, man, if you love her and you're happy, then hell yeah I'm happy for you. Of course, I'm not an asshole. You're my brother, and I'll always want what's best for you." He looked over at Eamon. "You too, for that matter."

Eamon and Xavier flashed him identical smiles. "Thanks, bro."

"Don't mention it." Jeremy reached for his beer. "Soooo I say that we officially need to make a toast to celebrate the occasion."

"Hear, hear," Eamon and Xavier chimed and then tapped their bottlenecks together. The three Kings then turned their attention to their cousin.

"You know, I fall under that technicality, as well. I'm just…" Q drew in a deep breath. "I have a problem with change. If this knucklehead here…" he said, tilting his head toward Jeremy, "…bails on me, I'm going to have to wrangle up some new cousins from some place."

Xavier set his bottle down and stood up from the table. "Come here." He opened up his arms.

"What?"

"C'mon," he coaxed. "Let's hug this out."

Quentin's bottom lip quivered as he stood up from

his chair. "That's all a brother wanted, a hug." He opened his arms as well and the cousins came together.

"Aww…" Jeremy tossed his napkin down and then stood up from the table and threw his arms around both of them.

Quentin peeked over Xavier's shoulder at Eamon.

"You've got to be kidding me," Eamon said.

"You don't feel the love?" Q asked.

Jeremy glanced back with a cocky smile. "C'mon, man. We're all family."

Exhaling a long sigh as he glanced around the crowded restaurant to see that his crazy *family* was indeed the center of attention, Eamon reluctantly got out of his chair and wrapped his arms around all of them. After all, the sooner he did, the quicker the little bonding episode would end.

"Ahem," a throat cleared.

One by one, the men dropped their arms and went about pumping out their chests to reestablish their image of masculinity.

When Jeremy turned to see who had interrupted their family moment, his face exploded into a huge grin. "Well, I'll be damned. Look who's here. Roy, my man. How the hell are you?" He now threw his arms around his boyhood friend.

"I'm good. I'm good." He nodded at Eamon and Xavier. "I see you guys are still thick as thieves."

"You know it," Jeremy said, standing back so that he could take another look at Roy. "I just can't believe it. It's been years."

"Well, it's not like we haven't invested a healthy sum in long-distance phone calls. What are you doing here?" he asked Jeremy.

"The same reason everyone else is here. I came to get something to eat." He laughed.

"C'mon. You know what I mean. Wait." He looked around and then grabbed a chair from the next table and crammed it next to Jeremy's.

"Join us. Have a seat."

"For a few minutes. I'm having a business dinner, but I don't see them just yet."

"Cool, cool. You can just hang out with us until they get here," Jeremy said, excited.

His brothers and Quentin had sat down by then.

"Oh, so does this mean that you're being traded to the L.A. Razors, Roy?"

"It looks that way, but don't tell anyone just yet. We haven't made the official announcement."

"Cool. Oh, I don't believe that you've met my cousin here, Quentin Hinton."

"Hinton?" Roy repeated. "As in your rich cousin you used to brag about?"

Quentin smirked. "Guilty as charged."

Jeremy laughed. "I did brag about that."

"Yeah, like that changed the fact that you were eating fried bologna sandwiches and drinking purple Kool-Aid like the rest of our broke butts."

Jeremy nodded. The King family didn't have much growing up in their small house in Atlanta, but they had plenty of love. "But you were like the king of the neighborhood because your pop built a tree house in your backyard."

"Yeah, perfect for kids that ran away from home with a boxful of puppies."

The table erupted with laughter.

Quentin's brows crashed together as he tried to keep up with the conversation. "Do what?"

"Oh, you didn't tell your cuz about that?"

Jeremy propped his elbow up on the table while his entire body trembled with laughter.

"It was a long time ago," Eamon started to fill Q in on the story.

"Yeah," Xavier agreed, shaking his head. "I tell you one thing, it certainly wasn't funny at the time."

"What wasn't funny?" Q grew anxious, waiting on the story.

"You want to tell it?" Xavier prompted Jeremy.

Jeremy struggled to wipe the grin off his face. "Aah... I think I was six years old and I found this box of puppies that someone had abandoned in the woods."

"So genius here decided to bring all of them home," Eamon cut in.

Xavier bobbed his head. "Only our dad said that we couldn't afford to keep them and that we would have to take them to the pound."

"Only I didn't like the idea of them going to the pound, so I ran away with the whole box of puppies and was gone for, like, two days." Jeremy continued shaking his head.

"It sent the whole family into an uproar. We were all over the news and everything."

Q frowned, thinking back. "Yeah, I think I do remember something like that happening. My mom was really upset and was convinced that Atlanta had another serial killer, snatching up little boys."

Roy jumped into the story. "Only, Jeremy and his puppies were hiding out in my tree house."

"Yeah, and you squealed me out," Jeremy reminded him.

"No, I didn't," Roy said, defensively. "My mother got a little curious about all the peanut-butter-and jelly sandwiches I kept making and sneaking off with and taking to the backyard. You know I would never drop dime on a friend—let alone a blood brother."

"Y'all are blood brothers?" Q asked.

The men held up their hands and showed tiny identical scars across the center of their wrists.

"Blood brothers for life," they said together and then looked at each other.

"Oh, there goes my agent." He stood up.

Jeremy was disappointed to cut their reunion short. "Well, we're going to have to get together and play catch up."

"Most definitely." They smacked palms and then gave each other a one-shoulder hug. "Oh, as a matter of fact, you should come to my engagement party."

Jeremy's eyes rounded. "Do what? *You're* engaged?"

"And the epidemic continues," Quentin mumbled, and then received a quick jab from Xavier's sharp elbow. "Oow."

"What woman did you knock over the head and convince to put up with your Milk-Bone-addicted ways?" Jeremy asked.

"Aah, man. You ain't never lied. I had to bust out the ring or lose the best thing that ever happened to me."

"Meet her on the road?" Jeremy asked, knowing Roy's propensity for groupies.

"Nah, nah, man. This is my good girl. Salt of the earth, the kind you want to start producing a string of Mini-Mes to continue the family name."

"Aah, don't tell me it's that one chick you been seeing off and on for, like, forever."

Roy dipped his head and blushed a bit. "The one and only."

"Aah, snap. So you're really going to make this legit and become a one-woman man?"

"Whoa, now. I didn't say all that. A playa is always gonna have a little dirt on him. You just have to wipe your feet off before you walk through the family door."

Jeremy's and his brother's smiles shaved off a few inches.

He elbowed Jeremy. "You feel me?"

"Yeah, yeah. I hear you."

"Well, I better go. I'll catch up with you later." Roy turned to leave but then stopped. "Wait. Tell you what. I'm going to make sure that I shoot you an invitation to the engagement party. I'd love for the future Mrs. Roy DeShawn Carter to finally meet my best friend."

Jeremy's smile bounced back. "I certainly can't wait to meet this woman."

Chapter 8

Sheree Matthews tossed up her hands. "Oh my God, Leigh. Would it kill you to smile? How am I'm going to be able to picture how you'll look coming down the aisle if your bottom lip is constantly dragging on the floor?"

"I'm sorry, Momma," Leigh whined. "It's just that we've been at this for weeks. I must've tried on a thousand gowns."

"And you haven't liked any of them," her mother reminded her. "I don't know why you just don't wear my wedding dress," she said, pressing a hand against her chest. "After all, that's supposed to be the tradition."

"No offense, Mom, but your dress is kind of dated."

"Yeah," Ariel said, closing a copy of *Bride* magazine. "Those shoulder pads alone would make her look like the bride of Frankenstein."

"Ariel," Leigh hissed, but it was already too late to remind her best friend to think before she spoke.

However, her mother just thrust out her chin. "That was *the look* at the time. Besides, the '80s are back in style."

The two friends shared a look.

"Fine." Her mother's hands flew back into the air. "I'll just save it for my grandbaby. I'm sure she'll have more appreciation for a timeless classic."

Leigh scoffed. "Grandbaby? You're getting ahead of yourself, aren't you? Who said anything about children?"

"First comes love, then comes marriage, then comes my grandbabies in the baby carriages," her mother said confidently. "DeShawn has already told me that he wants five—at minimum."

Leigh's stomach flopped. "DeShawn said what?"

"You heard me—five." She held up her hand in case Leigh needed a visual aid. "And he promised me that you two would get started on the first one as soon as possible."

"Humph. I like his nerve." Her frown deepened as she settled her hands on her hips. "We haven't even talked about children."

Sheree waved off her daughter. "Chile, get your hands off your imagination and go take that hideous dress off." She sauntered over to the upholstered chair next to Ariel where her flute of champagne waited on a mirrored coffee table. "Looks like we're going to be here all day."

"Mmm." Ariel shook her head while she planted her nose back into the magazine.

Leigh felt dismissed. "Wait a minute. I'm serious.

Is anyone at all interested in whether I want to spit out *five* kids?"

Her mother sighed. "Not particularly."

"Gee, thanks, Mom."

Sheree rolled her eyes. "Leigh, baby. I already know that you want to do a whole laundry list of things, and I'm sure at the top of the list is 'take over the world' in all caps and bold letters. But now we're talking about marriage, and with marriage come certain duties. And at the top of that list should be, 'have babies.'"

Ariel looked up from her magazines. "You can't be serious."

"I'm dead serious," Sheree said. "Look, you can call me old-fashioned—"

"Old-fashioned," Leigh and Ariel chorused together.

"But children are a blessing…" She stared Leigh up and down, adding, "…on most days. All this other stuff out here is a distraction. No one on their deathbed ever wished that they could've spent more time at the office or broken through one more glass ceiling. In the end, it's going to be *family*—and the time you did or didn't spend with them. Hey, I used to want to be superwoman. I could bring home the bacon and fry it up in a pan. It was the late seventies—and we were kicking butt and taking names. I thought I could wait and do the whole family thing on my timetable. Then I got those cysts on my ovaries and the doctor told me if I was going to have children, I needed to start having them right away. I made a decision, got off the pills and had you. A few months after that, I had to have a hysterectomy—no more children. There're not too many days that I don't think about those eight years that I made your father wait, and wonder if you might not have had an older brother or sister. You can't tell me that it wouldn't have been nice to have siblings."

Leigh dropped her gaze. She remembered all too well wishing that she had just that.

"Family! It's the most important thing. It's what endures. As a race, it was once taken from us—our family—our names—our birthright. Now—" she shook her head "—it's all about *self*—not family. That's why I've never missed one of your dance recitals, Leigh, or any of your track meets. I value being a good mother and a wife above everything else. I'm not saying that you can't have a career, but everything has its place."

Leigh swallowed her attitude.

Ariel rolled her eyes. "Well, shut my mouth. I didn't know that the Stepford wives' club was that much fun. I guess I better run out and nab me a husband, too."

Surprisingly, Sheree cracked up at the glib comment. "Girl, go on now. You are a fool."

Ariel laughed off Sheree's sermon.

"I didn't say that I didn't want children," Leigh said. "I just don't know about having a tribe…or having them right now." Her stomach flopped. Could she handle a house full of little DeShawns? And with him on the road so much, could she handle being essentially a single mother? "I'd better take this dress off. It's starting to make me itch." She turned and rushed back into the fitting room. When she was safely behind the closed dressing-room door, she bent at the waist and tried to chug in some much-needed air. She glanced up at the mirror. "God, Leigh. Do you know what you're doing?"

Knock. Knock.

"Leigh?" Ariel inquired softly. "Do you need any help?"

She pulled herself up and then pinched her cheeks to put some color back into them. "I, uh…"

"Open the door," Ariel ordered.

Rolling her eyes, Leigh did as her best friend asked, and moved aside so that Ariel could enter the small space.

Ariel took one look at her and was instantly concerned. "Are you all right? You look pale."

"Yeah. Of course. I'm fine." Her friend stared her down. "It's just…everything is coming at me like a speeding locomotive, you know?"

"You're not having second thoughts, are you?"

"No… Well, just a few."

Ariel smiled. "That's okay. It's normal."

"How do you know?"

"Are you kidding? How many girlfriends of ours have gotten married? How many of them almost ran screaming from the church before the ceremony? Hell, Maxine Jones hyperventilated the whole way down the aisle and then burst into tears after she said 'I do.' Now she's been happily married for six years with three kids."

"Yeah." Leigh nodded. "You're right."

"Of course I'm right." She blew on her nails and then buffed them on her chest. "They don't call me Ms. Know-It-All for nothing."

Leigh drew in a deep breath and then felt her nerves settle down a little.

"You know what? I know what will cheer you up," she lowered her voice to a conspiratorial whisper. "How about tonight we ditch the old lady and start planning the bachelorette party?"

"What?"

"Yeah. C'mon. As your maid of honor, I'm in charge of making sure that your last night in singlehood is one that you'll never forget."

"Oh, I don't know. I just want to go home and dive into bed and just sleep for a couple of weeks. I think I'm coming down with something."

"Uh-uh-uh. I don't want to hear it. I'm taking you out, and we're going to check out some good spots for the bachelorette party."

"Strip clubs? You want to spend the evening checking out strip clubs?"

"C'mon. Clearly you're not into dress, cake and venue shopping, so let's do the fun stuff tonight. Find the hot strippers." She started shaking her booty. "You know you wanna." She cheesed all up in Leigh's face and started bumping her hips against hers.

Leigh couldn't withhold her smile any longer. "All right. All right. We can go."

"Woohoo! Now let's hurry up and get you out of that dress."

Chapter 9

"*Booty, booty, booty, booty, rockin' everywhere, rockin' everywhere.*"

Quentin's head bobbed to the infectious beat, which happened to be the same rhythm that Caramel Swirl twirled her hips to as she slid her oil-slicked body down the stripper pole and tossed him a wink. "Damn, girl. You make me want to buy your momma a house."

"My daddy might have something to say about that." Caramel smiled and then edged closer so that he tucked two Benjamins into her tiny thong strings.

"That's all right. He can stay there too, for his fifty-percent genetic share." He winked. "So what are you doing later?"

"Spending time with you?"

"You read my mind." He leaned over and elbowed Jeremy. "Care to join us?"

"Uh, what?" Jeremy lifted his head from the doodling he was doing on the club's cocktail napkin. "What did you say?"

Quentin frowned. "All these luscious bodies bouncing in your face... What the hell are you doing?" He glanced down at the napkin and saw a woman's face sketched in remarkable detail. Recognizing that it was the same image his cousin had been sketching on practically every damn thing in the office over the past few weeks, he huffed out a long breath. "You have got to be kidding me."

"Q—"

"What's this? Are you obsessing over this girl?"

"What? No," Jeremy said, defensively. "I'm just... Well, you know, just passing the time."

"Are you kidding me?" He plopped back down in his chair and spread out his arms. "Look around you. You're a King on a throne and look at all the toys at your disposal."

When Jeremy sighed, Q hopped up from his chair and wrapped his arm around his cousin and tried to give him the big-picture perspective.

"What's your flavor, cuz? Dark chocolate, milk chocolate, maple sugar, butterscotch or even vanilla? There's just no way with all these flavors surrounding you. You should have a face so long, it's about to hit the floor."

Jeremy shook his head. "Look, cuz. I really appreciate what you're trying to do, really. But you can pump the brakes. It's not what you think. It's just...mysteries intrigue me." He tossed his napkin back onto the table. "And so far, she's the biggest mystery I've ever come across."

Q grabbed the napkin and took another look. "All right. She's cute, I guess."

"Ah, but Baby Girl was also stacked."

"Yeah?" Quentin perked up but then watched as that same tired look glazed his cousin's eyes. "Look, man. You know there's a good chance that your brick house was just some bored housewife who needed to get her rocks off, you know what I mean? It happens sometimes. Don't get your ego all caught up. Just be glad that she didn't leave any money on the nightstand. *That* would've been humiliating. Trust me. I've been there."

Jeremy cocked his head. "Really? I thought you loved your life when you had a fleet of sugar mommas trying to take care of you."

Quentin thought back. "Oh, yeah. That *was* really nice. Never mind. Scratch what I said. Order another drink and then let's set out finding you a chick who can pass for a look-alike for your mysterious Baby Girl. Role-playing can be fun too."

Jeremy thought that he could live a thousand years and never really understand his cousin or his demons, and he certainly had a number of those.

"Heeeey, Jeremy," a string of Dolls cooed as they sashayed their way toward the champagne room.

"Evening, ladies."

"What? Y'all don't see nobody else?" Quentin complained.

"Heeeey, Q," they chorused, flashing him the same blinding white smiles.

"That's better." Q puffed out his chest. "I don't want to have to start docking nobody's pay around here. You girls need to work on your hospitality skills."

"You're not a customer," Jeremy pointed out.

Quentin turned toward him, frowning. "Would it hurt you to have my back?"

"Sorry." Jeremy grabbed his glass and then tossed back his brandy. "So, um. Mind if I ask just how long you're planning to stay out here?"

Quentin's brows leaped. "Sick of me already?"

"Nah, nah, nah. I didn't say that."

"But you were thinking it?"

Jeremy dropped his head and made a rare prayer for patience. "Is this how it's always going to be, man? You, always trying to bait me into an argument?"

His cousin shrugged. "Maybe. I always thought that it was our thing."

"No. It's *your* thing…especially when someone asks a question you don't like."

"You'd think people would take the hint and just stop asking questions."

"Hey, man. It's only because we care." The cousins' eyes locked. "Whatever it is, you can't keep running."

For the first time in a long while, Quentin didn't have a snappy reply. Instead, his face turned really somber. "Have you ever done something that you wished you hadn't—something that you can never take back?"

"Sure. Everyone has—at some point or another." Jeremy cocked his head as he studied his cousin. *What did you do?*

Quentin shuffled around on his chair, but for some reason he couldn't get his mouth to work. Then the moment was gone, and the confession, that was just on the tip of his tongue, vanished.

"Well, what do you know?" Quentin picked up his glass and drained the rest of his whiskey sour in one gulp. "I think there is a hole in this glass." With that, he stood and then made his way to the bar.

Jeremy watched him go, regretting the moment that was lost just seconds ago. He still couldn't help but wonder, *What did you do?*

However, he was pulled from his thoughts when his BlackBerry vibrated in his pocket. *Duty calls.* He leaned over and scooped out his phone. Seeing the name on the caller-ID screen, he smiled and answered. "Eh, yo, man, what's up?"

Roy laughed. "Damn, man. You got it crunk up in there, ain't you?"

"We got to make it do what it do." Jeremy laughed, climbing out of his seat and strolling off toward the main floor and the club's office. "So what can I do for you?"

"Well, man, you now know what time it is. I'm gonna need you to do a couple of favors since pretty soon I'ma be putting a ring on my lady."

"Damn, man. I'm still trying to wrap my brain around that one." Jeremy shook his head as he pushed through the doors, leading toward the back. "Married. That means that you'll be a grown-up."

"You're telling me?" Roy's laughed. "But I have to do it, man. Sometimes, one has to piss or get off the pot—and I had a feeling my shawty was about to bolt."

"I don't think I've heard anyone use that term to describe their relationship before," Jeremy said, strolling into his office and then launching himself onto the black leather chair. "So if I understand you right, you're getting married to *tie* her down."

"Got to. Shawty is waaay too fine to be wandering the streets alone. I let that go and another brother would scoop her up before the next sunset. Plus, she got class and a damn good head on her shoulders. But more importantly, she's loyal."

"Well, I guess one of you has to be," Jeremy jabbed.

"Right," DeShawn agreed. "Anyway, man. I got to thinking after I saw you and your brothers the other day."

"I knew I smelled something burning."

"Ha. Ha. But I want us to be serious for a minute, bruh."

"All right."

"Like I said, I was thinking. You know me and you have been through a lot over the years. We've damn near known each other since we were in diapers. You mean a lot to me, man."

"Damn. Are you about to propose to me, too?"

Roy chuckled. "Nah, but I do want you to be my best man."

Jeremy's eyes rounded. "Really?"

"Yeah. Like I was *trying* to say, you're like the brother that I never had. I want you to be standing next to me when I take this big leap."

Touched, Jeremy nodded. "I'd love to stand up there with you man. Count me in."

Leigh twisted up her face when Ariel pulled her silver Mercedes into the parking lot of The Dollhouse. "What are we doing here? I thought we were going to an all-*male* strip joint. This is a *gentlemen's* club."

"I know what it is. I can read," Ariel said, shutting off the engine. "We have plenty of time for that later. I just want us to pop in here real quick."

"Why?" Leigh folded up her arms. "Is there something that you want to tell me? No judgment."

Ariel jabbed a fist up against her hip. "Gurl, stop frontin'. You know it's strictly dickly with me."

Leigh tossed up her hands. "I didn't know. You've been complaining about how bad the dating the scene is. I thought for a second that you were switching teams."

"Well, get that nonsense out of your head. There's a big buzz with some of the fellas in my office about how this place throws the best bachelor parties in town."

"And? Are you trying to hook me up or DeShawn?"

"Chile, please. I don't want to even think about the shenanigans that are gonna be going on at that man's party—and I suggest you don't, either. Nah. We came here for you."

"You're still losing me."

Ariel sighed and then spoke to Leigh as if she was a toddler. "If this place can throw great bachelor parties, then they can throw a bachelorette party. The premise is the same. To refuse us is like sex discrimination."

"And you would just love to sue their pants off for that," Leigh finally concluded.

"Well, I didn't get a law degree just so that I can dust it off on weekends. C'mon." Ariel turned and climbed out of her car.

Shaking her head, Leigh turned and followed suit. "How long do we have to stay here?" she whined, marching up behind her friend. She really was looking forward to drooling over some naked, muscled *men* tonight—for her party.

"Humph, humph, humph." One dude headed toward the front door damn near giving himself whiplash when

Ariel and Leigh walked by. "Please say you two are dancing tonight. I cashed my paycheck today and it's burning a hole in my pocket."

Ariel turned with her hand on her hip. "Paycheck? Bruh, where's your boss at? Tell *him* to holla at me." She swiveled her head and then switched her hips past the bouncer at the door.

"You're a hot mess," Leigh said, pulling up the rear. "What's wrong with a dude pulling a paycheck?"

"Girl, please. That knock-kneed-beer-belly-need-to-get-his-grill-fixed brotha better leave me alone. Shoot, a brother can't get a dime piece on credit. No more dates at Taco Bell, sitting on twelve-inch rims in a hatchback. From here on out, if a brother wants to be with me, he's got to bring what I'm bringing to the table. Period."

"All right, then, girl. Do you."

"Damn skippy."

They finished their short stroll through the lobby and when they hit the main floor, both of their mouths nearly hit the floor.

"Oh, my," Leigh said as she glanced around the place. She took in the strobe lights, falling glitter and the most incredibly stacked bodies writhing on gold stripper poles. "This place is like a man's fantasy world."

"Shawty said l-l-lick like a lollipop / She said l-l-lick a lollipop."

There was one chick on a stage with silver airplane propellers on her breasts. A customer stuffed hundred-dollar bills down the front of her thong while leaning close enough to her twirling blades to cool off.

"I think we hit the jackpot," Ariel said before moving farther inside the club.

Leigh remained fascinated by everything. It was like they had crashed some secret club and she was taking notes on everything she saw. "So who do we talk to about planning the party?" she shouted over Li'l Wayne's infectious beat.

"I'm not sure." Ariel turned and nearly collided with a waitress in a sheer nude outfit. "Oops. Sorry."

"It's all right, sweetheart," the woman said, flashing a genuine smile. "I can keep this tray up during a 7.0 Richter-scale earthquake."

The women laughed.

"Wait. Maybe you can help us," Leigh said. "Who do we talk to about booking a bachelorette party?"

"Oh, we don't do bachelorette parties," she said apologetically. "Wish that we did. I wouldn't mind a little change in scenery from time to time."

"And why not?" Ariel challenged.

"Well, because we don't employ male strippers, honey." The waitress thought about it. "But I guess if a lesbian couple wanted a party—"

"Who's the boss around here?" Ariel demanded. She was already putting on her lawyer hat.

"Well, there's one of them sitting over there. His name is Quentin Hinton. Good luck—and watch out for the dimples. They have a way of seducing you into bed."

"Thanks for the warning," Ariel said, straightening her shoulders and then marching off to war.

Leigh rolled her eyes and rushed after her. "Ariel, this is not a big deal. We can just go to the clubs that—"

"Excuse me." Ariel tapped the tall gentleman at the bar on the shoulder. "Are you Mr. Hinton?"

The man turned around smiling. "That all depends on who's asking."

That waitress wasn't kidding about those damn dimples. They winked at Ariel and suddenly she was standing as still as a statue.

"Can I help you with something?"

Leigh looked at her girl, and then became concerned. "Ariel?" She elbowed her and jarred her out of whatever system malfunction she was experiencing.

"Um, yeah. I wanted to book a bachelorette party," Ariel said, forcing resolve back into her voice.

"Aw, getting married. My condolences." He held up his glass in a lone toast.

"I take it you don't believe in marriage," Leigh said.

Hinton shifted his gaze from Ariel over to Leigh and his brows climbed an added notch. "As a matter of fact...I don't." He cocked his head. "Hey, don't I know you?" His eyes narrowed as they roamed over every inch of her body. "Face is familiar, but I'm *certain* that I've never been acquainted with that body. I'd remember."

Leigh smirked. "We've never met."

"No?" he asked, dubious.

"I'm positive."

"Do you want to remedy that?"

Ariel coughed to clear her throat.

"The three of us?" he amended.

Another woman, clearly one of the dancers, eased up behind him and slid her arm around his shoulder possessively.

"Make that four," he amended again.

Both Leigh and Ariel stared at the handsome gigolo, stunned at the offer.

"Don't worry, there's plenty of me to go around," he promised.

"I think we'll pass." Leigh grabbed Ariel's arm. "Let's go."

Ariel refused to budge.

"Now, I know that you're not actually considering taking this dude up on his offer."

Ariel's face flushed with embarrassment, but then she seemed to remember herself. "The party. We want a bachelorette party," she demanded.

"Well, that might entail a lot more women than I'm used to, but I guess that I could give it a try. I hear there's this little blue pill on the market."

Leigh laughed. She was actually starting to find him amusing. "We're not trying to hire you, silly. We're trying to hire your club. Apparently, word around town is that you're the best."

"I happen to think so."

"The *club* is the best."

"Oh, yeah. Well, that, too." He set his drink down on the bar. "Emilio, hit it again," he said to the bartender and then returned his attention to them. "Ladies, I would love to help you out, because that's the kind of guy I am. I love putting smiles on women's faces. But The Dollhouse simply doesn't do bachelorette parties."

"And is there any reason why your *business* establishment actively practices discrimination?"

Mr. Hinton groaned. "Lawyer?"

Ariel smiled. "How did you guess?"

"The shark teeth gave you away." He smiled to soften the insult and it worked.

Ariel just smiled back.

"I tell you ladies what," Quentin said. "I'm going to help you out."

"Oh?" Ariel crossed her arms.

"Yeah. And it's not because of the threat of a lawsuit. That happens from time to time around here. Nah, I'm going to do this because I think I like you two, despite your reluctance to join me and Caramel Swirl here in a night of sexual bliss. So I'm going to introduce you to my close cousin and business partner." Hinton turned toward the beautiful dancer. "Pardon me, sweetheart. I'll be back in a jiffy." He winked and then turned his attention back to Ariel and Leigh. "Ladies, follow me."

Jeremy cut the security cameras on by remote in his office as he continued his conversation with his best friend. "You know, as your best man that puts me in charge of the bachelor party, right?"

"You don't say?" Roy laughed. "Why, that thought never occurred to me."

"Uh-huh. You cheap bastard. You just want a free party."

"Free or not. You're going to do it up, right?"

"You can count on your boy," Jeremy said just as his gaze caught a familiar image on the screen. *Is that...?* He hopped up from the couch and used the remote again to zoom in. Despite experiencing so many false alarms over the past month, his heart still leaped to the center of his chest at the possibility of having found his Baby Girl.

It's her.

"I was thinking that we could do a whole Comic-Con theme," Roy said on the other line. "We can get The Dollhouse Dolls to dress up as—"

"Um, Roy. Let me call you back. Something just came up." *Why is she talking to Quentin?*

"Huh? Oh. Okay. Sure, man. Hit me back later when you get a moment."

They're on the move. Where are they going? "Cool. Later." Jeremy disconnected the call, and then raced out of the office. *No. No. No.* The last thing that any brother should ever do is leave their woman alone with his cousin. A pair of panties was just not safe within a three-mile radius of that man. *Hurry. Hurry.*

Jeremy threw his weight into the door leading back to the main floor at the same moment that Quentin was about to push the door from the other side. The result was Q being knocked back on his ass, holding his nose. "Ah, man. I'm sorry about that," he said, though truly he wasn't all that concerned about his cousin at the moment. His attention was completely focused on his Baby Girl.

"Hey."

Eyes wide, she gaped at him. "What are *you* doing here?"

"A little help here," Q said.

"You two know each other?" Ariel asked, swinging her gaze between the two of them.

Quentin pulled his hand away from his face. "Uh, I think I'm bleeding here."

Baby Girl looked about ready to faint. She turned to her friend. "We need to go."

"What? No. We came here to get them to host your bachelorette party."

Jeremy heart dropped. "Bachelorette party? You're getting married?"

Chapter 10

Leigh's brain struggled to process with what felt like an alternate reality. How was it that this man was standing here in front of her—and why was her heart trying to hammer its way out of her chest? "I, uh…" She glanced over at Ariel as if somehow her best friend could help her out of this mess, but how could she when she didn't know the torrid details of the situation?

"You know what? Don't bother," Hinton said, struggling to get back to his feet. "I'll help myself up." He pulled himself up off the floor and then straightened his clothes. "What a selfish ass—"

"How do you two know each other?" Ariel pressed, crossing her arms in her cross-examination mode.

Leigh turned toward Ariel. "Let's talk about it later. Let's just go," she hissed, but her low voice was drowned out by Beyoncé's "Hip-Hop Star."

Ariel cupped her ear and leaned over. "What?"

"Wait," Hinton said, now swinging his own gaze like a pendulum. "Now I know where I've seen your face."

"Ladies," her one-time fling said authoritatively. "You don't have to leave. You came here for a service. Um, I'm sure my cousin and I here—" he slapped Quentin on the back and passed a look at him "—will be able to work something out?"

Hinton blinked and then nodded as if some subtle message had been received. "Uh, absolutely!" He turned toward Ariel and turned up the charm. "I take it that you're the maid of honor in charge of planning the bachelorette party."

Ariel puffed out her chest. "I am."

Hinton's smile widened and his dimples winked. "No ring. Does that mean there's no man in your life?"

Ariel's back loosened as she shook her head.

"Would you like one to be?"

Ariel blushed. "Well…"

Leigh couldn't believe what she was witnessing. This man had effortlessly cast her hard-nosed, take-no-prisoners best friend into some kind of deep trance.

"Ariel?" Leigh stretched a hand in front of her girl's face and waved. She couldn't break the spell.

Hinton moved forward and eased an arm around her waist. "Tell you what, why don't you and me head over to the bar and you can tell me what you envisioned for your girl's party?"

"Oh, okay," Ariel said robotically, and allowed him to pull her away from Leigh's side.

"Ariel," Leigh snapped. "Ariel!" But her girl strolled off, stuck to the side of that charmer as if their bodies had suddenly been superglued together.

"Don't worry," the man whom she had once called Big Daddy said. "My cousin will take good care of her."

"I think that's what I'm afraid of," Leigh said. "If I hadn't seen that, I don't think I would've ever believed it."

"Yeah. Q is quite the ladies' man. When I saw you on the security cameras, I thought that you were seconds from being snared by him, too." His dark gaze roamed over her face. "I can't have that."

Seconds ago, Leigh thought the bass bumping through the club's speakers would shatter her eardrums. Now, staring into his face, her heartbeat took on that thumping sound.

"Why don't we go into my office and talk for a moment?" he offered.

"I don't…" She glanced around in need of a rescue.

"Don't worry. I don't bite—unless requested." He smiled.

Don't do it. Don't do it. Despite the voice in the back of her head shouting as if the words echoed through a megaphone, Leigh nodded. *Wait. Was he casting the same spell on her as that Q guy had just done to Ariel?* Regardless of whether she was aware of what was happening, she still let him wrap his arm around her waist and lead her into his office.

Once there, she was instantly impressed by what could've easily doubled as a bachelor pad. Black leather couches, wet bar, huge plasma screen—a Ping-Pong table and an adjoining bathroom. There was another door. But it was closed and she had a sneaking suspicion that it was, in fact, a bedroom. "Nice office."

He chuckled. "Thanks. I figured if you're going to spend a lot of time at work then you might as well make yourself comfortable." He flashed a smile and then closed the office door behind them. "Would you like to have a seat?"

Leigh glanced at the extremely comfortable-looking sofa. "Thanks. But I think I'll stand."

"Scared?" He *locked* the door. "What happened to the woman I met in Malibu with all that swagger? Don't tell me that you're afraid of little ol' me?" He moved in close and invaded her personal space and sniffed her hair. "Surely you know I'm harmless."

Leigh's knees buckled as she inched away. "I'm not afraid, I just try to avoid traps." She glanced around. "I don't always succeed." Her gaze was drawn to his wide chest as it shook from his rumbling laughter. She remembered vividly how it felt to lay her head against it *and* drag her nails across it.

"You know I should be bending you over my knee right now," he said seriously.

"What?" Her eyes traveled up from his chest to his twinkling onyx gaze. "It wasn't nice of you to leave me sleeping in a stranger's house." He cocked his head. "Thanks for getting me arrested."

"Oh." Leigh dropped her head as guilt rushed through her. "I'm sorry about that. There was a…communication glitch with a friend of mine."

"Yeah, that *glitch* nearly broke my jaw."

Leigh winced and forgot about the danger, moving closer to inspect his face for visible damage. Her recklessness led to her seduction by his devastating smile. "Glad to see that you're concerned for a brother. Should I take this to mean that you care?" He closed another inch between them.

A warning siren went off in her head. Bells, whistles and bullhorns tried to snap her back to reality. But for some reason, she was unable to tear her eyes away from his mesmerizing gaze. "Now, why would I want to cause you any harm? I enjoyed..." She realized what she was about to confess, but had the presence of mind to realize that maybe it wasn't such a great idea to make out in a locked office in the back of a gentlemen's club.

His lips spread wider as he erased the last inch, and bumped his chest up against hers. "You enjoyed what?" he whispered. "Or rather, which part?"

"I, uh..." She tried to get her legs to move, but instead she ended up leaning back until she fell against the door.

Her predator just smiled and planted his left hand on the side of her head and leaned in until his cool, minty breath caressed her face.

"Should I tell you what I enjoyed?"

The air thinned in Leigh's lungs and she could have sworn her legs were slowly turning into Jell-O.

"I enjoyed all of it. From the moment I joined you on the dance floor..." he said, wrapping his right arm around the curve of her left hip. "Hell, even before then when I watched you move this incredible body—" he moved her hips forward so that they connected with his own "—all around the dance floor," he continued. "I knew then that you were an exceptional woman." He started moving their bodies to the music that just barely sounded through his office's walls. His gaze lowered. "I knew by the way your breasts, your hips and your ass were talking to me that we would have wonderful—" his gaze roamed back to her face "—hot, sweaty—" he dipped and ground his hips *and* erection against her "—sex together."

After another dip and grind, Leigh emitted a weak moan. Even through their clothes, his cock was rubbing her in all the right places.

"I especially liked when you pressed your finger up against my mouth and told me that you didn't want to know my name or zodiac sign. You just wanted to go some place where I could just screw your brains out."

"Ahhh." She could feel her body's honey dripping like fresh sap from a maple tree.

"You remember that, Baby Girl? Hmm?"

Dip. Grind.

Leigh nodded her head weakly.

"Did I do a good job?" He leaned his head against the side of hers and started nibbling on her ear. "Did I give you what you were looking for?"

Dip. Grind.

"Y-yes."

He scraped his teeth against her lower earlobe before whispering, "Then how come you snuck out of there the way you did, Baby Girl? Hmm?"

Dip. Grind.

"I—I…" Heat rushed up her body as her clit started throbbing and tingling.

Dip. Grind.

"You know, I would've loved to taste you and feel myself deep inside your body one last time before you left." He abandoned her earlobe to sweep kisses across her collarbone. "I still do."

Dip. Grind.

"Oooh."

His hands moved from her hips to slide over her ass so that he could squeeze and press her ever closer against his dips and grinds.

"I don't know what you did to me that night," he whispered. "But I loved it," he confessed. "And I want you to do it again."

Dip. Grind.

Leigh was on the verge of coming. She was now matching his dips and grinds with a growing desperation. She just wanted to reach that magical place. She thought of nothing and no one else. There was only this dangerously sexy man doing wonderful things to her.

"I've been dreaming about you since that night," he confessed. "I keep thinking that I smell your scent and see your face everywhere I go. It's been driving me crazy." His small kisses led him to the long column of her neck. "And now you come in here and tell me that you're about to marry another man?" He shook his head. "You really think that I'm going to let you do that?"

Dip. Grind.

"I don't think so. Besides, if he could do to you what I'm doing to you right now, you wouldn't be here right now."

Dip. Grind.

"Ooooh. Please." She was quickly turning into a ball of fire and she clung to him, preparing for what was just around the corner.

"Look at you," he panted. "Begging me to let you come." He chuckled and brushed the lightest, sweetest kiss against her lips. "You want to come, don't you, Baby Girl?"

Dip. Grind.

"Hmm?"

"Y-Yes."

"Yes, what?"

"Y-Yes. I want to come. Pleeeeaaaase."

"Then why didn't you just say so, Baby Girl? You know I'll give you exactly what you want." He slanted his mouth against hers, sending her mind spinning through space while their bodies continued their frenzied bump and grind.

It wasn't long before she reached a crescendo. But when she screamed out, he was there to swallow it. At long last she fell limp against him, and a smile crept up the corners of her lips.

"That's my Baby Girl. Daddy knows how to take care of you." He brushed kisses against her fevered brow.

But reality had this pesky way of seeping in and she realized what had happened. "Ohmigod." She shoved him away. "What did you just do?"

"Me?" He laughed jovially. "The last time I checked, it takes two to tango—and, sweetheart, we are officially the reigning tango champs."

Leigh slapped a hand across her mouth in horror. "I've got to get out of here."

"Now, wait a minute." He stepped toward her as she threw her hands up like a stop sign. "*You* stay away from me!"

His hands gestured in surrender. "Okay. Calm down."

"And stop talking," she barked. "I can't think when you talk or...touch me." Leigh stretched one hand behind her back to unlock the door. "I didn't come here for this."

"No?" His brow jumped. "Are you sure?"

Leigh wasn't sure, but she did manage to get the damn door unlocked. "Just—just stay away from me. I mean it." She jerked open the door and raced out of the office.

"Yo, wait!" Jeremy gave chase. "I still don't know your name." After rushing out the door behind her, he was surprised to discover just how fast this chick could move. She bolted through the double set of doors and raced to find her friend.

Before he even got halfway to the club's four bar stations, she had already grabbed her friend by the arm and snatched her off the cozy stool next to Quentin.

"Q, stop her," he shouted. By the time his words sank in and Q turned his head, Baby Girl had dragged her friend halfway to the exit. "Damn!" *Don't let her go or you'll never see her again.* He redoubled his efforts to catch up. But threading through customers that were either shouting at him or grabbing his arm for attention slowed him down.

Finally he raced out of the front door shouting, "Wait!"

She jumped into a silver Mercedes. And when he neared the parking space, the reverse lights came on and Baby Girl's maid of honor nearly mowed him down.

"Wait!"

Tires screeched, and then the car took off.

"Wait," he groaned, helplessly watching as they turned onto the main road. Two seconds later, the bouncer that was planted at the front door and Quentin reached his side, out of breath.

"Is there a problem, boss?" Roland asked.

"Yeah, did we get robbed or something?" Q huffed with his face twisted in confusion.

"Nah. Nah. Nothing like that." He suddenly turned toward Q. "What was her name?"

"Uh, Ariel," Q answered. "Not her, her friend. Did she mention her name?"

Q blinked and then struggle to recall. "I think she kept saying Leanne-Leah—or Princess Leia—I don't know. It was loud."

Jeremy huffed out a frustrated breath. "Damn."

The Girl Is Mine

Chapter 11

Dr. Turner set her pen down. "So let me get this straight. Jeremy's Baby Girl was actually his best friend Roy's fiancée?" she asked.

"Yep." Quentin shook his head. "What are the chances, right?"

"And they had never met each other—even though Jeremy and Roy had been best friends most of their lives?"

"Apparently. As I understand it, Roy met his girl in college when he went to Ohio State. Jeremy went to college in-state at Georgia. He only heard about her around the way—and since Roy is a playa after my own heart, he followed the golden rule of never *ever* carrying your girl's picture in your wallet. Women love to go through a man's stuff when they think you're not looking." Quentin glanced over his shoulder. "Except for you. I'm sure that you completely trust Reliable Reggie."

Dr. Turner's back stiffened. "As a matter of fact, I do. A relationship is doomed if it's not built on a foundation of trust."

He rolled onto his side and propped his head onto his hand. "And how long have you and Reggie been laying this foundation?"

She opened her mouth and then caught herself. "Nice try, Quentin. These sessions aren't about me. And I'm beginning to feel uncomfortable about your interest in my private life. It's not healthy."

"What? We're just two friends talking. There's nothing wrong with that."

"Except for the fact that we're not friends," she said gently. "We have a doctor-patient relationship, nothing more."

Quentin's sly smile vanished as he plopped back onto his back and rolled over. "All things being equal, Doc, that whole doctor-patient thing sort of makes me uncomfortable too."

"But it is the truth."

"You know, Doc, the one thing that I do know is that everyone has their own perspective on what the truth is. It's all just a fragile belief system. Your truth today may not be true tomorrow. That's why who you are today is not who you were ten years ago—or who you'll be ten years from now. So why do we cling to something so malleable, so short-lived?"

"That's actually very profound," Julianne Turner said, cocking her head to the side and reassessing him.

"Don't look so surprised, Julianne. I'm smarter than I look." He glanced across the room where Alyssa sat, staring out of the window. "It's just that sometimes I do stupid things."

"If that's the case, then you do them intentionally."

He found his smile again but didn't respond.

"All right. So what did Jeremy do when he found out that he was dating his best friend's girl?"

"Whoa, slow down. There were a few things that happened before that blockbuster went down..."

Chapter 12

"Heads up!"

Jeremy belatedly emerged from his reverie and turned toward his right instead of his left, and was popped in the mouth by a basketball. "Damn!"

Roy laughed. "Why don't you pull your head out of your ass and get in the game?" He pulled up the bottom of his wife beater and wiped the waterfall of sweat off his face. "What is it with you anyway, man? You're out here half-ass paying attention and we're losing."

The Hoopstar laughed. "Not paying attention? Hell, I haven't noticed. His game has always been suspect to me."

"Ha. Ha." Jeremy flashed him the bird. "Sit and rotate, my man."

The boys cracked up as Jeremy rushed to the sidelines to grab the ball that had just assaulted him. It was one of those rare times that he and his boys got together for a game, since Roy, The Hoopstar and Drake Jennings were usually on the road playing professionally.

"Yo, time," Roy shouted.

"Time?" The Hoopstar barked. "What, you girls need to powder your faces or something? What's with this 'time' crap? We're winning."

"I know such a thing is rare for you two, but I need to check on my man here. Clearly, his mind ain't in the game."

"Yeah, whatever." Drake waved Roy off. "The only reason you two want a time-out is so that you both can come up with a lie for why you had to take this beating we're putting on you."

"You know what?" Roy said, turning and flashing them two middle fingers. "My boy was right. Sit and spin, baby."

Their two opponents cracked a smile but waved him off.

Roy turned his attention back to his boy. "Seriously man, whassup? I don't think I've ever seen your game this *weak* before. You got to tell me something or I'm going to seriously consider getting my ass a new partner. What gives?"

Jeremy tossed him the ball. "Ah, man. It's nothing. I just got a few things on my mind."

"A few things like what? How much baby oil to stock down at the club or how much more you're going to jack the price of those watered-down drinks y'all serve?"

"Ah, man. Get the hell off that."

Roy laughed. "I'm just saying. It's not like you have to make too many hard decisions at that place you call a job."

"Oh, you want to talk about real jobs? I hardly think

playing basketball qualifies as a job. It's just a hobby that pays well."

"Hey, don't hate on me," Roy said. "You should've stuck with it in college. Lord knows you had as good a shot if not better than me of getting in the NBA. You have skills—though you can't tell by the way you're playing out here today. So why don't you break it down for me? What's on your mind so we can get back in this game and shut these fake-ass ballers down?"

"I got your fake-ass baller right here," Drake said, grabbing and shaking his crotch.

Roy shook his head. "I swear, some of these young-bloods' mommas ain't raised them right."

Jeremy's lips hitched in a smile. "Nah, man. I'm good. I'm good."

"Boy, you're far from good. You just got popped in the mouth with a basketball and you haven't even checked to see whether you were bleeding yet."

"Uh? Oh." Jeremy reached up and touched his lip. He was bleeding. "Damn."

"Uh-huh. So now will you cut the crap and spit out what's bothering you?"

Jeremy hesitated.

"C'mon. It's me, your boy."

He had a point. Jeremy sucked in a deep breath. "Well it's this one girl."

"What?" The Hoopstar barked. "Female troubles? I guess that means unlike Jay-Z, your ass got a hundred problems."

"Do you mind?" Roy barked. "I'm trying to have a private conversation with my man here."

The Hoopstar's hands shot up. "All right, Dear Abby. We'll let you two have your *Cosmo* moment."

Send For
2 FREE BOOKS
Today!

I accept your offer!

Please send me two free Kimani™ Romance novels and two mystery gifts (gifts worth about $10). I understand that these books are completely free—even the shipping and handling will be paid—and I am under no obligation to purchase anything, ever, as explained on the back of this card.

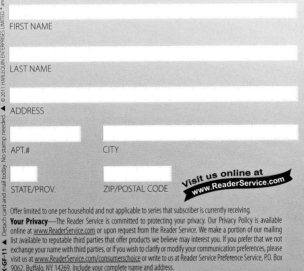

168/368 XDL FJKP

Please Print

FIRST NAME

LAST NAME

ADDRESS

APT.#   CITY

STATE/PROV.   ZIP/POSTAL CODE

Visit us online at
www.ReaderService.com

BUSINESS REPLY MAIL

FIRST-CLASS MAIL   PERMIT NO. 717   BUFFALO, NY

POSTAGE WILL BE PAID BY ADDRESSEE

THE READER SERVICE
PO BOX 1867
BUFFALO NY 14240-9952

NO POSTAGE
NECESSARY
IF MAILED
IN THE
UNITED STATES

Send For
2 FREE BOOKS
Today!

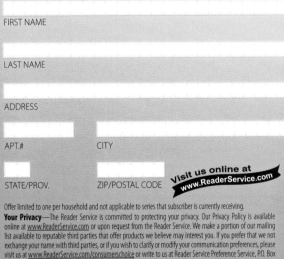

I accept your offer!

Please send me two free Kimani™ Romance novels and two mystery gifts (gifts worth about $10). I understand that these books are completely free—even the shipping and handling will be paid—and I am under no obligation to purchase anything, ever, as explained on the back of this card.

168/368 XDL FJKP

Please Print

FIRST NAME

LAST NAME

ADDRESS

APT.#   CITY

STATE/PROV.   ZIP/POSTAL CODE

Visit us online at
www.ReaderService.com

Offer limited to one per household and not applicable to series that subscriber is currently receiving.

Your Privacy—The Reader Service is committed to protecting your privacy. Our Privacy Policy is available online at www.ReaderService.com or upon request from the Reader Service. We make a portion of our mailing list available to reputable third parties that offer products we believe may interest you. If you prefer that we not exchange your name with third parties, or if you wish to clarify or modify your communication preferences, please visit us at www.ReaderService.com/consumerchoice or write to us at Reader Service Preference Service, P.O. Box 9062, Buffalo, NY 14269. Include your complete name and address.

© 2011 HARLEQUIN ENTERPRISES LIMITED. * and ™ are trademarks owned and used by the trademark owner and/or its licensee. Printed in the U.S.A.

K-GF-11 ◄ Detach card and mail today. No stamp needed. ▲

"Chill out with all those chick references," Roy warned. "You know me and my boy have wiped your rusty butt all up and down this court plenty of times. The mere fact that you two are up a couple points proves something is up. Now fall back before you get knocked back. Besides, it not like you and yours aren't already having problems."

Jeremy's head popped up. "What? You and wife number three on the rocks already?"

Now that his business was on Front Street, The Hoopstar quickly backed down. "Whatever, man. Shoot me the ball. We'll just play some one-on-one until y'all ready."

"We appreciate that," Roy said sarcastically, and then threw the ball over in his direction. "Here. Now take your freakishly tall ass on somewhere."

The Hoopstar and Drake peeled off, laughing while Roy turned his attention back to Jeremy. "A'ight. Now you have my full attention. What's up, Dr. J?"

"I think it's time to retire that nickname."

"Nah. You earned it. You must've played doctor with every girl in a ten-mile radius of our neighborhood when we were young."

"Man, you're still hating on that?"

"No hate. I was just happy to be around to pick up your leftovers."

"Yeah, I think they like to call boys like you *scrubs*."

"Please don't. Those days are long gone. Now I'm pulling my weight with the ladies."

"Now it's *lady*—one."

"A'ight. You ought to know better than that."

Jeremy shook his head again. "Haven't you ever heard that anything worth doing is worth doing right?"

"C'mon, Jeremy. You're not new to the game. You know it's impossible for brothers like us to be tied down to just one woman. One? For forever? *Forever ever?*" he said in his best Outkast remix. "It's not going to happen—and it certainly ain't going to happen with me. Don't get me wrong, I love Leigh. That's my heart. But a leopard can't change its spots."

"Sooo. You guys are just going to have an open marriage?"

"*I'm* going to have an open marriage. She is going to lock those knees together."

Jeremy laughed.

"Look. Leigh isn't new to the game. After college, we somehow managed to stay together even with my butt being traded to three different teams. She knows the life. Every pro athlete's wife does. Hell, I've even been caught a few times. A couple of kisses, some flowers, and—you know—the apology tour. And everything is good to go. We'll just play the game. Hopefully I'll be better than my boy Tiger, and everything is gonna be all good. You feel me?"

Jeremy tossed up his hands. "My name is Les and I ain't in that mess. You do you."

"Always." Roy smiled. "Now we're supposed to be talking about you. And frankly, I don't think that I've *ever* heard you say that you were having problems with the opposite sex. Has the world been turned upside down or something?"

"It feels that way," Jeremy said. "The baby girl that got my mind spinning, I met at Freedman's bachelor party."

"Freedman—Dylan Freedman? Hell, I didn't know

he was getting married. How come I didn't get an invitation?"

"Probably because he doesn't like you."

"Not like me? What's there not to like?" Roy said, trying and failing to sound hurt.

"I don't know. It might have had something to do with you always beating him up back in junior high."

"Oh, please. Talk about carrying a grudge. Anyway, you met ol' girl at the party, and…?"

"No, no. Not just any girl. I'm telling you that this chick really had it going on. She had the face of an angel and her body was just sick."

"Let me guess, you recruited her to be a Dollhouse Doll and now she's at the club driving you crazy?"

"Nah. Nah. It's nothing like that. Though if Baby Girl was ever looking for a job she definitely wouldn't have to audition. I mean, she had a lot of dudes up in there stuck on stupid—tongues rolling out on to the floor. Brothers were getting checked and dismissed on the dance floor."

"Damn. Shawty sounds hot."

"Trust me. You would've liked this girl. We probably would've fought to the death over her."

"Aw. Damn. Now I really hate that I didn't get an invitation to that nerd's party." Roy's lips stretched. "So I know you stepped up and showed the fellas how a real playa put it down."

"Well, I don't want to brag." Jeremy pretended to pop his collar. "But I tell you, man, I don't know what the hell she did to me, but I can't get Baby Girl off my mind. I mean it's all the time. When I wake up in the morning, when I'm at work—" he gestured to the basketball court "—or even when I'm playing."

"Did she cook for you? She might've put some roots on you," Roy said, suspiciously.

Jeremy laughed. "Maaaan."

"Nah. Check it. You'd be surprised what some of these females out here will do to land a successful brother—and you definitely have a big target painted on your forehead, baller."

"Boy, squash that. Everything was all good and then the next morning Baby Girl was gone."

"Did she leave money on the dresser?"

"What? No. What's with you and Q with that?"

Roy shrugged. "I'm just saying that would've been really jacked up."

"No money on the dresser."

"A'ight. So y'all hit it and quit it. What's the problem? Your butt is surely familiar with the term *one-night stand.*"

"I told you. I can't get the girl off my mind," Jeremy said, frustrated. "Twenty-four-seven—and I don't know her real name. Then, check this, out of the blue she pops up at The Dollhouse with her girl—"

"Ahh. She swings both ways." Roy bobbed his head. "I get you. You want advice on how to steal her from her lesbian girlfriend."

"What? No. Damn, man. Will you stop interrupting and let me finish?"

Roy shot his hands up in the air. "My bad, my bad. Continue."

"Baby Girl and her friend showed up wanting to hire the Bachelor Adventures to do *her* bachelorette party."

He frowned. "I didn't know you guys did bachelorette parties."

"What am I, talking to an idiot? We don't. That's

not the point. The point is that she's *engaged*—about to marry some clown out here."

"Ahh." A light finally shone in Roy's eyes. "I see. Daaammmn. So what are you going to do?"

"Normally?" Jeremy shook his head. "I'd fall back and play my position. I try not to play ball in another brother's court, you know what I mean?"

"True dat. True dat."

"But I don't know, bruh. I got the girl alone in my office...and she's definitely still feeling me...and I'm sure as hell feeling her." Almost ashamed for even contemplating trying to steal another brother's girl, Jeremy dropped his head. "Baby Girl got me twisted. And what's crazy, I *still* don't know her name. I don't know what I'm going to do."

"Now that you mention it, you kind of look fevered around the eyes."

"Can you be serious?"

"Aw, man. Don't let it get you down," Roy said, slapping him on the back. "These things happen."

"That's the best you got?"

Roy shrugged. "'This too shall pass'?"

"Gee, thanks. I'm starting to remember why I don't come to you for advice."

"A'ight. How about this, 'all in love is fair'?" he said, and laughed. He sobered looking at Jeremy's expression. "You like this girl, go get her. Engaged isn't the same as being married—right? Engagements fall apart all the time. Why the hell you think I'm trying to get my girl down the aisle as soon as possible?"

Jeremy reflected on the advice and liked what he heard. "You're right." He bobbed his head. "Thanks, man."

"Heeey. That's what I'm here for. Now that we got your bottom lip up, let's go mop the floor with these clowns."

"You got it."

Chapter 13

"Positive!"

Leigh shook her head. "That just can't be. It can't be." She pulled in a deep breath, said a prayer and then slowly peeled her eyes open again. The results of the pregnancy test were still the same. "Positive." She doubled over and collapsed onto the bathroom's tile floor. The headaches, the nausea and the missed period suddenly all clicked into place. "I'm pregnant." Her announcement echoed off the bathroom walls and hit her with resounding force. "I can't believe this. I can't…" Just the thought of being someone's mother seemed so foreign to her. She couldn't even begin to process what the rest of the news meant.

Slowly but surely, those other questions started creeping into her head. "No. I can't think about that right now. I just can't." However, her mind rebelled against her declaration and the needles started getting bigger and sharper. The memories tumbled faster until they rewound back to the moment during her torrid one-night stand when the condom had broken.

"Don't go there, don't go there," she told herself. She didn't want to be in this position. But reality kept slapping her around pretty hard.

Knock! Knock! Knock!

Leigh jumped, and then quickly pulled herself off the floor. "Just a minute." Her eyes rounded when she saw the doorknob twist. She scrambled to grab the four boxes of pregnancy tests from off the counter and shoved them into the wastebasket. Thank God she apparently had the good sense to lock the door.

"Yo, Leigh. What's taking you so long in there?" DeShawn asked. "We're going to be late to our own engagement party."

Leigh sighed. Just the idea of spending the entire night smiling and forcing herself to make small talk with a room full of people triggered another wave of nausea. She quickly slapped a hand across her mouth.

Knock! Knock! Knock!

"Leigh, honey. Are you all right?"

Finally, she managed to stave off the rising bile in the back of throat and answered. "Yes. I'm fine. Just... give me another minute."

On the other side of the door, she heard DeShawn exhale a long, frustrated breath before turning and walking away from the door.

Once he was gone, she exhaled as well and turned toward her reflection in the mirror. The perfect flat-ironed hair, perfect makeup and soft, flowing, body-hugging Herrera gown in no way resembled the turmoil raging inside of her.

"How could this have happened?" Tears glossed her eyes, but she blinked them back before they could ruin her hour-long makeup job.

"Yo, Leigh!" Deshawn shouted. "Shake a leg!"

She rolled her eyes, but she knew that DeShawn had a thing about being late. "All right. You can do this," she told herself, then forced the pregnancy-test results to the back of her head. After straightening her dress and inhaling several deep breaths, she finally emerged from her bathroom and joined DeShawn, who was pacing a hole in the living-room floor.

"Well, it's about time." DeShawn glanced at his platinum Cartier watch. "If we leave now and I drive at warp speed we may—just *may* get there twenty minutes late."

Leigh's thin veneer crumbled on the spot. "Fine. Then we won't go." She slapped her hands to her sides and spun around to head back to her bedroom. "You can let yourself out."

"Whoa, whoa, whoa." Deshawn rushed and grabbed her by her arm. "It's all right. It's cool. I was just buggin'. I'm sorry." He flashed her a smile to try and patch things up. He raked an appreciative gaze over her gown. "You look beautiful, by the way."

She crossed her arms, her irritation far from being alleviated. When she failed to recapture her smile, De-Shawn got the hint that he was walking on eggshells.

"Again, I'm sorry. I didn't mean to upset you." He switched over to his puppy-dog face.

Leigh sighed and gave him a "whatever" look. "C'mon. Let's go. The sooner we get there, the faster we can get back."

That answer probably wasn't what her fiancé was looking for, but, again, "whatever."

DeShawn rushed to help her into a light jacket and opened the door. "I mean it, baby. When the fellahs get a look at you, I'm going to be playing defense the whole night." His smile broadened as if by doing so it would encourage her to do the same.

It did. After all, there was no reason for him to be in a good mood if she wasn't.

"I don't think that I've ever been a dude's plus one before," Quentin cheesed, snapping on his cufflinks. "I think that it's only fair for me to tell you now that I'm not a cheap date."

Jeremy rolled his eyes and checked his watch. "Are you ready, yet? Damn, cuz. I swear that you're worse than a woman getting dressed."

"Don't hate just because my regime is a little more than cocoa butter and ChapStick."

"Funny. Can we go now?"

Quentin struck a pose on both his left and right sides before finally giving the go-ahead. "Let's roll."

"Finally," Jeremy mumbled and turned to leave. When they reached his front door, he opened and held it. "Your highness."

"Don't be an ass, Junior. Just point me toward the groupies."

"It's an engagement party. There're not going to be any groupies."

Q laughed. "Oh, my naive li'l cousin. Where there are ballplayers, there are groupies. I believe it's one of Newton's laws of physics. Look it up."

Jeremy shook his head. "Where do you get this stuff from?"

"I told you, me and Wile E. Coyote are suuuper geniuses."

Jeremy laughed as they finally left the house.

A half hour later, the cousins arrived at Vinoteque on Melrose. Jeremy tossed the keys to his Porsche to one of the young valets with a warning, "You break her, I break you."

"Yes, sir," the kid said, with a curt smile.

Strolling into the lush European-style restaurant, Jeremy noted that Quentin had indeed been correct. His groupie radar was beeping off the charts as he spotted pockets of leggy-and-toothy women clustered together just outside or near the restaurant lobby.

"Name?" a tall brother draped in black asked.

"King—Jeremy King."

After running his finger down several pages on a clipboard, dude bobbed his head. "And you?" he asked looking at Quentin.

"Actually, I'm his plus one."

"We're cousins," Jeremy quickly added.

However, Q swung his arm around Jeremy's shoulders and pressing their faces together. "Kissing cousins."

"Cuz, if you don't get off me—" Jeremy warned only for Quentin to crack himself up laughing as he strolled into the restaurant.

"You two enjoy yourselves," the maître'd said, rolling his eyes over Jeremy.

He just shook his head and followed behind Quentin. "You know I'm going to get you back, right?"

"I'll sleep with one eye open," Quentin said.

Jeremy shifted his attention around the crowded posh restaurant. "So many women, so little time."

"Ahh. It's been a minute since I've heard that line from you. Does that mean that you're officially finished obsessing over your Baby Girl?"

"Let's just say that things are put on hold until I can at least find her again."

"Well, in a city of 3.8 million people that shouldn't be too hard."

"Thanks for the vote of confidence."

"Anytime." Quentin popped him on his back. "Now let's find some women and some alcohol—preferably in that order."

The cousins melted into the crowd and easily struck up conversations. Before long, they rolled up on The Hoopstar and Drake Jennings.

"Well, it's good to see that you two clean up well—especially after that ass-whooping me and Roy put on you."

"Will you stop with that?" Roy said, suddenly popping up from behind. "How many times have I told you that Roy is my father? People call me DeShawn now."

"Sorry, man. Old habits die hard. You didn't start being *DeShawn* until you grabbed the spotlight in college."

The best friends laughed, and then slapped palms and bumped shoulders.

"Thanks for coming, man."

"Wouldn't miss it for the world," Jeremy said. "I see you spit-shined yourself up as well. I'm impressed."

Roy struck a couple of *GQ* poses. "Please. I always stay ready for my close-up."

"I guess that means things do change. I thought all through fifth grade that your butt was color-blind."

"Oh, you're going to roll up in here and crack jokes?"

"You make it easy, man."

"A'ight. You know I know a few embarrassing tidbits about your butt, too."

"We're going to brick wall that, bruh, because I don't know what you're talking about."

"I just bet you don't."

They laughed during another shoulder bump.

Truly enjoying the evening, Jeremy got down to the question of the night. "So when can I finally meet this imaginary fiancée of yours? Hell, maybe there's still time I can talk some sense into her."

"Better fall back. You scare this one away from me and I'm going to have to take you out back."

"Oooh. All right." Jeremy bobbed his head as his smile blossomed. "It's like that, huh?"

"Just keepin' it real."

"Then mum's the word." He pounded Roy on the back.

His boy turned and surveyed the crowd. "I know that she's around here somewhere. Yo, there she is." Roy signaled Jeremy to follow him. They maneuvered through the growing throng.

Jeremy snatched a flute of champagne from a waiter's tray without breaking his stride. But as he tossed back some of the bubbly liquid, he noticed a familiar backside—the height, the hair, the unbelievable curves.

It can't be.

Then Roy tapped the woman on the shoulder. "Leigh, sweetheart. There's someone I'm just dying for you to meet."

Suddenly, the universe shifted into slow motion. Well, everything except for Jeremy's heartbeat. It more than quadrupled in speed.

She turned beaming a beautiful smile—until her eyes landed on him.

Baby Girl.

Chapter 14

The night was officially a nightmare.

Leigh forced herself to blink several times, but the man in front of her remained the same. Judging by the look on his face, he was equally stunned to see her. That didn't help calm the nauseating feeling inside her. To make matters worse, his cousin Quentin, at least she knew his name, strolled up to the small circle.

His face fell, as well. "Well, I'll be damned."

DeShawn's smile rivaled the Joker in a Batman cartoon. "I know. I told you she was a dime piece, didn't I?"

Silence.

"Hey," DeShawn said with a note of warning. "Don't look so hard, I don't want you two doing those Jedi mind-tricks you do that cast women under your spell." He laughed, but no one joined him. After another beat, DeShawn swung his arm around Leigh's waist. "Leigh, honey, I'd like for you to meet my best friend in the whole world, Jeremy King. Jeremy, this is *my* baby girl, Leigh Matthews."

"*You're* Jeremy King?"

"*You're* Leigh Matthews?"

DeShawn laughed. "It's crazy I'm just now introducing you two. But as soon as I sign with the Razors by the trade deadline, L.A. will be my home and we'll be spending a whole lot more time together."

This isn't happening. Leigh blinked one more time, but Jeremy King was still standing there.

"Well, damn, y'all. Say something." DeShawn laughed, swinging his gaze between them.

At long last, Leigh forced a smile and extended her hand—hopefully no one would notice it was shaking. "How do you do? It's a pleasure to *finally* meet you."

Jeremy glanced down, but then followed her lead. "I assure you the pleasure is all mine, *Ms. Matthews.*"

"Aw, man. There's no need to be so formal. Just call her Leigh."

Only one side of Jeremy's mouth curled upward. "Certainly. *Leigh.*"

"I have to warn you, honey," DeShawn said. "My boy here is quite the charmer. Half the state of California is in love with him."

The other corner of Jeremy's lips hitched upward. "That might be a slight exaggeration," he said.

Somehow, I doubt that, she thought. Their hands remained locked, despite the scorching heat rushing up her arm. Not only that, she was having a hard time trying to pull her eyes away from his smoldering gaze.

"You know, I was beginning to think that you were

just a figment of Roy's imagination." Jeremy made his first attempt at small talk.

"No. I assure you that I am real."

His gaze finally dropped to roam over her figure. "*That* you certainly are."

Surprisingly, it was his cousin who stepped in and rescued them from themselves.

"Quentin Hinton. I'm this knucklehead's cousin." He thrust out his hand and forced Jeremy to break contact smoothly.

Leigh accepted the handsome cousin's hand. "A pleasure." Their grip fell quickly away.

"And on that note—" Quentin turned, and continued "—I need a drink. Why don't you join me, cuz?"

"Actually, you go ahead, Q. I think I'd like to get to know Leigh a little better."

Quentin shook his head and mumbled something that sounded like "Fools rush in" before strolling off.

When it was just the three of them, Jeremy tossed back the rest of his champagne, and then started the interrogation. "So remind me again how you two met?"

"College," DeShawn said, puffing out his chest. "My girl here put all the other chicks at Ohio State to shame and she had the whole hard-to-get thing on lock. It must've taken me most of my senior year to convince her to go out with me." He hugged her hip. "Said that she didn't want to date athletes."

The storm roiling inside Leigh was quickly turning into a hurricane.

Ariel rushed to her side and hissed into her ear, "Leigh, you're never going to guess who I just saw over at the bar. It's that..." Her gaze crashed into the man standing in front of them. "Oh, my—"

"Hello," Jeremy said, shifting his eyes toward Ariel. "I don't think we've had the pleasure." He extended his hand. "Jeremy King."

"I, uh—"

DeShawn chuckled as he warned his friend, "Careful, my man. She's one of those loan-shark lawyers."

Ariel turned her confused look toward Leigh.

"Ariel, this is DeShawn's best friend from Georgia that he's always talked about and I've *never* met before today." She felt Jeremy's eyes zoom back toward her at the bald-faced lie. "Jeremy King. He's also going to be DeShawn's best man."

Ariel's eyes doubled in size. "*You're* Jeremy King?"

"Have been since the day I was born." Jeremy turned up the wattage on his smile.

Leigh leveled another quick glance at her girl. *Please, please, don't blow this,* Leigh telegraphed through her eyes.

Ariel nodded as if she understood the message loud and clear. But it was clear from her face that she was also having a hard time processing the night's latest development. She finally slid her hand into Jeremy's. "Ariel Brooks. Pleasure to meet you—for the first time—Mr. King."

Just shoot me now. Leigh glanced at DeShawn and noted that he frowned for a moment, but then shook off Ariel's comment.

"You know what?" Ariel said. "*I* need another drink."

Leigh seized the moment. "And I need to make a quick trip to the ladies' room." She smiled at DeShawn. "Excuse me, won't you, sweetheart?" She also tilted her head at Jeremy, and then made her escape. Her feet moved so fast that it was amazing she didn't leave skid marks on the hardwood floors. Even Ariel had a hard time keeping up with her.

When she bolted through the doors, she breathed a sigh of relief that the only person in the ladies' room was just leaving. Wasting no time, Leigh raced to an open stall and doubled over to empty her belly of the champagne and hors d'oeuvres.

"Leigh, are you all right?" Ariel asked, catching up with her.

"How can I be all right?" she asked between heaves, and then dropped down to the floor.

"Hold on." Ariel turned and rushed to one of the sinks and started wetting paper towels. When she returned to the stall, she placed them along Leigh's fevered brow. "Okay. Deep breaths. It's going to be all right."

"No. No. You don't understand," Leigh moaned.

"It looks bad. I understand that, but…" Ariel said, determined to find a silver lining. However, when she couldn't find one, she abandoned her sentence all together. "Well, at least he didn't blurt out about your…" She glanced back out into the bathroom to make sure no one was around to hear their conversation. "Affair," she said in a whisper in case double security was needed.

"It was just one time. *One* time I sleep with someone else in five years and look what happens. I've been cast in some horrible Greek tragedy."

"Calm down. At least no one has died."

"Yet," Leigh corrected her. "When DeShawn finds out he's going to kill both of us."

"There's no reason that he needs to find out. I seriously doubt that *he's* going to tell him. And I know that you're not crazy enough to. Besides, it happened when you and DeShawn had broken up. You two were technically on a relationship break."

"Yeah—and I *technically* used that break to unknowingly screwing my now fiancé's best friend. His best friend! Of all the men in the world, why did it have to be him?"

"Yeah…that is unfortunate."

"And that's not the worse part."

"Oh, honey, I don't think it could get any worse unless…" Their eyes locked and then shock slowly rolled across Ariel's face. "No." She shook her head. "Stop playing."

Leigh struggled to swallow the lump bobbing in the center of her throat. "I took the test before I came here tonight. Actually I took several of them."

"And they're all—"

"Positive," Leigh answered.

Ariel joined her on the stall's floor. "Sweet Jesus. Well, maybe it's not…"

"I haven't slept with DeShawn since we got back together. I told him I wouldn't until after the wedding. I was still punishing him for having caught him cheating on me in the first place." She shook her head. "We should never have gotten back together. But then you reminded me of all the time I've invested in this relationship."

"What? Wait. Please don't drag me into this."

"No. No. I'm just saying that I'm confused. I think I was forcing something that no longer even feels right to me."

Ariel blinked. "Are you thinking about breaking the engagement?"

"I don't see that I have a choice anymore. Eventually, I'm going to have to tell him about the pregnancy. I sure as hell am not going to try pass it off as his."

"Yeah. I guess that would be wrong?" Ariel said.

"Of course it's wrong!"

Ariel held up her hands in surrender. "All right. All right. I'm just saying that there are plenty of secrets out there that women have taken to their grave. Not everyone opts to 'do the right thing' and tell the truth."

"Well, I'm not like that and I could never do something like that. I'm surprised that you would even think that I would."

"Fine. Forget that I even said it." Ariel lowered her hands, trying to process how fast things were changing. "But whatever you do, don't tell DeShawn here— tonight. There are over two hundred people here. Have your Spike Lee moment when you get home. But not around any sharp objects."

"Got it." The tears that she'd managed to suppress for most of the night suddenly surged forward and blurred her vision.

"I think we *both* need a drink." Ariel attempted to get up, but Leigh grabbed her arm and pulled her back down.

"Are you crazy?" She popped her on the back of the head. "I can't drink. I'm pregnant!" Hearing her own declaration was like another punch in the stomach. "Oh God." Her shoulders deflated as she repeated softly, "I'm pregnant."

"Not only that, but you have to get through this night

sober?" Ariel shook her head. "Well, I definitely need one."

"Wait. Don't leave. I'm not ready to go back out there and face those people just so I'll have to send out regrets in the next few days that the wedding is off. My parents are out there, practically floating on air."

"I know, sweetie. But you can't hide and throw a pity party in here."

"Why not?" she whined. "I need one."

"Because I think that it's considered bad manners," Ariel joked and then swung her arm around her friend. "But I'll tell you what. We'll compromise. We'll stay in here another ten minutes, have a mini pity party, and then paint on fake smiles and get through this night."

Leigh poked out her bottom lip and laid her head on Ariel's shoulder. "I like that plan." She sighed and then allowed her tears to flow.

"Congratulations," Quentin said, raising his glass in a toast.

Jeremy's gaze remained locked on the women's-bathroom door as he helped his cousin hold up the bar. "For what?"

"I think that your life is officially more screwed up than mine."

That comment finally got Jeremy to pull his eyes from the door to stare at his cousin. "Nice try, but I don't think that's even possible."

Quentin thought it over some more, and then acquiesced. "Yeah, maybe you're right." He drained the rest of his whiskey sour. "So when are you going to tell your boy?"

Jeremy pressed his lips together, and then turned his head back toward the closed ladies'-room door.

"You are going to tell him, right?" Q pressed.

"I need to talk to Leigh first."

"Talk to her about what?" His cousin's voice dipped into the serious territory. "What is there to talk to her about? She's out here creeping on your boy—while he's telling the whole world about how she's such a *good* girl."

"Q, man, I need you to back off. Right now, I'm trying to get to the bottom of this situation."

"I'll help you. The situation is that both of y'all's baby girl has been running game on both of you. Not surprising, given what I know about women."

Jeremy closed his eyes and shook his head.

"What? You're saying I'm wrong?"

"Yes, I'm saying you're wrong," Jeremy snapped. "And right now I'm not in the mood for you to turn my situation into *your* situation. Believe it or not, everything is not about you. When the hell are you going to get your head out of your ass and just move on? Huh? Sterling and Alyssa have been married for *three* years. Aren't you tired of singing this same pathetic song? I know I'm tired of hearing it." He leaned into his cousin. "Your problem isn't what Alyssa did or even what Sterling did. You can't own up to what *you* did."

Quentin leaned back in shock.

"What? You thought I didn't know? You thought none of us knew?" From the corner of his eye, Jeremy saw the bathroom door swing open before Leigh and Ariel emerged.

"Do yourself a favor. No, do me a favor," Jeremy said, standing up from his bar stool. "Stop tossing out your so-called wisdom to people who don't ask for it. Fly your ass back home, get on your hands and knees and beg Sterling and Alyssa for forgiveness. After you do that, then maybe I'll listen to what you have to say about my love life." Jeremy slammed his glass down on the counter and made a beeline toward Leigh.

The fact that she was now smiling and laughing with guests only intensified his already hot temper to volcanic levels. When she turned and saw him fast approaching, her eyes widened and she started to make a retreating step. He latched on to her arm before she had a chance to bolt. "We need to talk."

Chapter 15

"Oow! Let go of me," Leigh hissed, struggling to snatch her arm out of Jeremy's death grip as she tried to plant her feet in one place. But nothing stopped him from pulling her across the room at a dizzying clip. He did nothing to quell the renewed panic washing over her. The last thing she wanted was to be alone with this man. How in the hell did she know that he wasn't taking her somewhere so that he could wring her neck?

"I'll let go once I get some answers," he growled. "And I warn you, they better be damn good, too."

Leigh made another attempt to pull her arm free. But it felt like he would rather rip the sucker off than let her go. "Please," she begged. "Let's not do this here."

"Oh, no. You're not in charge of this show anymore, sweetheart. We're done playing games."

His stride quickened and Leigh feared that she would

trip over her shoes. "Well, can you at least slow down? You're going to draw attention."

"Like I give a goddamn." He jabbed at the swinging door to the kitchen, but it was more like he punched it. The door went flying backward with a whack. And the next thing Leigh knew, she was being jerked through the restaurant kitchen.

A few curious workers' heads popped up.

"Everything's all right. Nothing to see here," Jeremy told the staff, and surprisingly they returned to their work.

"Where are you taking me?"

"Why? Are you scared?"

She swallowed, but he seemed to read the answer in her expression.

"Good," he spat, and then punched open another door as he hollered over his shoulders, "We'll be out in a moment, folks."

Leigh's fear skyrocketed at seeing that he had dragged her into a walk-in freezer. At least she didn't see any meat hooks in there. Yet she might as well have been naked given the freezing-cold air circulating around them, slicing through the thin fabric of her dress.

"All right. Talk!" Jeremy whipped her around so fast she nearly lost her balance.

"I—I—I don't know. What do you want me to say?" *Or where to begin, for that matter.*

"You don't know what to say?" he growled murderously. "You can't be serious!"

"Ow!" She reached over and tugged on his arm. "Let me go! I'm not your damn property!"

"No. What you are is a liar and a cheat," he sneered.

Stunned, Leigh stopped pulling on his arm and instead backhanded him across his steely face. She didn't even mind the stinging in her hand. "How dare you. You don't know me!"

"I know that you haven't been faithful to my best friend out there. A man who seems to think that the sun rises and sets on you."

The bark of laughter was out of her throat before she had a chance to stop it, but she quickly sobered. "Look, I'm not discussing my relationship with DeShawn with you. It's none of your business."

Jeremy ground his teeth so hard that his veins popped out along his neck. "Well, I think what happened between you and me is very much Roy's business. What do you think about that? At least, it would show him how much of a fraud you really are."

Narrowing her gaze, Leigh studied his hard features and tried to make a judgment call. "You wouldn't."

Unbelievably, his death grip tightened to the point that she gasped. "Don't even think about calling my bluff, Baby Girl! Trust me. He'll believe every word I have to say. So you might as well start getting your lies straight now because your dream of marrying an NBA baller is over."

"What? I'm not some groupie and I haven't lied to anyone." *Technically, at least that was true.*

"Oh, really? So we can just march right out there and tell Roy exactly how we met? Is that what you're telling me?"

She hesitated.

"Good. Let's go." Jeremy jerked her arm to head back out the door.

"Wait," she cried, and then tried to pry her arm free.

"What's the matter?" he asked, in a patronizing tone. "Did you suddenly remember that maybe a few things might have slipped your mind? Maybe, a few *more* one-night stands floating around?"

"Fuck you!"

"Fuck me?" he thundered incredulously. "Tell you what, I'll go out there and let my boy know what time it is. Unlike you, I don't have anything to hide."

"But you do have something to lose," she tossed back.

He cocked his head.

"What? You think that you can just walk out there and drop something like this on him and you two will remain *boys?*" When he hesitated, it was the opening that she needed. "You have no right to threaten and bully me. And more importantly I don't *owe* you an explanation for anything."

"I have the right to some answers," he barked. "What was that night—just something you do on the weekends or when the rich, clueless boyfriend is out on the road?"

Leigh unleashed the second backhand. Her hand hurt worse the second time and she left a glowing handprint on the side of his face. "I don't like what you're implying." She seethed.

Jeremy's eyes narrowed as he leaned into her space. "The only thing that I'm implying is that you're either a gold-digger or a ho—"

Slap! Slap! Slap!

Leigh couldn't stop swinging. "How dare you! You self-righteous asshole!"

Jeremy sustained the first couple of blows, but then he finally had to try and ward them off. "Stop it. Stop it." He made a grab for her free hand, but missed.

However, Leigh spotted other objects in the freezer that would help her win her fight. In the next second, she hurled vegetables, chicken, fish and any damn thing she could get her hands on.

"Men can cheat. Men can do whatever they want— hurt anyone that they want. Well, I'm sick of it. You hear me? Sick! Sick! Sick!"

"Will you stop it? Are you crazy?" Jeremy barked.

"Oh! So now I'm a *crazy* ho. Is that it?" Her arms and hands became a windmill as she pelted him everywhere. "For your information, I didn't go to that party looking for a one-night stand. It was just a stupid, impulsive thing that I'll regret for the rest of my life!"

"Ha!" Jeremy's head popped back up. "I'm supposed to believe that? I remember that night. You were a woman on the prowl and you were no rookie," he charged.

"I don't give a damn what you believe!" Tears rimmed her eyes, but she fought like hell to keep them in check. "I just know that I wasn't supposed to see you again. But so far you've been like something stuck on the bottom of my shoe that I can't get rid of."

"And you're *never* going to get rid of me," he swore, knocking the bunch of produce from her hand and moving in close. "It'll be a cold day in hell before I let you marry my best friend—even if it costs me my friendship. Now, you look me in the eyes and tell me if you think I'm bullshitting."

Leigh angled her chin upward in a last bid of defiance, but she believed that Jeremy absolutely meant what he said.

Jeremy nodded. "Good. We understand each other.

You have forty-eight hours." With that he turned and stomped out of the walk-in freezer.

Leigh watched him exit and had the urge to swing a good rump roast at the back of his head. But in the end all that was left were tears and a fresh wave of nausea. Heads turned when Jeremy marched out of the kitchen freezer. He ignored most of the stunned and shocked faces even when he stopped to pass the chef his business card and told him, "Send me the bill for the mess." After that, he straightened his back, brushed a few leafy vegetables off his shoulders and then headed back into the party. Even then everyone who saw his stormy face scrambled out of the way.

"Jeremy," Roy called out, and then rushed to catch up with him. "Is there a problem, man? You look ready to kill someone."

"No, man. I just—had something come up and I really need to get to it," Jeremy said, avoiding eye contact but, more importantly, not breaking his stride toward the door.

"So you're heading out of here?" Roy asked, surprised.

"I'm afraid so, man." Jeremy swung an arm out and briefly whacked his buddy on the back. "Sorry. I have to cut out. It's a nice party, but I'm going to have to catch you later."

"Oh, okay, then," Ray responded, clearly unable to hide his disappointment. "Well, at least you finally got the chance to meet my old lady," he boasted.

"Yeah, finally." Jeremy strolled out the front door of the restaurant, but Roy remained by his side as he stopped at the valet. "Sorry. I didn't get a ticket, but I'm driving the—"

"I remember who you are, sir," the young kid bragged, and then reached for his keys. "Be right back, sir."

"Thank you." While Jeremy waited, for the first time in his life he dreaded having to make small talk with his best friend.

"Well?" Roy prodded.

Jeremy frowned. "Well what?"

Roy laughed. "Well, what the hell do you think? She's something else, ain't she?" His friend's grin exploded, doubling in size. "I'm a lucky son of a bitch, ain't I?"

Jeremy's darting gaze finally settled on Roy's smiling, hopeful face. *What was he supposed to say to that?* He was kind of hoping to keep his quota to one lie tonight. "Yeah, man. You're real lucky."

Roy shoved his hands in his suit pants' pockets and rocked back on his heels. "Look, because we're boys, I don't mind telling you that I'm a bit nervous about all this."

That piqued Jeremy's interest. Maybe if his boy was experiencing some doubts then there was some room to maneuver in this drama.

"Nervous about what?"

Jeremy's Porsche pulled up to the curb.

"Well," Roy hedged and shrugged his shoulders. We don't have to talk about it now. I don't want to keep you from handling your business. Another time." He turned and started to head back to the party.

Jeremy caught his arm. "No. I can—"

"Here you go, sir." The valet stepped in front of them.

Jeremy quickly gave the kid a folded bill from his

pocket and turned his attention back to his best friend. "Now, what were you saying about doubts?"

Roy blinked. "Well, I didn't say doubts—" He stopped to think about it. "I guess there are *some* doubts. But that's just to be expected, right?"

"I wouldn't know."

"Oh… right." Roy bobbed his head. "Mr. Bachelor-for-Life. How could I forget?"

Jeremy's patience was wearing thin. "So—what are you nervous about?"

"I guess the whole thing," he said, lowering his voice to make sure no one was listening to their conversation. "Don't get me wrong or anything. I love Leigh and everything. I mean, look at her. She's hot to def, right? It's just… I got to thinking about what you said the other day."

What had he said?

Jeremy's brows dipped. Roy reminded him, "You know, the whole conversation about my still creeping and keeping my dirt on the low?"

"You're paraphrasing, but yeah, I remember the conversation."

"See, it's not that I *want* to cheat on Leigh or anything. But out there on the road, you don't know, man. It's like being a kid in a candy shop and my ass is addicted to sugar."

"Are you kidding me? Did you forget where I work?"

"Yeah, and how many women fall into your bed?"

Good point.

"The truth of the matter is, if I get caught again, I'm pretty sure Leigh isn't sticking around. Hell, I had to wage a whole campaign to get her family and friends to help me get back in her good graces. And to tell you the truth—" he glanced around again "—when I popped open the ring box, Leigh actually said *no*."

"What?"

Roy nodded as his nervous confession continued to pour out of him. "Yeah, man. We had actually broken up and old girl got a little taste of freedom. I'm thinking she realized that she didn't have to put up with my bullshit. You know what I mean? For the first time I was really scared of losing her. It took me damn near two weeks to wear her down—and I still haven't been able to get her back into the bedroom."

"So you two are not…"

Roy shook his head. "Clearly I'm on restriction until after the 'I do's!"

"*You* are not having sex until the wedding night?"

A mischievous smile curled Roy's lips. "*We* aren't having sex. Trust and believe I'm handling mine out here."

"But—"

"That's what I'm saying." Roy stepped closer. "It's just not in me to be a one-woman man. But at the same time, a brother doesn't come across a woman like Leigh every day. Not only is she fine, she's smart and she not impressed with the money and the fame."

Jeremy felt a sickening twist in his gut as his recent tirade in the kitchen freezer scrolled through his head. Hadn't he just pretty much called her a gold-digging ho? No. Scratch that. A *crazy* gold-digging ho.

Cars pulled up and around the valet. Everyone was clearly trying to work around Jeremy's car blocking the curb.

"Damn, listen to me," Roy said, shaking his head. "I'm just spilling my guts when you got to get going.

You go handle your business, man. We can talk another time."

"No. It's okay."

"Nah. We'll hook up soon," Roy said, backpedaling. "I really appreciate you coming out tonight. I'll holler at you later."

Before Jeremy could mutter another word, Roy spun on his heels and went back inside the restaurant to the party.

Jeremy's shoulders deflated. Now he felt like an ass. It wasn't too hard to put the pieces of this puzzle together. Leigh and Roy were broken up at the time he met her in Malibu. The rendezvous that had him so shook up was likely an impulsive revenge hook-up on her part and... "She had said *no*." He didn't know why that small detail filled him with so much hope, but it did. Upon further reflection, he wondered what he was so hopeful about. He didn't have a shot in hell with her now or ever.

While his thoughts and feelings tumbled over one another, he strolled to the driver's side of his Porsche and eased behind the wheel. However, a second before he could pull off, the passenger door jerked open and Quentin hopped in.

Jeremy blinked as if the sight of his cousin jarred him. Then another layer of guilt attacked him.

"Well?" Q said, folding his arms. "I'm waiting."

Jeremy nodded at the olive branch. "I'm sorry."

"That's it?" Quentin asked, hiking up brow.

"I'm *very* sorry. I shouldn't have attacked you. You were just trying to help."

Q's head swayed as he weighed whether to accept

the apology. "All right. Apology accepted." He twisted up his nose. "Why do you smell like fish?"

Jeremy laughed and managed to let slip his first genuine smile in the past hour. "It's a long story." Still, he just had to get in the last word. "But I still think you should call Sterling."

You Give Love a Bad Name

say that you needed to talk to your

Chapter 16

"What did he mean by that?" Dr. Turner interrupted, braiding her fingers together.

Quentin tried to play dumb. "What did who mean by what?"

"Come on, Q. Let's not play games. A few minutes ago you said Jeremy alluded to something that happened between you and your brother Sterling. Care to elaborate?"

Quentin shifted around on the chaise.

Alyssa pulled her gaze away from the window and finally turned her attention to them. "Tell her," she urged.

But Q's tongue suddenly felt like lead in his mouth and the room's temperature surged to sweltering heat.

"Q?" Julianne Turner leaned forward in her chair sensing that she had hit a nerve. "Why did your cousin say that you needed to talk to your older brother?"

Did she think he hadn't understood the question the first time? "It's..." Quentin shook his head.

"Take your time," she encouraged softly.

"I was hurt," he started. "And so damn angry."

"Of course you were. Your brother married the woman you thought you were in love with."

"I *was* in love with her," Q corrected.

"You weren't in love with me," Alyssa accused, and then rolled her eyes in frustration.

"You don't know what you're talking about," Quentin snapped, jumping to his feet and yelling at someone who wasn't there.

"Excuse me?" Dr. Turner asked, alarmed.

"I know plenty!" Alyssa charged. "After all, I am your subconscious. You weren't in love with Alyssa!"

"I was!"

"No!"

"Yes," he thundered, and then realized the absurdity of the situation. "Look at me. I'm arguing with myself."

"You're pissed because you lost! You can't stand that Sterling supposedly took something that you thought belonged to you. And in your own sick way, you thought my adoration belonged solely to you. Why not? You had it for years. But the truth of the matter is if you had loved me you never would have married her," his subconscious Alyssa said.

"Who?" he thundered. "She has nothing to do with this!"

"Who are you talking about?" Julianne Turner asked, fascinated by Quentin's breakthrough—or meltdown—the jury was still out on which one it was.

"She has everything to do with this!" Alyssa shouted. "When you love something—or someone—

you fight for that love. That's what Sterling did—he fought for what he wanted. He didn't let *you* or anyone else take away what he wanted. He wanted me. Let's face facts. When you had your chance, you chose your precious inheritance—damn whoever got in your way."

"That's not true!"

"No? Have you even told her why you got married? Does she even have a clue? Or did you just forget all about her or what she might have been going through once you got your money and your annulment?"

Quentin's shoulders slumped in defeat as he finally admitted the truth.

"Face it. You were a selfish bastard then and you're a selfish bastard now. You can't even allow yourself to be happy for your brother—or for me."

"Quentin?" Dr. Turner spoke softly. "Are you okay?"

He shook his head. "Not really."

"What's going on?" she asked.

Quentin glanced around the room. Alyssa was gone—and something in his gut told him that he wouldn't see her image ever again.

"Q?" Julianne Turner tried again to get through to him.

"Uh, yeah. I guess I just realized something."

"And what's that?" she asked cautiously.

"That I am a real asshole."

Silence followed his announcement as his head flopped back on the chaise.

"Can I get you something?" Dr. Turner asked, standing. "Would you like some water or something?"

"Water would be nice," he said, suddenly exhausted.

Julianne Turner walked over to a small refrigerator by her desk and retrieved the bottled water. As she twisted open the top and grabbed a small glass, she looked over her shoulder at him.

"It's okay," he said. "I'm not cracking up. At least I don't think I am."

She smiled as she walked back and handed him the glass. "Why don't you leave the diagnosis to the professional?"

Quentin flashed his dimples. "All right, Doc. Am I cracking up?"

Dr. Turner's lips stretched wide into a smile as she returned to her chair.

"I guess that means that the jury is still out," he joked.

"Tell me about your breakthrough."

"Only that love is more foreign to me now than it has ever been. But maybe now I think I understand Jeremy's situation a little better."

Chapter 17

"Girl, are you all right?" Ariel asked, rushing to her side when she finally emerged from the kitchen. Leigh was far from being all right, but she put on a brave face anyway. "Yeah. I'm okay." She glanced around the room and was both relieved and disappointed that Jeremy King was gone.

"He left," Ariel filled in.

"What?"

"Your baby's daddy," her girl said flippantly. "That is who you're looking for, right? He blazed out of here a few minutes ago. So what's up? Did you drop the news on him or what? And why are you shaking like a leaf?"

"Because Jeremy hauled me into that huge freezer in the kitchen."

"What? He tried to kill you or something? We can probably sue him for that."

"No. But I can't swear that the thought didn't cross his mind."

"Girl, the drama at this damn party is off the hook. So what are you going to do?"

"Right now? Go home." Leigh glanced around the room again. "Where's DeShawn?"

"Uh." Ariel grimaced.

"What now?"

"He rushed outside—with Jeremy."

Leigh felt too exhausted to panic anymore. At this point she would quietly march in front of a firing squad if it meant that this nightmare would be over.

Ariel, however, remained rapt with anticipation. "So what do you think they were out there talking about?"

"I assure you I have no idea."

"You don't think that your baby—"

"Please, stop calling him that. I don't know what they are talking about, nor do I care. I just want to go home."

"But your party—"

"I don't care about this party, either," she hissed, while tears burned the backs of her eyelids like acid. "Take me home."

"But—"

"Ariel, if you're my friend, you'll jump off my last nerve and get me home before I completely lose it."

Ariel blinked.

"Please," she added as those same tears now threatened to roll down her face.

"All right. All right. Sure. Let's just get our jackets."

Leigh bobbed her head and proceeded to follow her girl to the coat check of the restaurant. As they stood in line to hand over their tickets, Leigh's gaze drifted toward the glass front door. There she saw Jeremy King and DeShawn standing by the parking valet talking. She couldn't help or stop herself from comparing the two.

Both men had no trouble turning women's heads, but Jeremy King's effortless style and suave good looks were truly second to none. Looking at him, it was clear he was a manly man. And having had the experience of what it was like to rake her hands down his massive chest *and* to have him buried deep inside of her, she knew, for her, who was the better man.

Judging by the body language and the fact that DeShawn was doing all the talking, Leigh thought it was safe to conclude that no bombshells were being dropped. But if she wasn't mistaken, Jeremy did look surprised about something. She wondered what it was that DeShawn was telling him.

"Here you go, girl," Ariel said, handing over her jacket.

Leigh accepted it without pulling her gaze away from the two men—well, from Jeremy. *Why couldn't I have met him first?* There was such a longing in her question that her chest hurt. And there were other parts of her body aching for his touch.

"Are you ready?" Ariel asked.

"Huh, what?" Leigh jerked her head around to face Ariel, but it was too late. Her friend had already turned around to see what had captured her attention.

Ariel folded her arms. "I thought we didn't care what they were talking about."

"I don't care."

"Right. Is that why you're drooling like someone was waving a dog biscuit in front of your face?"

"Please, Ariel. Don't start. Not now."

Sympathy saved her butt, because Ariel looked as if she was far from being satisfied. "All right. Let's get you home."

"Honey?" Leigh's mother's voice drifted over to her.

Mustering the strength that she must've had stored somewhere deep in her bones, Leigh forced a smile and turned toward her mother. "Hey, Mom. Dad. I'm not feeling too good right now. I think it might've been something I ate."

Her mother instantly pressed the back of her hand against Leigh's forehead. "What are your symptoms?"

"I'm just a little nauseous."

"A little?" Ariel chuckled before she could stop herself.

Leigh rolled her eyes.

Her mother's brows jumped as a tiny smile quirked her lips. "Really, now? How long have you been feeling like this?"

Realizing what the hopeful light in her mother's eyes meant, Leigh tried to course correct. "Just today, Mom. I probably ate something that didn't agree with me." She tried to smile through the lie.

Her mother nodded her head, but she'd clearly dismissed Leigh's explanation. "And are you experiencing any mood swings or breast tenderness?"

Yes and yes. "Mom, I don't think we should be discussing my breasts right now."

"I'm just saying that signs of pregnancy are—"

"Mom, we're not talking about that."

"Humph." Ariel glanced up and suddenly became interested in the ceiling.

With a friend like her, who needed enemies?

"Would you like me to take you home, sweetheart?" her father said, towering above her mother. He glanced around. "Where's DeShawn?"

"Oh, he's outside talking to a friend at the valet and—"

"You're both leaving?" Her mother cut in. "What about your party? Everyone came to wish you well on your engagement."

"I know, Mom. DeShawn can stay here. Ariel can take me home."

"Nonsense," her mother interjected. "Your father and I can take you home. There's no need to pull your friend away from the party."

"Oh, it's no trouble," Ariel said, smiling. "Besides, it's on my way home."

"What's on your way home?" DeShawn said, walking up behind them.

Leigh's mother's smile faltered. "Leigh says she's not feeling well."

"She's not?" DeShawn turned his attention to his fiancée. "What's the matter, sweetheart?"

Feeling the heat of the spotlight, Leigh cleared her throat. "I'm just feeling a little nauseous—probably indigestion. That's all. No big deal."

"Leigh, if you want, your father can go out and get you something for your stomach ache."

Leigh couldn't believe how difficult this was. "Mom, I really would like to go home and lay down."

"Darling, you don't just run out of a party because you have a *little* indigestion. Now, if there's something else..."

Leigh's patience was wearing thin. "Please, stop

trying to turn this into a federal case, Mom. I'd just like to go home and lay down. Is that too much to ask?"

Sheree blinked at her daughter's sudden outburst and then that tiny smile returned. "Are you sure that you're not—"

"Mommm," Leigh warned.

Her mother tossed up her hands. "Fine, I have nothing else to say."

Wouldn't it be nice if that were true? Leigh closed her eyes and searched her soul for patience. Turns out, she was fresh out. "You know, everyone can just stay here and I'll hail myself a cab."

DeShawn eased his arm around her shoulder. "Baby, don't overreact. Your mother was just trying to help. I'll take you home."

Leigh shrugged his arm off her shoulder. "Please, don't patronize me. I told you I didn't even feel like coming here tonight." A wave of nausea hit her and she just wished that everyone would stop staring and interrogating her half to death.

DeShawn's expression twisted in confusion before he leaned in close and asked, "Did you get your period or something?"

"Aw, hell." Ariel rolled her eyes and jabbed her hand on her hip.

Sheree Matthews shook her head disappointedly.

The one thing Leigh would've welcomed right now was her period.

"Son," her father said, shaking his head. "Bad move."

It was a bad move, because it took everything Leigh had for her head not to spin around and fly off. "As a matter of fact, I *didn't*. But have you *lost* you ever-lovin' mind?"

DeShawn shrugged his shoulders. "What? I was just asking. You're acting really strange this evening. You've been snapping my head off since before we got here."

"Before?" Her mother latched on to that tidbit as her eyes grew to the size of saucers.

Leigh went from anger to being on the brink of tears in the blink of an eye. "Can someone, *anyone,* just take me home? Tell the guests whatever you want. I don't care."

"I'll take you," DeShawn volunteered. But he looked scared, as if something might happen to him in the car.

Her mother leaped back into the fray. "But, De-Shawn—"

"It's okay. I'll take her home and come right back. No big deal."

Her mother gave a look that said it was a very big deal and something that one simply didn't do at your engagement party.

"How does that sound, sweetheart?" he asked Leigh as if he expected to get a cookie. He took another chance and wrapped his arm around her shoulder.

Despite wanting to snatch it off, Leigh left it there. Her mother had her under surveillance. "I'm sorry for snapping. I really don't feel well."

"Uh-huh," her mother nodded, looking like she knew exactly what time it was. "I'll come by your place in the morning and check on you."

Great.

Her father drew closer. "You just make sure that you get plenty of rest. Don't worry about the party.

We'll take care of everything." He pressed a kiss to her forehead.

"Thanks, Dad." Leigh turned toward Ariel. "And thanks, girl. I'll call you later."

"Not if I call you first."

"Let's go." DeShawn escorted her out of the restaurant. After the valet retrieved DeShawn's bright blue Gumpert Apollo, they slid into the comfortable leather seats. After pulling away from the curb, the couple rode for miles in silence. DeShawn hoped that she would say something to fill him in on what the hell was going on with her, and she was hoping that he would remain quiet the entire ride.

She did think that maybe she should go ahead and end things with him now. But knowing that he would be going back to the party, she decided that it would just make things too awkward for him.

Tomorrow. I promise I'll tell him tomorrow.

"Are you feeling any better now," he asked tentatively.

So much for silence. "Yes," she lied. Hell, she was doing a lot of that tonight. "Thanks for taking me home."

"No problem. I just wish that I knew why you weren't feeling like yourself. I don't like it when my baby is sick." He reached over and grabbed her hand.

Leigh pulled her hand back.

Silence filled the car again but DeShawn's persistence returned. "You know, they say that planning a wedding is extremely stressful. What do you say we hire a wedding planner to help take some of the stress off you?"

Silence.

"Is there something else wrong? I feel like there's something you're not telling me."

Those damn tears threatened again. Was the entire nine months going to be like this? She'd go mad if it was.

"Leigh?"

"DeShawn, not tonight. Please. We'll talk tomorrow. I promise."

"I don't know how this is going to work if you refuse to talk to me."

Now he wants to talk. Not when he's on the road and I'm blowing up his phone. Now, on the one night I need to process my thoughts, everyone is treating like a criminal. She turned and stared out of the window.

"Ooookay." He huffed out a deep breath.

Tell him. Tell him.

"Please. Tomorrow, okay?"

"Okay."

She could feel when his gaze shifted to the back of her head. And like before, she prayed that he would drop it. Tomorrow, she would put an end to this. Tomorrow, she hoped to have some kind of plan going forward. Jeremy King's handsome face floated to the forefront of her mind, but just as quickly, she shook it right out. She could only handle one problem at a time. Leigh turned back in her seat and glanced over at the man behind the wheel. This was one time that they shouldn't have gotten back together.

Another five minutes and DeShawn pulled up to her place. As hard as she tried, he wouldn't listen when she told him that he didn't have to walk her to the door. And once at the door, he needed to come in to use her bathroom. For the first time, she sensed that he didn't trust her.

How ironic. She let him in to use the bathroom. He chattered nonstop as he walked down the hallway to the bathroom. She tuned him out as she removed her jacket and high-heel shoes. Once he was in the bathroom, she headed to the kitchen for a bottled water, but then she nearly jumped out of her skin when she heard a loud whoop from the bathroom.

"What on earth?"

"Now I get it!" The bathroom door jerked open and DeShawn rushed out, waving a stick. "Baby, why didn't you tell me we were pregnant?"

Chapter 18

"Oh my God! I can't believe we're about to have a baby," DeShawn declared, rushing toward her like a linebacker.

Before Leigh knew it, a pair of strong arms wrapped around her and lifted her off the floor.

"I knew something was up. You're acting so strange. You should have told me." He bounced her up and down.

Leigh's eyes bulged as the tumultuous waves in her stomach increased. "DeShawn, honey. Please, set me back down."

"A baby," he shouted. The bouncing transitioned into her being swung around the kitchen. "I'm going to be a father. I can't believe this!" Then just as suddenly he stopped and put her feet down back on the floor. "I'm going to be a father," he repeated, somberly. "That means that I'm going to have to be…" He sucked in a deep breath as though someone had just handed him his maturity pills. "Okay…" He bobbed his head. "I can do this. *We* can do this."

Leigh wasn't sure whether he was trying to convince her or himself.

You have to tell him now. There was no way around it now. She couldn't have him leaving there thinking that she was carrying his child. In fact, any second now he was going to start asking questions so that he could do his own calculations.

"So how far along? Two months—three?"

Oh, Lord.

Smiling, DeShawn glanced down at her belly, and then pressed his hand against it. "I bet it's a boy."

"DeShawn." She stepped away from his hand. "We need to talk."

"I'll say. How long have you known?"

"Please, just hear me out. I—" A sudden violent wave of bile gurgled up her throat. Leigh slapped a hand over her mouth, spun and then made a mad dash to the bathroom.

To Leigh's dismay, DeShawn rushed in behind her as she upchucked most of the water she'd just drank since she hadn't eaten at the party and her stomach was empty. "Oh my God," DeShawn said excitedly. "This is really happening. We're really about to do this." He turned toward her medicine cabinet. "What do you need, baby? Can you take Pepto-Bismol?" He rummaged around the cabinet some more. "What about some Alka-Seltzer?"

Leigh moaned as she sat next to the toilet. *This cannot be happening.*

"A daddy," DeShawn said. "Me."

"DeShawn," she said, lifting her head with tears streaming down her face. "Sweetheart, I don't know any other way to say this, but—"

"You know what? I'll just call the team doctor— well, I'm not officially on the team *yet*—and he's technically not a pediatrician—or do you need to see one of those gyno-people for this? I can't remember." He was rambling on badly.

"DeShawn," Leigh tried again. It was clear that there was no way that he was going to take any of this well.

"Hold on, baby, let me just call and—" He was still smiling and shaking his head. "Wait until everyone hears about this. A father!" He pulled his cell phone from his ear and looked at the screen. "Now, I know I've got the right number in this thing."

"DeShawn, please! Listen to me!"

"I'm listening, baby." He dragged his eyes from the phone and smiled. "You just don't realize how happy you've made me. Hell, I didn't know how happy I would be hearing something like this. A father!" He still sounded stunned. "And, baby—" he knelt down on the floor next to her by the toilet bowl. "I promise you— I *swear* that you're going to see a changed man from here on out."

"DeShawn—"

"No, baby. Please hear me out. I know that I've put you through some unnecessary changes, but that's over now. You hear me? From here on out, I'm going to be the best father and *husband* I possibly can be. And—"

"Shh…" Leigh cupped his face in her hands. "DeShawn, this is soooo hard, but…I can't marry you."

He blinked and then shook his head as if there was something wrong with his hearing. "What?"

Leigh's guts twisted inside of her. "I'm sorry. But I should have never accepted your proposal. And you've got to believe me that I didn't know I was pregnant until today."

His smile wavered, but then it brightened again as if he figured out what the problem was. "Leigh, honey, I know that you've been having some doubts. I mean, even I had some. But I'm telling you now, this news changes all that. I swear I'm going to do right by you. I'm going to—"

Leigh's patience snapped and she just blurted it out. "DeShawn, it's not your baby!"

Chapter 19

"You dragged her into the freezer?" Quentin asked, kicking his feet up on the corner of Jeremy's desk. "Ha! If you don't mind my saying, that's pretty *cold*-blooded.

"It was the only place I could think of at the time that we could be alone and not worry about being overheard," Jeremy offered weakly, tugging off his tie and tossing it onto the small glass coffee table. Next he started unbuttoning his shirt while he continued to replay the night's events in his head.

"You know, this whole thing just blows my mind," he said. "For years I'd heard about my boy's chick. But he always kept her on the sidelines and we never actually met. And then suddenly—boom! This is craziness!"

"Of course he kept her on the sidelines. That's a true playa move."

Jeremy frowned. "What do you mean?"

"Come on. If you had to guess between you and your

boy, which one of you pulled the most women, who would you pick?"

Jeremy tilted his head with a cocky grin, giving Quentin the "well, I don't want to brag" look.

"Exactly!" Quentin grinned. "A playa never introduces his serious girl to a bigger playa than himself. That's just asking for trouble. Funny thing is your man still fumbled the ball—and she wandered into someone else's court. And here we are." Q tossed up his hands. "One big-ass mess!"

"You're making sports analogies now?"

"I use whatever I have on hand." Quentin stretched back in the leather chair and folded his arms behind his head.

Jeremy plopped down onto the leather sofa and watched the security cameras that monitored the club's main floor. He saw all the swirling hips, popping booties and bouncing breasts, but none of it moved him. All he could think about was Leigh's angry face and how she'd tried to pelt him to death with frozen food.

God, she was breathtaking.

A smile hitched the corners of Jeremy's mouth. All the while he was trying to breathe fire, there was still a very strong part of him that wanted to drag her into his arms and smother her ruby-red lips with a passionate kiss. He missed her. Missed kissing her lips, smelling her skin, and definitely missed the feeling of what it was like to be buried deep inside of her.

The truth of the matter was Jeremy needed that freezer to stop him from embarrassing himself. Even now, it pained and disgusted him that he was actually attracted to his best friend's fiancée. Sure, he was mad—but if he was going to be honest, he was jealous, too.

"I need a drink." Jeremy popped up off the couch and strolled over to the bar. "Want one?" He reached for an extra glass.

"Nah, I'm good."

Stunned, Jeremy glanced up.

"What?" Q asked, shrugging. "I know how to say no."

"Learn something new every day," Jeremy said, pouring himself a brandy.

"So have you decided yet?" his cousin asked.

Jeremy lips twisted. "Decided what?"

"Have you decided whether you're going to steal your best friend's girl or not?"

The question surprised Jeremy so much that he spewed out half his drink. "What?"

"Come on, man. I don't stutter and your ears don't flap. I can take one look at you and see that right now you're thinking about Baby Girl, and it has nothing to do with whether or not she's going to break things off with Roy. You still want her for yourself."

A voice in the back of Jeremy's head told him to deny it, but he couldn't get the words out of his mouth. Had he been thinking about that?

Q shook his head. "Fascinating. Now I get to see how the other side works."

"You're talking in riddles." Jeremy refreshed his drink.

"No. I'm speaking English." Jeremy flashed him an annoyed look.

Quentin's hands shot up. "Don't worry. I get it. No

more lectures. Just think of me as a casual observer of this D-list Shakespearean tragedy."

"Have you ever heard the saying, 'People in glass houses shouldn't throw stones'?"

"Touché." Q tapped his temple and then watched as his cousin finished off his drink in one gulp.

Jeremy grew uncomfortable under such scrutiny. So much so that after he drained his glass, he quickly poured himself another one.

"Fascinating."

"Don't start."

Q's hands came up. "No judgment."

"Who are you kidding? You haven't stopped judging me since I found out that me and Roy were in love with the same girl."

Q's eyes nearly popped out of his head. "*Love?* Who said anything about anyone being in love? I thought you just wanted to screw the girl's brains out again. You're in love?"

"No!" Jeremy shook his head to clear his thoughts. "I meant *like*. We like the same girl." Quentin's thunderstruck look remained. "Yeah, because I get those two words confused all the time." He smacked the palm of his hand against his head. "Damn—you hardly know the girl. Does it happen *that* fast?"

"Q—"

"No. I mean, really. You just learned her name tonight. Did you fall and bump your head? Are you sure she didn't slip something in your drink when you weren't looking? How about voodoo? Did you see any strange dolls lying around with pins in them?"

"It was just a slip of the tongue," Jeremy persisted,

mainly because he couldn't believe he'd said it himself. "My bad. It won't happen again." *Love. Please.*

Quentin's eyes narrowed as he studied his cousin. A worry line creased his brow. "I swear, you Kings are going to turn my hair gray. I should have found more reliable business partners. He lowered his feet from the desk and then headed off to the bar. "You know what? I think I will take that drink now."

"Be my guest."

"I'm just going to have one," Q said.

Pause.

"Are you monitoring how much I drink now?"

Jeremy watched his cousin. "Who are you talking to, Q?"

"Huh? What?" Quentin glanced around. "Oh. No one."

Jeremy made a note to himself to renew his effort to be careful about what he said around his emotionally fragile and potentially unstable cousin. *Damn. Maybe I should have a heart-to-heart with him. I'm really starting to worry about him.*

For a few minutes Jeremy's thoughts were pulled away from Leigh, as he contemplated whether he should be concerned—*really* concerned—about Q's mental state.

"Now, back to your little problem," Quentin said, making his whiskey sour. "Do you believe what she told you tonight?"

The question caught Jeremy off guard. And for a second, he didn't know what his cousin was talking about.

"Was your little freak fest a one-time thing or is her game tighter than you two knuckleheads realize?"

"I don't know."

"You think she's really going to break off the engagement?"

"I don't know."

"You think she'll tell your boy about the two of you?"

"I don't—"

"Better hope not."

"I don't— Wait, why? It's not like I knew—"

"But now you've also missed your opportunity to come clean *first*. By the way, I want to be on record that I told you to do that. If she tells him and you didn't— trust and believe there's going to be a misunderstanding and some furniture moving around."

"I like these no-lecture sessions we have."

"When you see a baby reaching for a hot stove, you smack their hand away."

Jeremy wanted to say something slick, but unfortunately Quentin was making too much sense. His directive to Leigh was for her to end the engagement. He wasn't specific about how. "I know the risk," Jeremy mumbled and then wandered back over to the sofa and plopped down.

Quentin had a hard time trying to hide his irritation. "Just so that I understand, you're seriously willing to risk the friendship of the man you have known your *whole* life, a man who's practically like a brother to you—a real blood brother—for a woman?"

"Roy deserves to know the truth."

"Then why didn't *you* tell him?"

Jeremy opened his mouth but was cut off.

"And before you blow smoke up my ass, let me warn you that we're waaay past the B.S. now. This isn't about an accidental one-nighter. This is about you wanting your boy's girl. You're rooting for the bust-up of this engagement, just so that you can swoop in and steal his girl for yourself!"

"That's not—"

"Don't do it!" Q shouted. "Don't you dare lie to me! And before you bark at me about this having nothing to do with *my* problems, remember there are waay too many similarities in our situations. And I'm not going to be beaten into feeling guilty just so you can sit there wrapped in some fake-ass, moral-superiority robe to justify your jacked-up decisions. *You* should have told your boy—your *blood brother*—the truth. The girl is irrelevant. This is about brothers—and what you *do* and *do not* do to each other!"

Knock! Knock! Knock!

Jeremy jumped, thankful to whoever it was at the door for saving him. "Come in!"

The door swung open. A blast of music from the main floor filled the office as an angry blur stormed through the door.

Jeremy jumped up. "Roy!"

Chapter 20

A million thoughts raced through Jeremy's mind as he stood with his feet bolted to the floor. He thrust his chin up and tried to prepare for anything. As a sign of unity, Q sprang up from his seat to stand beside him. The gesture touched Jeremy. It didn't mean that they weren't about to get their butts kicked, but it touched him all the same.

Roy slammed the office door and then proceeded to pace around like an angry, fire-breathing dragon.

"Roy," Jeremy began cautiously. "What are you doing here? Aren't you supposed to be at your engagement party?"

"Screw that damn party!" Roy said, tossing up his hands. "Screw all those fake-ass friends…and screw *her!*"

Jeremy jerked and then cut a look over at his cousin.

Quentin stood, bobbing his head as if he was bonding with Roy's pain.

"Would you like a drink or something, man?" Jeremy asked, even though he knew that there was a fifty-fifty chance that the alcohol was going to either calm or escalate this fragile situation.

"Somebody better give me something," Roy said, pacing like a caged lion. "'Cause I swear that I'm really ready to set it off in this damn town."

Jeremy turned to go back to the bar, but Q caught him by his arm and said, "I got this, cuz. You see about your boy."

The look his cousin gave him said for Jeremy to toss all his cards on the table and do the right thing.

Reluctantly, Jeremy nodded, but wondered where in the hell he was going to find the right words that could help this situation. Should he start off with humor, as in, "Hey, man, I have a funny story for you." Or apologetically, like "Sorry, dude, but I accidentally hooked up with your girl. And, oh, by the way, is there any way for you two to break up so that I can date her?"

Sucking in a deep breath, Jeremy suspected that there really wasn't any right or good way to about this. "Roy...would you like to sit down?"

"Hell, no, I don't want to sit down." Roy punched a fist into his palm. "I'd rather smash a brother's face in."

Jeremy touched the side of his face. "Now, c'mon. Violence has never solved anything."

Quentin chuckled from behind him.

He mumbled. "Well, it hasn't."

Roy was in his own world as he tried to wear a hole in the floor with his pacing. "I can't believe this, man. I can't believe this!"

Wait. Why isn't he already trying to pound my face into the ground? "I'm not quite sure what it is you're mad about," Jeremy said, tilting his head.

"I can't believe this woman straight up played me. I feel like a damn fool!" He punched his hand again. "Me!"

Something wasn't right here.

"Do you know how early in the morning you have to get up to pull something over on me?"

Jeremy shook his head.

Quentin took a guess. "About six?"

Both Jeremy and Roy cut a look at him.

Quentin shrugged. "What? He asked a question."

Jeremy rolled his eyes.

"Well," Roy said, disgruntled, "pretty early. And Ms. Leigh Matthews has been getting up at the booty crack of dawn for a while, 'cause this woman…" Roy slammed his eyes shut and shook his head.

Jeremy still wasn't quite sure what they were talking about. He glanced back over his shoulder and gave Q a questioning look. Maybe he was having a better time deciphering what the hell Roy was talking about. Leigh told his boy something, but clearly not the whole truth. The last thing he wanted to do was rush headlong into a five-alarm fire armed with just a bucket of water.

Since Quentin didn't have a dog in the race, he asked, "Did something happen?"

Roy laughed. The sound bordered on demonic. "Oh, something has been happening, all right. All this damn time, Leigh has been riding my back about how much of a dog I am—how I can't walk by a set of tits without getting my howl on—and what has she been doing?"

"Clearly not out trying to get a fenced-in yard," Quentin chuckled, plopping ice cubes into a glass.

No one laughed at the joke.

"Nah. She's been out here roaming the streets without her own damn flea collar on." Roy shook his head. "I can't believe I fell for that straitlaced, girl-next-door bullshit!"

Jeremy dropped his head. "I'm sorry, bruh." And he was sorry, but it didn't mean that he still didn't want her for himself.

Roy kept trying to rationalize how he got caught up. "You know what it was?" He stopped long enough to wave a finger. "I think I liked her because she wasn't another one of those chicks that always had her hand in your pocket because she needed to keep her hair whipped and dipped. A lot of these females spend enough money on wigs and weaves to run a small country—saying nothing for what it costs to keep them in the right labels and shoes. Not once did that girl ever ask me for nothing. She had her own, you know what I mean? But not in that bourgie, I-don't-need-a-man kind of way. She was cool. She was honest…." The anger gave way to confusion. But it wasn't long before he was shaking his head again. "I need to get my B.S. detector fixed."

"We all do," Quentin said, stepping from behind the bar.

Q was the lone amen choir today.

"Fell for it—hook, line and sinker," Roy continued. "Joke's on me."

"Here, have an Irish car bomb," Q said, handing him his drink. "Should hook you right up."

Roy snatched the drink and then tossed it back like

it was water. "Thanks, man. But in all honesty, I don't think even a horse tranquilizer could calm my nerves," he said, handing the glass back to Quentin. "Right now, I just want to find this sneaky son of a bitch that's been creeping with my girl behind my back." Another fist pound. "Might even catch a case, you feel me?"

Quentin glanced at his cousin and winced.

Jeremy ignored him while he processed this information. *So she told him about the affair, but not who it was with.* That tidbit gave him a pinhole of hope. Why? He had absolutely no idea. After his argument with Leigh in the freezer, he doubted that he was very high on her list of eligible bachelors.

"Well," Q said. "Since I'm fresh out of horse tranquilizers, how about I just fix you another drink?"

"Thanks, man." Roy bobbed his head and then resumed his pacing.

Jeremy struggled with his guilt. It wasn't like he had originally set out to steal Roy's girl, regardless of what Q's beady-eyed gaze seemed to accuse him of. He met a woman at a party. He liked her. They had a fling and tonight he discovered that she was his buddy's girl. How did that make him the bad guy?

"Look, Roy. Maybe you shouldn't just jump to conclusions," he backpedaled. "Maybe this dude didn't know she was your girl."

Roy stopped. "What? You're defending this dude now?"

"Nah. I'm just saying…" He shrugged his shoulders. *What am I saying?*

"What are you saying?" Quentin pressed, folding his arms.

Jeremy cocked his head. "I thought you were about to make Roy another drink."

"Fine." Q headed back to the bar, but as he walked past Jeremy he added, "I was just trying to help you out."

You call that help?

"All I know," Roy said. "Come tomorrow, I'm going to be a laughingstock. We bust up on the night of our engagement party. You know how that's going to look in the papers? Hell, I turned my whole life upside down to get traded to L.A. Why? So we could be closer—so I can spend less time on the road."

"And less time in someone *else's* bed," Quentin added, nodding. "That's a huge sacrifice."

"See?" Roy gestured to Q. "He gets it."

"That's a scarier thought than you know," Jeremy said.

"All I know is there's no way I'm signing those papers come Monday morning. I can't stay in this town. What if I run into her again?"

"So you're going to blow up a huge multi-million deal over a woman," Q marveled. "Damn, that is love."

"Oh, c'mon," Jeremy said, strolling over and pounding Roy on the back. He needed to try and fix this. "I wouldn't take things that far. This sort of the thing... happens—intentionally or unintentionally."

Roy frowned.

Jeremy gave him an awkward laugh. "I mean...take me for example..." A rock suddenly lodged itself in his windpipe so he started coughing to try and dislodge it. "Now, you know that I would never try to...intentionally hurt you, right?"

"Yeah...and?" Roy was clearly lost as to where

Jeremy was trying to go with this. From the corner of his eye, he saw Q set the bottle down and lean over the bar, resting his elbows on the counter, like he was watching reality TV.

"And...who knows, it might have been the same way for Leigh."

"What? You're going to tell me that she accidently fell on some dude's dick? Bruh, c'mon, now. Stop playing."

"No. No. I'm just—"

"Look. All I know is that I don't ever want to see that woman again. And if I *ever* catch wind of who this brother is, I'm going to stomp him into the ground. That man is *dead*. And to think how close I came to actually raising that man's child!"

Jeremy's head jerked up. "What?"

Roy sobered as his jaw squared. "Yeah. To top everything off, Leigh's pregnant!"

Chapter 21

Leigh couldn't stop crying.

When she didn't answer Ariel's fifty back-to-back calls, her best friend hauled butt out of the party and rushed over to Leigh's place to check in on her. Seeing her girl sprawled across the bed and crying her eyes out, Ariel actually breathed a sigh of relief.

"Shhh. It's going to be all right," she consoled, rubbing her girl's back and stroking her hair. "It wasn't pleasant. But you did what you had to do and now you can move on."

Leigh lifted her head off the pillow. "But you weren't here. You didn't see his face. He was soo excited one second and the next…I don't think I've ever seen him that mad. *Ever*."

"Are you having regrets?"

Leigh sniffed. Her guilt only doubled when she confessed, "No."

"Then see? That just proves that you did the right thing. Sure, it's painful now, but soon all this pain will go away."

She could only hope so. "You know he'll hate me forever."

"Maybe. But why don't we just try to concentrate on the things that we can control?"

Leigh smiled weakly at her friend. I'm so happy that you came over."

"Aww." Ariel curled up next to her on the bed. "That's what best friends are for. Tears, chocolate and alcohol. Not necessarily in that order."

Leigh laughed.

"See. That's better." Ariel smiled.

However, Leigh's good feeling was only temporary. "I still don't know what I'm going to do about Jeremy."

"Humph. If you don't know, then you're more than welcome to pass his fine butt over to me—or at least his cousin, Quentin. I'd loved to spread that man over a Ritz cracker any day of the week."

Leigh's laughter rumbled pretty steadily. "Girl, you are a mess."

Ariel shrugged. "Maybe—but I ain't lying."

Leigh propped her head on her girl's shoulder and told herself that she was just going to have to rest her eyes for a few minutes. Next thing she knew, she was fast asleep and dreaming of a different party...

She was happy, nestled in the center of a large, white couch with equally large and overstuffed pillows. An army of women surrounded her. They were all laughing and smiling. A couple of them would tug on her arm only so that they could remind her of just how lucky she was.

"I know," she'd tell them, one right after the other.

And she believed it—felt it—even though a part of her was still aware that this was all just a dream.

"Okay. It's time to open this one," Ariel said, passing her a giant box. However, it was awkward to maneuver the present around her incredibly big belly.

"Do you have any idea what you're having this time?" Cathy asked, pushing back her perfect honey-blond hair.

A deep baritone interrupted the women's conversation. "We want to be surprised—again."

All eyes turned toward the door, where Jeremy stood holding a little boy on one hip, and on the other a beautiful even younger little girl dressed in an adorable pink dress. Jeremy bent over and set them down on the floor. "Say hello to your mommy."

The kids took off running toward her on the couch. "Mommy, Mommy!"

All of her friends looked as if their hearts were melting at the picturesque maternal image.

"All I know is that I'll be thrilled as long as the baby has ten fingers and ten toes," her mother bragged. "And then they can get right back to work on the next one."

Jeremy's face lit up as his gaze shifted back to Leigh. "I think I can handle that."

Leigh's eyes popped open. She was back in her bedroom with Ariel, who was lightly snoring beside her. When she glanced at the clock, she guesstimated that she had only been asleep for about twenty minutes. Yet when she tried to recall the dream, it was like trying to capture a puff of smoke. Whatever she'd been dreaming, it certainly made her feel good.

Pregnant.

Stunned, Jeremy stared at Roy. It was the only thing

he could do, especially since the room was spinning and the blood rushing to his head sounded like a freight train. After a moment, he managed to open his mouth, and in the next, he closed it. *Open. Close.* Surely if he kept it up, words would eventually start flowing—but he wouldn't bet his house on it.

Pregnant.

Q was the first to get over the shock. "Now, when you say 'pregnant' do you mean with a child?" Okay, maybe he wasn't over the shock.

"Crazy, huh?" Roy said, shaking his head. "But an hour ago, I was bouncing off the walls, thinking that I was about to be a father." He resumed his pacing. "You should've seen me. There I was blabbing on like an idiot about how I was going to be a better man and predicting that we were going to have a boy. He stopped and a wave of sadness washed over his face.

"You know what, man, I got to get out of here. I need to go for a drive or something." He glanced up.

Jeremy struggled to pull his thoughts together. "Roy, we need to talk." He turned toward Quentin. "Cuz, can you give us a moment?"

"Some other time," Roy interrupted. "I need to try and get my head right or at least get it wrapped around this whole situation."

"Yeah, but—"

"Look. I really appreciate you letting me come over here and blow off some steam. I know that when the chips are down, that I can really count on you to come through for me." He locked gazes with Jeremy. "In fact, I love you for that."

More rocks piled onto his windpipe. "And I love you, man—which is why I have to tell you that—"

"Tomorrow," Roy said, turning toward the door. "I promise tomorrow we'll hook up and finish this convo, a'ight? Right now I can't really handle anything else. I got to do some serious thinking and make a couple of moves. Cool?"

Jeremy hesitated, but then after a moment of reading his friend's expression, he nodded. "Cool. Tomorrow, then. I'll call you on your cell."

"Bet. I'll catch you later." Roy jerked the door open and a loud burst of music flooded the office again. "Yo, Q. Thanks for the drink."

"Anytime." Quentin gave him a two-finger salute.

"A'ight. Later." Roy winked at Jeremy and then jetted out.

Jeremy stared at the door halfway expecting his boy to return and yell "April Fool's." But once one, then two, then three minutes passed, reality started settling in. He turned and Q stood next to him.

"Congratulations?"

"She's pregnant," Jeremy said, still stunned.

"I heard. Maybe next time you'll start buying condoms that fit. Here you go." Q handed him a drink. "You look like you could use this."

Jeremy took the glass and, just like Roy, tossed it back like it was water. "Thanks. I needed that."

"Don't mention it." Quentin folded his arms. "Look. I know that this may not be the best time to bring this up, but in the most-screwed-up-life category, you just pulled ahead by a hair."

"Noticed that, did you?" Jeremy said, as he rolled his eyes and went back to the couch. On his back, he stared up at the ceiling. "You know, this means she knew when I hauled her into the freezer and practically showed my ass."

"Guess that means that your daddy weekend visitations will have court-appointed supervision."

Jeremy groaned. "Why didn't she say something?"

"Would that conversation have happened between your being pelted with the chicken or the fish?"

Jeremy fell silent while the words *pregnant* and *father* tumbled around in his head. "Can I tell you something on the serious tip?"

"Sure."

"I think I'm scared."

Quentin's brows knitted together, but then he thought about what he'd do if he was in Jeremy's situation. "I feel you."

Jeremy sat up, but still squirmed around in his seat. "I mean…I've never really thought about being a father. I guess I knew one day that it would happen. But I never thought about what kind of father I would be, you know?"

Q nodded. "I don't think that I've given much thought to it, either. Heck. I'm having a difficult time just navigating being a son…and a brother."

Jeremy braided his fingers together and said, "I hope I'm as good a father as my dad."

Quentin glanced up. "Yeah. Jorell is cool. I remember a few summers when you guys would come up to the estate, and he would go out and play ball, wrestle or whatever you guys felt like doing. He was really hands-on," Q said. His gaze floated back down. "I don't have a single childhood memory of when my father wasn't wearing a suit." He shrugged. "But there was always Alfred, James and Antonio. There were plenty of times when they would feel sorry for the poor little rich kids and sneak in time to play with us. My playmates—the cook, the gardener and butler. What else could a child want?"

Jeremy's heart squeezed. "I'm sorry to hear that."

"Don't be. It was a veeeery long time ago."

"Still..."

"Well, instead of feeling sorry for me, do me a favor and make sure that you pay a little more attention to your kid than my old man. Maybe they won't turn out to be so screwed up."

"Deal." Jeremy sucked in a deep breath. "All I have to do now is break my best friend's heart and then hope that I haven't completely ruined my chances to not only be in my child's life, but in Leigh's, as well."

Quentin shook his head. "Maybe you should think about joining somebody's church because that's going to require a whole lot of praying."

Chapter 22

"Leigh, honey. Wake up."

Leigh woke to the gentle rocking of her shoulders and groaned. Unfortunately, her stomach joined the motion of her shoulders, and she immediately bolted out of bed and sprinted to the bathroom. All the contents of her late-night refrigerator raid came out.

"I knew it," her mother said excitedly from the bathroom doorway. "You're pregnant!" Sheree clapped her hands and started bouncing. "Wait until your father hears. He'll owe me a month's worth of breakfasts in bed. I told him last night that you were knocked up." She gasped. "You know this means we'll have to move up the wedding date." She started making new plans while she waltzed over to the linen closet and pulled out a small face towel. "I know it's a bit old-fashioned, dear, but having a noticeable baby bump on your big day is still considered bad form."

Her mother moved over to the sink, turned on the water and made a cool compress. "I know getting the caterer, baker and florist to commit to an earlier date shouldn't be a problem, but the venue may be a grand mal–inducing migraine." She shook her head. "But don't you worry about it. I'm all over it. Now, as for an obstetrician, I know this fabulous—"

"Mom," Leigh moaned.

"Yes, sweetheart?"

"There's not going to be a wedding." She reached up and took the cold towel from her mother's hands and pressed it to her forehead. "Thanks for the compress."

Sheree shook her head and tried to clear it. "Say that again, because it almost sounded like—"

"DeShawn and I are not getting married." Leigh struggled to her feet. "We broke up last night." She shuffled out of the bathroom, certain that she looked like the walking dead. In the bedroom Ariel peeled herself out of bed. "Morning. How do you feel?"

"Probably about as good as I look."

Ariel winced. "Damn."

"Wait a minute," Leigh's mother said, coming out of her shock and strolling out of the bathroom behind her daughter. "How could you two be broken up? Does DeShawn know about the baby?"

"Oh, he knows, all right," Leigh said, making it all the way to the kitchen and then stopping briefly to wonder whether she could stomach the strong smell of coffee this early in the morning.

"If you want," Ariel said, joining her, "I can make the coffee."

Leigh looked at her and then shook her head.

"Tea?"

Another head shake.

"Then how about orange juice?"

"I think I can handle that."

"Good. You can have the orange juice and I'll have a screwdriver."

"Hello?" her mother said, irritably. "Baby? Wedding? Somebody say something. I think I'm one minute from having a nervous breakdown."

Leigh turned toward her mother's wide and expectant eyes and felt a wave of embarrassment for having to make this confession. But putting it off really wasn't an option. "The wedding is off for a host of reasons. One, because I'm no longer in love with DeShawn. And to be honest with you I haven't been in a long while. Two, I told DeShawn last night that I had been with another man during the last time we broke up. And three..." She drew in a deep breath.

"And three?" Sheree pressed as she held her breath.

"And—and I'm having the other man's baby."

Her mother gasped, but then clearly realized that having a fit of apoplexy was not the way to go. "Okay, okay. Well...I am... Well—" She glanced over at Ariel who was pouring vodka into her orange juice.

"Ariel, honey. I think I'm going to need one of those."

"Coming right up."

"Well, okay, then." Her mother slumped into one of the stools at the breakfast counter. She waited until Ariel handed her the screwdriver before she attempted to speak again, and only then after she had taken a healthy gulp. "So...okay. DeShawn is out and this new young man—does he have a name?"

"Jeremy," Leigh said. "Jeremy King." She tried to

ignore the delicious quiver that raced through her at the mere mention of his name.

Her mother nodded and then stopped. "Why does that name sound familiar?"

DeShawn had talked about his best friend to her parents countless times. They, like her, just had never had the opportunity to put a face to a name—until last night.

"Didn't DeShawn have a friend named...?" Her mother's eyes grew even wider as she shook her head. "No! It can't be the same guy, is it?"

Leigh's good-girl image had officially crashed and burned.

"By some weird ironic joke...I'm afraid it is. I simply didn't know at the time."

"I guess it's a good thing that I'm sitting down." She looked at her drink. "And it's too early in the morning to have more than one of these...isn't it?"

"Mom, I know this is a lot to take in. And I understand if you're disappointed..."

"Now, Leigh, let's not confuse shock with disappointment. I'm your mother. I'm going to love you no matter what. And I refuse to believe that this child you're carrying is a mistake or an accident. He or she was meant to be and that's good enough for me."

Leigh smiled and then walked over to her mother's outstretched arms for a much-needed embrace.

Ring! Ring! Ring!

"Ugh. Who could that be calling so early?" Leigh asked, pulling out of her mother's arms and heading over to the phone. Once she read the name on the caller ID, she froze.

"Who is it?" her mother and Ariel asked in unison.

Beep!

"Hello?" Jeremy's deep baritone filtered through the speakers. "Yes, this is Jeremy King. (pause) I'm looking for a Leigh Matthews. I'm hoping that this is the right number. If so, I'd really appreciate it if you would give me a call back. I...know that there's a chance that you might not want to do that, especially after my appalling behavior last night."

Pause.

"There really isn't a good excuse for that...and I wish... I hope that you will give me the opportunity to apologize to you in person. So please, give me a call. My cell phone is—"

"Aren't you going to write the number down, sweetie?" her mother asked.

Leigh stared at her machine like it had just fallen from outer space. "How did he get my number?"

Ariel shrugged her shoulders. "I doubt that it's all that hard, especially now that he knows your name."

"Why wouldn't he have known your name?" her mother asked, trying to keep up with the conversation.

Leigh ignored the question while another horrifying thought assailed her. "You don't think—" she glanced over at Ariel "—that he knows?"

"About the baby?" Ariel said, and then gave her another shrug. "Anything is possible. You know men gossip worse than women."

"DeShawn could've left here and gone straight over there," she reasoned. "He could've told him about the breakup and about..."

"So I take it that the young man didn't know?" her mother asked.

"Heck, I didn't know until yesterday, Momma."

Leigh plopped down on the stool next to her and tried to process all of this. "Everything is moving so fast."

"Humph. You better get used to the pace, sweetheart. Once you become a mother, time starts ticking at warp speed."

A mother.

Ariel finally asked the sixty-four-thousand-dollar question. "Are you going to call him back?"

"And say what?"

Sheree cut in. "Well, you can tell him whether or not you accept his apology. I don't know about you, but he sounded pretty sincere to me."

Leigh thrust her hip out to the side and folded her arms.

"Or not," her mother amended. "I thought it would at least be a nice conversation starter. Can I risk asking what it is that he did that got you so upset?"

Leigh remembered Jeremy's rant vividly. And the last thing she wanted to do was to recite the entire ugly episode to her mother. *Especially the "crazy gold-digging ho" part.*

"You know what?" Leigh said, shaking her head. "I can't deal with him right now."

"You're going to have to deal with him sooner or later."

"Yeah. Well...I choose later—much, much later."

Jeremy couldn't shake the feeling when he hung up the phone that Leigh had just heard every word he'd said but had refused to pick up the phone. Not that he could really blame her. His behavior last night looked even worse when viewed in the light of day.

But somehow he had to figure out a way to fix all of this—with Roy *and* Leigh—*especially* with Leigh.

He'd slept in his office, his home away from home. He slept there not because he'd pulled an all-nighter at work, but because he was too shocked by everything that had happened to drive. All in all, he might have gotten about two hours of sleep. And then suddenly, his dreams were filled with babies and baby showers? *Weird.*

Yet somehow, the dream made him feel good. Now that the idea of becoming a father had had a chance to marinate, he discovered that he really wasn't all that scared. If anything, he was excited.

A father. The list of things that he wanted and could do with his child was endless. He was so excited that he popped up that morning, brewed some coffee and went online. After just a few clicks, he was able to find the Leigh Matthews that he was looking for.

But now what?

What if she didn't return his call?

What if she had already decided that she didn't want to have anything to do with him?

What then?

She'll call, he thought, trying to reassure himself.

The usually confident voice inside his head didn't sound so confident. If anything it sounded like an all-in poker bet at the blackjack table.

I hope she calls.

Hope. That tiny pinprick was still hanging in there.

After a quick shower and a fresh change of clothes, Jeremy made his next big phone call. Roy. Even before all the speed-dial numbers appeared on the cell-phone screen, Jeremy's heart rate had accelerated a good twenty percent. It was crazy, since it wasn't like he was about to drop his bombshell over the phone. He just wanted to nail down a time and a place where they could hook up and talk—preferably, somewhere public, where the chance of Roy committing homicide was less likely.

When the call went to voice mail, Jeremy was both relieved and disappointed. He left a quick message asking Roy to call back. He waited for a few minutes, hoping that Roy would call back quickly. When that didn't happen, he elected to go grab some breakfast from the café a few blocks down the street. As he walked through the club, the day crew was already cleaning and stocking up.

"Jeremy," Delilah called out. "You have a moment?"

"Sure." He glanced at his watch as he strolled back to work. The hostess's daytime look was a makeup-free face and a Nike running suit. "What's up?"

Her face pinched. "Well, actually… I don't really know how to bring this up."

He chuckled. "You?" He blinked in surprise. His opinionated hostess had never been tongue-tied before. "Well, it must be awfully serious."

"I think it is."

At hearing that, he sobered. "Okay. I'm listening."

"It's about Quentin."

The words hit him like a sucker punch. "All right. What about him?"

"Well—a few of us are a little concerned."

"How do you mean? Has he done something?"

She hesitated again. "Look. It's not like we don't all talk to ourselves now and then. But a couple of us—myself included—have seen Quentin sort of talking or arguing with himself. You don't think he's cracking up, do you?"

Jeremy first instinct was to say no, but then he remembered that brief incident in his office last night. Hadn't it seemed like Quentin was arguing with someone who wasn't there?

"Thanks for bringing it to my attention. I'll get to the bottom of it."

Delilah's shoulders relaxed with relief. She had clearly been nervous about approaching him with this. "Thanks. And I'm really sorry to have to be the one to tell you this, but we felt that we needed to say something."

"Don't worry. You did the right thing," he assured her with a quick smile.

He turned and headed out of the club. After more than a year of playing Pass the Cousin, Jeremy decided that it was time to change course. Sliding in behind the wheel of his Porsche, he scooped his cell out of his pocket and made one more call. "Hello, Quentin?"

Chapter 23

I'm not going to call. I'm not going to call.

Leigh kept her eyes closed standing under the hot shower while she repeated the mantra. She had hoped that the more she said the words, the more it would strengthen her resolve. So far, it wasn't working. It probably had a lot to do with the sound of Jeremy's voice on her answering machine. Sure. He sounded all humble and contrite now. But that probably had a lot more to do with him finding out that she was pregnant than anything else—and she was nearly a hundred percent certain that he knew.

Last night, she was the crazy gold-digging ho. Today, what—he found out that she was possibly having his child and wanted to change up? *Please.*

Leigh ground her teeth. What had she ever seen in him before—other than the obvious? Sure, he was handsome, charming and successful—but so was De-

Shawn. In fact, those two being best friends had to be another red flag. What did they say, "birds of a feather flock together"?

If DeShawn was a dog, then certainly his best friend, Jeremy, was too.

I'm not going to call. I'm not going to call.

He called to apologize for his appalling behavior. *Humph. Guess now I'm supposed to just forget everything he said last night so he can clear his conscience,* she thought. Leigh shook her head and tried to strengthen her resolve.

I'm not going to call. I'm not going to call.

By the time Leigh stepped out of the shower, her mantra was still holding fast. That is until she hit Play on the answering machine again and again. Jeremy's sexy baritone embraced her. It was difficult for her to ignore that she had more than a few heartstrings tugging at her.

Surprisingly, there was still a little part of her that wanted to forgive Jeremy for his explosive reaction last night. After all, every time she took a moment to try and see things his way, there was an argument to be made that he could've felt duped in this whole scenario, especially if he hadn't known that she and DeShawn had broken up during the time they met. Maybe DeShawn doesn't tell his boy everything.

In *that* case, she might have looked a little...sorta, kinda *loose*. And *maybe* the idea that she was stepping out on his best friend and had intentionally entangled him in a web that could potentially destroy their friendship, then maybe, just maybe, he did have the right to be angry.

That still did not make it okay to call her a crazy gold-digging ho.

Of course, there was also that scene in the back office of The Dollhouse. She flushed.

But he *knew* she was engaged, too. Was it okay for him to make a move on another man's woman as long as it wasn't someone *he* knew?

He had some nerve. For the past couple of months, she had been fantasizing about this man, and now she could hardly stand the thought of him.

That's not true.

It wasn't true now. But if she said it enough times, it might become true.

Maybe.

Hopefully.

Despite her constant rehashing of the events in recent weeks, and admitting that from Jeremy's perspective there was a *slight* chance that she looked like she was playing his best friend, Leigh still felt that he should have given her a chance to explain herself.

But no.

Instead, he dragged her out of her engagement party and threatened to expose her infidelity in a claustrophobic walk-in freezer.

But he did call to apologize.

And there she was—having come full circle—still not knowing whether she was going to accept his apology or not.

I'm not going to call him. I'm not going to call him.

An hour later, Leigh strolled into Dr. Norman's office with her stomach twisted in knots. Her mother pulled a few strings to get her the appointment on such short notice so that they could confirm what several home pregnancy tests had already told her.

After signing in, she and her mother found two seats in the waiting room and began the doctor's office ritual of scanning ages-old magazines, while waiting for her name to be called.

"In other news," the entertainment reporter said, from the mounted flat-screen television in the corner, "NBA star DeShawn Carter is officially off the market. In a statement released by his publicist, the star basketball player has recently tied the knot with his longtime gal pal, and exotic dancer, Sydney Russell, a.k.a. Caramel Swirl. The statement also states that the couple is expecting their second child later this year."

Sheree gasped, while Leigh stared at the screen. There was something wrong with her hearing. The reporter couldn't have possibly said what Leigh thought she'd said.

The reporter's handsome co-anchor turned his head and asked, "DeShawn Carter and Caramel Swirl? I thought he was engaged to another woman, an L.A. screenwriter?"

The reporters smiled benignly. "Who can keep up with celebrity couplings these days?" She turned back toward the camera. "On to the Middle East…"

After a few seconds, Sheree turned toward her daughter. "Who on earth is Caramel Swirl?"

Leigh shook her head. She knew the name well. It was the same woman who had always come between her and DeShawn. "Don't worry about it, Mom. Let's just hope he's happy." *Bastard.*

"Married? What do you mean he's married?" Jeremy asked Quentin, who sat across from him at the Breakfast Café. This wasn't the reason he asked his cousin to join him for breakfast. But after Q dropped the latest bombshell, he was rendered speechless.

"It says so right here," Quentin said, flipping over a thin newspaper and shoving it toward Jeremy. "I heard it on the radio on the way over here. Couldn't believe it until I bought the paper right outside, and bam! There you go—your man cheesing in the gossip section. Recognize the chick under his arm?"

Jeremy leaned in and blinked. "Is that—?"

"Caramel Swirl," Q said, shaking his head. "You know, it's about time I rolled my butt up out of this city. All this woman-sharing is starting to creep me out—and that's saying something."

Jeremy couldn't stop shaking his head. "Roy referred her to me, but he never said anything about them being in any relationship. And…a *second* kid? What the hell?"

"Seems your boy has a hell of a lot of secrets."

"Yeah, but *this*—this is something else altogether. And last night he seemed so crushed about Leigh not being pregnant with his baby."

"I don't know. I guess I can see where he's coming from."

Jeremy glanced up. "You can?"

"Yeah. I mean, he kept the good girl on his arm and the freaks on the side. But if the good girl can flip the script on you like that, then why not just marry your freak and save yourself the trouble? Plus, he was awfully concerned about being a laughingstock last night. Maybe he just didn't want the sun to rise today, and the grapevine be all about him getting played on the night of his engagement party. This way, it looks like Leigh was the one that got dumped. Brilliant playa move—I'm impressed."

"What—is there some playa handbook out there I don't know about? How come you know all these supposed moves?"

"Nah. Nah. Nobody is crazy enough to write this stuff down. You do, and the whole system collapses. Women get hold of something like that and it's a wrap." Q trembled at the thought.

Jeremy's gaze returned to the article. When he was through reading, he read it again. Despite all Q said, he still had a hard time wrapping his head around why Roy would make such an impulsive move.

"C'mon. Stranger things have been known to happen, especially in L.A."

Jeremy tossed the article down and slumped back in the booth. "This is probably going to crush Leigh." He tried to imagine her reaction to all of this.

"Or not," Q said, signaling for the waitress. "Do you think that she's still in love with him?"

Jeremy shrugged his shoulders. He was forced to admit, "I honestly have no clue. It's not like we've ever had the chance to talk about it."

"Yeah, you two have that whole cart before the horse thing going on."

Jeremy nodded. "Maybe. But right now, I'd be happy if she just called me back." He scooped out his Black-Berry to see whether he'd somehow missed a call.

Q chuckled. "Maybe you should swing by one of those sports stores and see about picking yourself up some knee pads. If you're seriously going to pursue this, then you're going to be groveling for a minute. You might as well make yourself comfortable."

Sighing, Jeremy nodded again. "Yeah, I've been having that same feeling myself." He reached for his coffee. At least now, he knew why Roy hadn't returned any of his calls. He was on his honeymoon.

Married...with kids.

"Heeeeey, Jeremy. Long time no see."

He glanced up and smiled. "Hey, Ella. What's the day's special?"

Ella smiled and twirled her hips as she recited the breakfast specials.

Jeremy listened, but they both knew what he was going to order. "I'll have my usual."

"Your order is already in." She winked, letting him know just how well she knew his routine. She then turned her attention to Quentin, and gave him the same flirtatious smile.

Q winked. "I'll have whatever he's having."

"You got it." Ella winked back before pivoting and strolling back toward the kitchen with an extra oomph to her walk.

"All right. Now that I've dropped my little bombshell on you this morning, pray tell, what the hell am I even doing up at this ungodly hour?"

Jeremy sighed. He really didn't want to have this discussion.

"You do remember calling me and telling me that you needed to talk, don't you? You're a little too young to be having memory problems."

"Yeah, I want to talk to you about something that has been brought to my attention."

"Oh?"

"Yeah. I talked to Delilah this morning and she

brought up some concerns that she and some of the other employees were having about you."

"Me?"

"Your health."

Quentin laughed. "What? I'm fine. I'm the very picture of good health—mainly because of my mother's genes."

Jeremy smiled. "Yeah, well, it's more about your *mental* health."

Q's brows arched up as his tone dropped a notch. "Oh?"

"I have to admit that I've been a little concerned, as well." He paused, but Q remained silent. "Have you been feeling okay? How's your stress level?"

"Stress?" Quentin found his humor again. "Stress and overexertion are two things I try to avoid at all cost."

Jeremy studied his cousin. But since he wasn't a doctor, he wasn't sure what he was looking for. "Last night. You were sort of talking to yourself—more like arguing."

"Oh—that?"

"Yeah—that."

Quentin waved him off with an awkward laugh. "It's nothing. I'm fine."

"But you are aware that you do talk to yourself?"

"And you don't?" Q spun the question back on him. "Everyone talks to themselves from time to time. It's no big deal."

That was true, but there was still something a little off about it.

"So that's it?" Q said. "I dragged myself out of bed

because I had a debate with myself over whether to have a drink or not?"

"And the concerns of the employees." Jeremy sucked in a breath and tried again. "Look, man. Maybe you should just go talk to someone. Get a lot of that stuff that you're carrying around off your chest."

"What? You mean like a therapist or something?"

"Yeah." He shrugged. "Why not?"

"Because I'm not crazy," Quentin snapped.

Jeremy held up his hands, surrendering. He'd stated his case. That's all he could do.

Ella arrived with their food and Quentin's tense features softened. He went back to flashing his deadly dimples at the waitress.

"You boys enjoy your meals," she said, winking.

"Absolutely," Quentin said and then watched the sway of her hips as she strolled off. He started to turn his attention back to Jeremy, when someone coming into the café caught his eye. "Yo, cuz. Isn't that your future baby momma over there?"

Chapter 24

I'm going to be a mom.

That news trumped the news of DeShawn running off to Vegas to marry an exotic dancer. From what she understood, that sort of thing happened all the time. Her mother, however, was having a harder time with it, and judging by the number of times Ariel was calling her cell phone, she was, too. However, for Leigh, DeShawn's elopement had a more liberating effect. The guilt she woke up with that morning was gone. And the confirmation she'd received at the doctor's office literally had her floating on air.

A mom.

This was definitely one of those times when she didn't know how much she'd wanted something until it was right there, staring her in the face. Perhaps the circumstances weren't ideal, but her joy triumphed over everything else. She was nowhere near showing, and yet she couldn't stop touching her belly and smiling.

I'm going to be a mom.

"Hello, Leigh."

Leigh jerked her head up at the unexpected, but still very sexy and familiar baritone. *Annnnnnd here's the father.* She sucked in a deep breath and tried her best to level him with an annoyed glare. "Hello."

He amped up his smile, and then turned it on her un-suspecting mother. "Hello. Jeremy King. I don't believe we've had the chance to meet."

Sheree's eyes sprung wide with shock. "Oh, you're Jeremy King." She slowly slipped her hand into his, as if she was in some sort of trance. "I'm Sheree Mat-thews, Leigh's mother."

"Nice to meet you." He tried to release her hand, but it was her mother who hung on. "My, what large hands you have."

"Why, thank you."

"Huh…um." She cocked her head and assessed the shoulder, chest and waist.

If Leigh hadn't gently kicked her under the table, she was fairly certain that she was about to tell him to turn around so that she could check out the rear view. "Mom," she hissed.

"Hmm, what?" Sheree dragged her eyes away from Jeremy's chiseled frame to meet her daughter's hard stare. "Oh. Right." She released Jeremy's hand and proudly…and inappropriately announced, "We're mad at you."

Leigh closed her eyes and tried to count to ten—she made it to three. "Is there something that I can help you with, *Mr. King?*"

"Actually, yes. I was hoping that we could have a few minutes alone so that we can talk." His smile turned apologetic toward her mother.

"We don't have anything to talk about," Leigh stated flatly.

"Leigh," her mother hissed, before her foot nearly took her daughter's shin out under the table.

"Ow!" Leigh said, glaring back at her mother.

Sheree Matthews flashed her daughter a flat, tight smile before picking up her purse and sliding out of the booth.

Leigh panicked. "Where are you going?"

"Just to the bathroom," she responded in an overly saccharine tone. "I'll be back in a minute."

Leigh had a sneaking suspicion that she'd be lucky if her mother was back in an hour. *Damn. Why hadn't she driven the car?* With only her sharp glare as a weapon against her mother, she sighed in another deep breath as Sheree stood and offered her seat to the enemy.

"Thank you," Jeremy said, and sat down.

When his dark soulful eyes leveled on Leigh's face, her body's mutiny began. Her tongue curled, her breasts ached, her mouth went dry and her clit hammered in sync with her speeding heart.

"What do you want?" she managed to ask before her throat tightened.

"I called you this morning...I don't know if you got my message...."

Leigh folded her arms and stared. She wasn't going to acknowledge a damn thing.

He knew what time it was and inhaled another deep breath. "About last night," he began. "I—"

"I don't want to talk about last night," she said, shaking her head and grinding her teeth.

"But—"

"In fact, I don't want to talk to you about anything ever again, if I can help it."

To her surprise, his head jerked back as if she'd just slapped him. She leaned in over the table. "You had some nerve manhandling and talking to me like that."

"I know, I—"

"Not only was I humiliated, but you had the audacity to call me a crazy gold-digging ho," she hissed.

"Actually, I said that you were either or."

She pounded a fist on the table while her eyes narrowed murderously.

Jeremy's arms flew up in surrender. "But your point is well taken." This time, he leaned over the table.

In response, she eased back.

"Leigh, I'm not proud of what I did last night. I have to admit that it had a lot to do with my anger and fear. And while my emotions were at levels that I've never experienced before, I have to say that I am truly, truly sorry."

He reached for her hands, but she jerked them back. His touch was the last thing that she could handle at this moment.

Leigh's eyes misted as she shook her head. "You're only saying that because…" She struggled to swallow the boulder lodged in her throat. "Because…" She turned and hopped up out of her seat. "I can't do this right now," she croaked. "Do me a favor and just go to hell," she said, and raced out of the café.

Two seconds later, her mother bolted out of the ladies' room after her.

Jeremy watched them race out with his throat tightening and a growing pain inside his chest. "I've really screwed this up."

Rolling in the Deep

Chapter 25

"Frankly," Quentin said, in an utterly sincere voice, "I thought it was a wrap for my boy. I mean, I ought to know. There are some things that there's just no coming back from."

Julianne Turner frowned as she cupped her chin and studied him. "You don't believe in forgiveness?"

"Well, there's forgiving and there's forgetting. In my opinion, a lot of people get the two mixed up. Most of the time when people ask you to forgive them, they are really asking you to forget. Nobody forgets. It's impossible except, I guess, when you're dealing with someone with memory issues. Other than that…" He shook his head. "It's not happening. And if you're unable to forget, you'll never truly forgive. It's all just lip service."

"You have an interesting belief system, Quentin. You claim not to believe in love—"

"Uh-uh-uh…" Q sat up and shook his head. "I said that I didn't *understand* love. I believe in it. After all, my parents are in love—or at least their version of it. *I* was in love with Alyssa—"

"Was?" Dr. Turner perked up. "You don't believe that you are anymore?"

Quentin blinked, but as he considered the question for a full minute, the truth tumbled out. "No." Once the simple answer fell from his mouth, he would've bet everything he owned that a huge weight had just been lifted off his shoulders.

"This is good," Dr. Turner said, bobbing her head. "I think that we may be getting somewhere here."

"Huh." Quentin remained silent as this revelation washed over him.

"How do you feel about it?"

After another minute to run that question through his mind, Q answered honestly, "I'm not sure."

"Okay." Dr. Turner bobbed her head and flashed a smile. "That's okay. This is still good."

Quentin smiled at the way her eyes lit up. "Reggie is a lucky man," he said, shaking his head. "I hope he knows that."

"Not that it's any of your business," she said sternly, but still holding on to a smile. "But yes, he does."

Their eyes locked for an indeterminate amount of time before Julianne Turner snapped out of her trance and cleared her throat.

"Uh, w-where were we?" She coughed to clear her throat, but when it didn't work, she hopped up. "Excuse me for just a second." She rushed over to the small refrigerator and took out a bottled water. She didn't bother with a glass.

"Are you all right?" Quentin asked, his dimples deepening.

"Yeah. Sure. I'm good." She waved off his concern, but she was clearly flustered. She tilted the bottle again and drained it. "Okay. Now, where were we?" she asked as she returned to her chair.

"Several places, actually," Quentin said, checking out the deep flush of embarrassment on her face.

"Forgiveness," she blurted, sliding back on her professional veneer. "Let's back up to that. I'm interested in knowing why you think one can't forgive without being able to forget."

It was his turn to become uncomfortable again.

"Forgiving a wrong simply means someone chooses not to let the wrongful deed have power over them— the power to hurt, the power to fester, the power to destroy love," said Dr. Turner, somberly. "Forgiveness can sometimes be just paying lip service, I agree. In society we toss around the word a lot. But it does happen. I see it every day."

Quentin was quiet for a long time. "I haven't."

"No?" she asked dubiously. "Didn't Victoria ultimately forgive Eamon for his omission? Didn't Xavier forgive Cheryl for her deceit?"

Quentin's brows crashed together.

"And what about Jeremy and Leigh? How did he ultimately win over his wife?"

"Well," Quentin reflected. "It wasn't easy."

Chapter 26

Two months later...

"You called her what?" Eamon said, abandoning the buttons on his tuxedo to cup his ear. "I *know* I didn't hear you right."

"You heard him right." Quentin smirked. "He should count himself lucky that she only slapped him around with a piece of fish instead of him sleeping with them."

Xavier just stood in front of the mirror holding his cuff links with his mouth visibly gaping open.

"I know. I know." Jeremy groaned while still fumbling with his Windsor knot. "I don't think she's ever going to forgive me."

"You and me both," Eamon said. "That's almost up there with the b-word. I think Victoria would smack the taste out of my mouth if I ever called her that."

"Of course she would. You're a borderline domestic-violence victim as it is," Jeremy shot back.

Xavier roared in agreement. "She does kind of have a temper on her."

Eamon waved them off. "My baby is just passionate—and as long as you see this smile on my face, just know that your big brother is satisfied."

Jeremy's face twisted. "Uh-huh. Has she learned how to cook yet—because you can count me out for family dinners at your house."

"Victoria doesn't need to learn how to cook. I handle all that."

Jeremy and Quentin exchanged glances with each other before they said in union, "That's a no."

Eamon refused to be fazed. Nearly a year into matrimony and he was still thrilled about the day his wife stormed into his life like an Amazon goddess, waving around a fifty-million-dollar lawsuit.

"Well, has she even talked to you about the baby?" Xavier asked, worried. "I'm sort of looking forward to being an uncle."

"No. Not yet," Jeremy said, trying to tamp down his own nervousness about that. "I don't mind telling you guys, but I feel like I'm dying over here, man. I can't sleep. I can't eat. I'm hardly at the club anymore. I'm at my wits' end about this. I'm scared to call her anymore because I'm just a couple calls away from having a harassment suit slapped on me.

"I've sent roses, daffodils, irises, sunflowers, daisies—you name it. Friday the florist said that Leigh started refusing my deliveries. And don't get me started on the chocolates—or the puppy."

"You sent her a puppy?" Xavier said, frowning.

Jeremy shrugged. "Who doesn't like puppies? Frankly, I think it's a good sign that she kept *that* delivery—but then again it was an adorable Yorkie."

His brothers shared a look.

"I know. I know. This is never going to happen." He glanced up, hopeful. "Is it?"

"I'm not one to rain on anyone's parade," Eamon said. "But maybe you just need to give her space. Sounds like she's been through quite a lot. Let all of this process first."

"Yeah. Yeah." Jeremy bobbed his head. "But patience has never been my strong suit."

"Check it out, li'l bro," his brother said. Xavier crossed the room and swung his arm around Jeremy's shoulder. "You know, Cheryl and I also had to rebuild from scratch. After finding out that she was a cop, I wasn't even sure that the person I thought I was in love with even existed. Lucky for me it turned out she did. I hate to say it, but you and Leigh have even less invested in each other than even we did at the time. Think about it. You guys really only had that *one* night. And she's never given you any indication that she wanted more than that. Am I right?"

Jeremy's heart sank as he nodded.

"I'm not saying that it can't happen for you. But I do think that you need to prepare yourself in case it doesn't."

"You're right." Jeremy sucked in another deep breath, and then forced a smile. "All right, enough with my pathetic love life. Let's go see if Cheryl is still crazy enough to take our last name."

They pounded each other on the back and finished getting ready. And never once after their brotherly talk did Jeremy let on to the rest of his family and friends that his thoughts were swirling around Leigh Matthews.

Cheryl and Xavier's wedding ceremony at Bradford Galleries was perfect. Cheryl's small family consisted of a younger sister, Larissa, and her son, Cheryl's only nephew, Thaddeus. There were a few of Cheryl's fellow officers from when she was on the force, including her partner, Detective Johnnie Walsh. The rest of the guests were from the Kings' large family tree—mostly out of Houston, Texas.

Their father, Jorell King, was also the youngest of three brothers: Ivan and Deon. To date, Uncle Ivan had produced the most children: seven boys and two girls, while Uncle Deon often complained about having to chase men away from sniffing around his five girls.

Having just seen them all at Eamon's wedding, everyone poked and prodded Jeremy about when he was going to tie the knot. His old cries of "Never" had now morphed into "Who knows?" And every time he said it, an image of Leigh racing from him on a moonlit night in Malibu surfaced in his mind.

"So when are you going to tell him?" Ariel asked, sitting across from Leigh on the back deck of their friend Cathy's Malibu home. "You're already past your first trimester."

"I know. I know." She glanced off toward the ocean and watched the rumbling surf take out a few exuberant surfers. As usual, the young and not-so-young guns would pop back up, looking like a cluster of bobbleheads, laughing and ready to take on another wave.

"I tell you what, I'm more than impressed by how long you've made the man grovel. A couple more weeks, and a deed to a house or the keys to a brand-new car might show up."

"I'm not trying to punish him. I just needed some time," she said. "Time for myself to reflect, to mourn, to grow—to plan."

"Do you think that you'll ever forgive him?"

"That's just it. I think I did that the day at the Breakfast Café. There's no doubt in my mind that his apology was sincere. At the time, I thought that I just wanted to hang on to my anger, but I just couldn't."

A strong breeze swept across the deck. Leigh closed her eyes and the let the wind comb through her hair. Once it died down, she sighed and opened her eyes.

"You know what's crazy?"

"What's that?"

"I miss him."

"Please say you mean Jeremy King."

Leigh nodded. "One night. One glorious, uninhibited night of pleasure and I can't get the guy out of my head. Everything from our dancing at the party to playing in the ocean and..." Her smile almost wrapped around her head.

"Damn. That good, huh?"

"Oh. The sex was out of this world—but there was something else, something I can't quite put my finger on." She closed her eyes just in time to feel the next breeze. But this time, she imagined that it was Jeremy who was running his fingers through her hair.

"In the end, I know it could never work. I learned the hard way that you can't take the play out of a playa. And men like Jeremy and DeShawn are not the settling-down type. They can never be content being a one-woman man. And I refuse to go back to a life where I always get this sickening feeling every time my man doesn't answer his phone, or he's always texting on the damn thing when he *is* around, or when he's looking me dead in my face, *lying*—and I *know* he's lying. With men like that, women are too readily available and willing, and are nothing more than eye candy or toys."

Leigh sighed. "No. It could never work, but it is time that I see him and talk to him about the baby. But that's it." She turned her head away from Ariel just as the threat of tears burned in the back of her eyelids. It was strange to mourn something that never existed. It was like mourning the death of something or someone you never knew—the death of possibility and of hope.

As the tide crashed onto the rocks along the shore, Leigh closed her eyes again. As she began to drift off, she could have sworn she heard Jeremy's deep laughter amid the sound of the ocean's waves.

Chapter 27

"You promised!" Quentin shook his head and fumbled to get the folded piece of paper out of his breast pocket. "I have it right here in writing. You cannot sell your shares in the business." He smacked the agreement down and pointed to Jeremy's signature.

"Sorry, cuz," Jeremy said, pushing away the paper. "I guess you're just going to have to take me to court."

Q's mouth fell open as a feeling of betrayal cut across his face.

"C'mon, man. Don't look at me like that." Jeremy slumped back in his chair. "I feel guilty as it is."

"As you should. You're breaking your word—and what is a man if he can't keep his word?"

It was Jeremy's turn to be shocked. "Damn. You're going hardcore on me like that?"

"You damn right I am. I'm tired of everyone thinking that it's okay to just skip out on me. You know, just because I like to joke and be the life of a party, doesn't mean that I don't have feelings."

Jeremy blinked. "What? I've never thought anything like that."

"Yeah, yeah." Quentin jumped up and snatched the paper off the desk. "You know, I should've known this was coming. If you could do your boy dirty, then planting a knife in my back was just something you'd do before taking out the garbage."

Jeremy had a hard time keeping up with the conversation. "What? Whoa. I didn't do anything to Roy."

"You slept with his girl," Quentin charged.

"I didn't *know* she was his girl!"

"But have you talked to him since you found out? Does he know that you're the one that knocked her up?"

"I've tried. I've called, texted and emailed him to try to set a date to talk to him. I've even rolled by his place, but he's never there. What else am I supposed to do? *Roy* won't talk to me. *Leigh* won't talk to me. Do you have any idea how frustrating it is when people won't even pick up the phone?"

Quentin dropped his head. "I might know a little something about that."

"All right, then! So what do you propose I do? I'm hoping like hell that Leigh talks to me soon because I'm not going to let her keep me from my kid—and I still have to tell Roy about the whole situation because it will eventually get out that Leigh and I have a kid together. I'm on a wire here and you're stressing me about *this?*" Jeremy tossed up his hands. "C'mon, cuz. Does that piece of paper mean that much to you?"

Q turned away to avoid revealing his hurt and disappointment.

"It does mean a lot to you," Jeremy said and plopped back against his chair. "All right, I won't sell."

Quentin shook his head, but refused to turn around. "That's all right. Don't do me any favors."

Jeremy frowned. "You're acting like this decision means I'm severing ties from *you*. We're still cousins, man. We're family. We don't need a document to hold us all together."

Quentin glanced back over his shoulder and found his cousin's gaze. *You mean that?* He didn't say the words, but it was the question that lingered his eyes.

Of course I mean it. Jeremy confirmed their bond with a smile.

Q's shoulders slumped in acceptance. "All right. But you've got to give me time to find another investor."

"You got it."

"And…" Quentin continued. "I didn't mean any of that other stuff. Truth is, you and your brothers are some of the best men I know."

Jeremy smiled. "Thanks. And back at you."

His cousin gave him a look like he wasn't buying the compliment, but it was true. Jeremy was certain that he understood Quentin more than most. Sure, he'd perfected the party-boy image, but it was a facade. His cousin was surprisingly sensitive, smart, gregarious and disarmingly charming. If Jeremy was a betting man, he'd wager that Quentin hadn't married so that he could get his inheritance back. But instead, he believed Q had given in to his father's demands to win his love and approval.

Only it just didn't seem to have worked.

Knock! Knock! Knock!

"Come in!" Jeremy shouted.

Delilah poked her head through the door. "Are you two decent?"

Quentin laughed.

She cracked a smile, as well. "Laugh all you want, but one never knows when you are in a dick-measuring contest around here."

"Speaking of which—" Quentin turned toward his boy "—you still owe me two hundred dollars."

"You've got to be kidding me?"

"Don't tell me you're going to renege on that, too," Q challenged.

"You know what? It's time to shut you up, old man." Jeremy hopped up out of his chair and started unbuttoning his pants.

"Bring it, Junior." Quentin went for his zipper.

"Whoa, whoa, whoa," Delilah shouted with her hands up. "Let me just give you this." She held up a set of keys. "Your real estate agent just sent them over a few minutes ago."

"Ah, the keys to my new crib." Jeremy perked up as she dropped them into his hand.

"You bought a new place?" Q asked.

"Yep. I bought Dylan's old Malibu pad."

Quentin smirked.

"What? It's a great place. I was just out there yesterday doing a final walk-through. It's perfect."

"Uh-huh." The twinkle in his cousin's eyes told Jeremy that he was on to him. "Maybe you should give her your Porsche, too?"

Delilah's brows dipped in confusion. "Give who his Porsche?"

"Nobody," Jeremy said, signaling to his cousin that

he didn't want his employees all up in his business. "Thanks for bringing this to me, Dee."

"All right. Fine, then." She jabbed a fist into her hip as she headed back toward the door. "By the way, there's someone out here on the main floor to see you."

"Oh?" Jeremy plopped the keys down on his desk. "Who is it?"

"Some pregnant chick named Leigh Matthews."

Chapter 28

Just stay calm. Breathe. And try to avoid making eye contact—or any contact. Leigh nodded at the instructions from the voice in the back of her head. However, it was already growing increasingly difficult to remember them since she'd started shaking like a leaf the moment she and Ariel strolled into the near-empty club.

She and Ariel opted to arrive two hours before the club opened for this very reason. There were still a number of employees around scrubbing, cleaning, stocking and waxing. The Dollhouse operated like a well-oiled machine. She was actually quite impressed.

"How much do you think this place pulls in?" Ariel asked, sounding equally impressed as she glanced around, while they waited.

"No clue," Leigh said, unconcerned. At the moment, she wanted to concentrate on getting through this meeting.

Ariel shook her head. "I think you're making a big mistake by not going through the courts to ensure—"

"Ariel, *please.*" Leigh slammed her eyes shut and counted to three.

"All right," Ariel said, shaking her head. "I still think that you're making a big mistake. There. I said it."

"Fine! You've said it, *again.* So can we just focus on doing what we came here to do?" Leigh opened her eyes. *"Please?"* she added one more time.

"Fine!" Ariel tossed up her hands.

"Great." Leigh sucked in another breath and then pressed a hand against her growing baby bump.

The door leading to the back of the club swung open and the hostess Leigh met earlier strolled out with a thin smile. At first seeing the woman alone made Leigh's heart drop. *Did this mean that he wasn't coming out to talk to her? Had she waited too long to come and talk to him?*

"Let's go." Leigh popped out of her chair and grabbed her purse.

"What?"

"He's not coming." But the moment she made that pronouncement, Jeremy's tall, muscular frame strolled onto the main floor. At the sight of him, Leigh's heart sprang from her stomach clear up to her throat, where it got stuck.

When his gaze landed on her, his full lips kicked up into a smile, which apparently detonated a switch attached to her knees given how fast they folded and made her butt plop back down into the chair. The rules that she spent all morning reciting flew right out of her head. Her pulse hammered and her breathing sounded like she'd just completed a triathlon. As for that no-eye-contact thing, Leigh couldn't have pulled her eyes away if someone had held a gun to her head.

It seemed as if his leisurely stroll over to their small table was happening in slow motion. If he had just been stripped naked and doused in some baby oil, he would have been the perfect romance-cover model.

Jeremy stopped at the table and tilted his head. "Hello, Leigh." He broke eye contact so that his warm gaze could roam over the rest of her body. "You look beautiful today."

The compliment disarmed her completely. "Thank you." It was on the tip of her tongue to return the compliment—because he, too, was a beautiful sight to see—but reality kicked in and saved her from herself.

Jeremy pulled out a chair as his gaze swung over to Ariel. "Ms. Brooks."

"Mr. King," Ariel said, responding in her professional lawyer voice.

It was the first time that his brows dipped in concern. "So what brings you ladies by today?" He braided his strong fingers together.

"My client here wants to formally notify you that she's pregnant."

Jeremy's gaze swung back to Leigh and she read in his eyes what she had long suspected he knew. "Congratulations," he said warmly.

"And that you are the father of the child," Ariel added, and then waited for a response.

He waited a beat and said, "I guess it's up to me to congratulate myself."

Leigh almost smiled.

"Congratulations," Ariel said stiffly and resumed her prepared spiel. "Ms. Matthews prefers for us, and your lawyer, if you'd like, to hammer out an agreement without involving the court system."

"Is that right?" he said, easing back in his chair as his jawline seemed to stiffen.

"Ms. Matthews would prefer that you'd stay involved in the child's life, but will respect your wishes if you choose not to."

"If I choose not…" He cut himself off, and then sucked in a deep breath. "Of course I want to be involved in my kid's life." His gaze narrowed on her. "That goes without question."

"Good. So that just leaves our working out support and visitation," Leigh said.

"Visit…"

Another deep breath. If Leigh wasn't mistaken, his eyes began to glisten.

"Let me guess. You expect me to just be a weekend dad now?"

"We're open to something like every other weekend, or once a month?"

His leg started bouncing and shaking the whole table. "Is that right?"

"Yes. And—"

"Excuse me," he said to Ariel. "Would you mind giving us a few minutes?"

Leigh started to panic.

"Well, I—"

"I'm sure that my cousin at the bar wouldn't mind keeping you company for a few minutes. Just a few."

Ariel glanced over at her girl again. Time stood still until Leigh gave her the signal that it was okay for her to go.

Unfortunately, the moment Leigh gave the signal she started having second thoughts.

"All right. I'll give you five minutes." She stood up from the table and gave Jeremy a look that said she would be watching him.

While she strolled away, Jeremy took several deep breaths. Judging by his stiff body language the exercise wasn't working.

"What is this, Leigh? Why are you coming at me like this?"

"Like what?" She coughed. "I just want us to come to some kind of arrangement."

"I want to be a part of *my* child's life. Weekend babysitting? Is this your idea of an arrangement?"

Silence.

"All right. So you hate me that much?"

"I never said I hated you," she said, shrugging her shoulders.

"You just act like it," Jeremy said.

She didn't have a response to that either.

"How did we get to this?" he asked, leaning over the table. "There was something there in the beginning, wasn't there? Or was it just me? Am I the only one who couldn't stop thinking about that night, dreaming about that night?" He cocked his head and studied her face even harder. "And when you came here and we went into the back office, wasn't that fire still there the minute we touched?"

To prove his point, he reached for her hand. At the instant connection, a spark shot up her arm.

Leigh jerked her hand back. Her eyes brimmed with tears. "All right. I admit it. It was a great night—a perfect night. But then the sun rose the next morning and it was over."

"It doesn't have to be over. Look where we are, look at what we're about to do. We're going to have a child together. Shouldn't we at least see whether there's a chance for more? I don't know you, but I love you. How crazy is that? And I readily admit that most of my anger in that freezer that night wasn't *just* because I found out you were my best friend's fiancée, but because I still wanted you anyway. That knowledge was eating me up inside."

Leigh shook her head as tears trickled down her face. "It could never work. Look. You're probably a really nice guy. But you and men like DeShawn are not the settling-down type. You could never be what I need you to be."

"That's not fair. You've never even given me a chance. I haven't settled down because I've never met a woman I ever contemplated settling down with— until I met you. Roy and I are friends, but we are *not* the same person. I'm an honest man and I'm just asking for an honest chance here."

"An honest chance to do what? Build a relationship off a one-night stand?" She shook her head faster, unaware that she was ripping his heart out. "You know what else I think about all the time?"

"What's that?"

"I think about what it would have been like if we could've met under different circumstances. If I wasn't out trying to prove something to myself and you weren't a guy who was just looking for a good time. Maybe we were a blind date, and you took me to a nice restaurant and we talked all night and learned everything there is to know about each other. We'd stay until the restaurant employees had to ask us to leave and then we'd still find some other place to go and just talk and talk until the sun came up." Tears streamed down her face. "I better go," she said, pushing back her chair.

"No. Wait." He grabbed her by the arm again. "We can't leave it like this."

"We can hammer out the details about the baby another time. I'm sorry—for everything. Probably for screwing up your life, ruining your friendship with DeShawn…"

"*Ruin?* What are you talking about?"

She paused as confusion filled her eyes. "I thought DeShawn was the one to tell you about the baby."

"He did but, wait…" Jeremy cocked his head. "You told him it was mine?"

"Of course I did."

Chapter 29

Jeremy didn't bother to call, text, email or even send smoke signals to try to get a hold of his best friend Roy. This time he contacted Calvin Strozier to find out what times his boy would be at the court practicing, and then arranged it so that he could get into the gymnasium with a guest pass. He made sure to arrive toward the end of practice.

He hung outside the locker room, leaning against the concrete walls. He could hear the players laughing and joking inside, Roy being the loudest of them all. As usual, he was talking smack about the team they were going to be playing the next night. His new teammates were clearly joining in on the fun.

About forty minutes later, the locker-room door swung open and the players streamed out.

Jeremy pushed away from the wall, and then hollered out, "Yo, Roy!"

A few of the Razors turned to see who had yelled, but it was Roy DeShawn who'd whipped his head around the fastest.

Almost instantly, Roy's jovial smile melted off his face.

"Hey, man. I need to holler at you for a minute."

Roy hesitated, and then jutted his thumb over his shoulder. "Nah, man. Now is really not a good time. I got some business I have to take care of right now."

"It can wait." Jeremy stepped forward. "We need to talk."

Roy's teammates continued to stream out of the locker room; a few of them hung around curious about what was going on.

Calvin Strozier exited the locker room, spotted Jeremy and then gave him an encouraging nod.

Roy correctly sensed that Jeremy wasn't about to let this go, so he huffed out a frustrated breath and started toward his childhood friend. It was clear from his body language that he didn't want to deal with this.

Too bad.

"What is it, man? I already told you that I have a lot of stuff to do," he said, as his voice seemed to reflect his rising irritation as he approached.

Jeremy planted his feet and thrust up his chin, and then prepared himself for what he knew was going to happen after his opening line. "You knew that I was the father."

As expected, Roy unleashed a right hook across Jeremy's jaw, snapping his head back.

"Whoa!" a few of the players who were left in the hallway hollered out.

One bold player stepped forward. "What's going on over here?"

Calvin leaped in front of the crowd and ushered them back. "It's all right. It's all right. There's nothing to see. Just two friends having a discussion. Everyone go on about your business."

They stepped back but hung around to see what would happen next.

Despite the hard blow, Jeremy remained on his feet, but could taste the small trickle of blood flowing from the corner of his mouth. He slowly and calmly wiped it off with his thumb.

"I oughta…"

Jeremy held up his hand and warned. "You only get one."

Roy hesitated. Undoubtedly, a slew of memories flooded and reminded him that Xavier wasn't the only King who knew how to land punches. At long last, he lowered his fist, but anger still radiated off him in waves.

"Help me understand," Jeremy said. "That night you came to The Dollhouse, breathing fire. If you knew, why?"

Roy continued to grind his back teeth for about a minute. "I wanted to—started to…but in the end, I couldn't." He shrugged his tight shoulders. "You're my brother, man."

"I didn't know," Jeremy informed him. "Not until that night."

"Yeah, she said as much. Plus…" He dropped his head. "I remembered you telling me about your Baby Girl, how you two met and it matched her version of events down to a T."

After concluding that there wasn't going to be any more fists flying, the rest of the players drifted out of the gym until it was just Roy and Jeremy.

Roy inhaled a long breath. "When I left her place, I was steaming. I wondered why you hadn't told me yourself. Then came the question of would you."

"You came to The Dollhouse to test me?"

"Needed to know whether you were going to man up."

"It was hard, I was trying…"

"I know. When I saw that you were going to go for it, suddenly I thought that I couldn't take hearing it."

"So you got the hell out of there?" Jeremy concluded.

Roy nodded, still having trouble maintaining eye contact.

"And all my calls?"

"Wasn't ready, man. I was beginning to doubt that I'd ever be." *Pause.* "I tell you what. It's true what they say. You never know what you got until it's gone." Once I left your place and started driving around, I knew that between the two of us—you were the better man. She deserves someone like you. Honest. Loyal. Reliable."

It was Jeremy's turn to drop his head. "I don't think I deserve such high praise, man."

"What do you mean?"

"That night…after I found out who she was, I still wanted her for myself." He sucked in a deep breath. "I was angry about finding out who she was. But I still wanted her."

Roy's eyes narrowed.

Jeremy glanced up and saw that his boy's fists were balling up. Shrugging his shoulders, Jeremy planted his feet and lifted his chin again. "All right, man. Go ahead."

Roy's fist snapped his head left.

Jeremy saw one or two stars after that one, but quickly held up his hand to make sure that it was the last one. By the time he focused his gaze back on his buddy, there was some satisfaction in seeing Roy having to wave his hand from the sting of the punch.

"So are we cool?" Jeremy asked, wiping away another dab of blood from the other side of his mouth. "Don't tell anybody else. But I think I'm starting to miss your big knucklehead."

The corners of Roy's mouth twitched. "Of course you do. I'm me."

Jeremy laughed, and then the two old friends and longtime blood brothers came together for a one-arm hug. "Come on. I'll walk you to your car."

"Thanks." As they walked down the long hallway together, Roy cut a sheepish look over at his friend. "So how is she doing?"

After testing his jaw to make sure that it wasn't broken, Jeremy answered the best way he could. "Fine. I guess."

Roy's head jerked up. "What do you mean you guess? Aren't you two together?"

Jeremy shook his head. "No, doesn't look like things are going to work out that way."

Roy's voice dipped and hardened. "What did you do?"

"What? Me? Nothing. The relationship was dead before I even got out of the gate good."

"She's pregnant. I think it's safe to say that you

cleared the gate," Roy joked, pounding his hand on Jeremy's back.

"True," he acknowledged.

"So?"

"So nothing. I said something to upset her at the engagement party. She didn't speak to me for a long time, and then when she did pop up, it was with her lawyer, talking to me like I was just some sperm donor with weekend visitation rights."

"What did you say to upset her?"

"No. You're not getting another excuse to punch me," Jeremy said. "Though I should deck you for not telling me you're already a father."

Roy shrugged. "She claimed they were mine. I accepted it, though nobody in my family has green eyes. But hey, the girl is a freak in the bedroom. It's enough to keep me happy for the moment."

Jeremy shook his head. "I don't think that I'll ever understand you, man."

"Me, either. But are you cool with your situation?"

"Honestly, no." He hunched up his shoulders just as they reached his boy's Range Rover. "I just don't know what I can do about it."

"All I know is, if you get the chance, don't screw it up like I did. Leigh was the best thing to happen to me and I was just too blind to see it."

"I guess she was the best thing to happen to the both of us—it's just too bad that she doesn't want either one of us."

Roy shook his head, feeling sorry for his best friend. "C'mon. Pick your bottom lip off the floor. I'm sure between the two of us, we can think of something to win your baby momma back."

Chapter 30

Leigh and Ariel's morning runs through the park had now been replaced with long walks along Malibu's sandy beach. Dolly, her Yorkie, and the one gift that she kept from Jeremy, spent most of her time barking at the waves than actually keeping up with her owner.

The sight of the small dog running toward the ocean, most likely because the lap dog thought all that barking would actually force the waves back, wasn't nearly as amusing as seeing her tiny little legs do double time getting out of the way when the surf came crashing in.

"I think your dog is missing a few marbles," Ariel noted, shaking her head.

"I don't think—I know." Leigh laughed. "But she's funny—and she's good company."

Ariel cut a long look over at her friend.

"What?"

"Nothing," Ariel said, shaking her head.

Leigh cocked her head. "So you just like staring a hole in my head for the hell of it?"

"I'm just...you know what? Never mind. It's none of my business."

"That's never stopped you before—or are you turning over a new leaf eight months after New Year's?"

"Nah. It's just that I recognize that I've given you bad advice before...and I probably lack credibility on this issue."

"*Again*—that's never stopped you before."

"Ha. Ha." For a few seconds her gaze fell back to trying to figure out what the hell her dog was doing. Neither one of them had a clue. But eventually, Ariel went back to glancing over at Leigh out of the corner of her eye.

"Damn, girl. Will you just spit it out?"

"All right. But you have me on record saying that I know that sometimes my advice has been a little suspect."

"Duly noted." Leigh combed her fingers through her hair.

"All right. Here goes." Ariel stopped walking and turned to her friend. "Are you crazy?"

"*That* is what has been bugging you?"

"I think it's a question that deserves an answer, especially in the cold way that you turned that man down yesterday. Hell, I was struggling to keep it together. I don't know what you did to that man or all that went down between you two that night, but, honey, it has definitely left a mark on that man."

"You just like him because he's rich and probably wouldn't bat an eyelash if you ordered extra cheese for your taco."

"Nooo…well, that *is* still an added plus. But it has more to do with how he looked at you."

"You mean when the steam was rising out of his ears?"

"No, before that."

Leigh dropped her eyes.

Ariel smirked and shook her head. "Yeah, you know exactly what I'm talking about. You're just trying to play crazy."

"No. It's not that. It's…"

"What?" Ariel pressed, but Leigh didn't immediately answer. She started shaking her head. "You know, I've always talked to you about how hard it is to get a decent date or how hard it is to find a man to act even half-right. But before yesterday, I'd never seen a man look at a woman the way Jeremy looked at you when he came out of that office—and it had nothing to do with just a physical attraction. That man is feeling you on a deeper level, girl. And I'd be lying to you if I said I wasn't jealous. I was—extremely jealous."

Leigh's gaze found its way back to her friend, but her eyes were trying to hold back as much water as the ocean they stood next to.

"At the end of the day, Leigh, I want you to get more than just your fair share of cheese on a taco. I want us both to find men who look at us—and truly see and love us in a way that Jeremy desperately wants to do with you."

A tear escaped through her lashes and had even made it halfway down her face before Leigh swiped it away. "What if I'm just scared?"

"Of?"

"Of being hurt—of being cheated on—of giving my

all and then getting nothing but lies in return. It's all too much."

"None of us likes to lose at love because, you're right, it hurts like hell. But if you fall down and stay down, soon you'll *forget* how to get up. I don't want you to stay down. I'm not going to stay down—especially now that I know what love truly looks like."

Woof! Woof! Woof!

Dolly continued arguing with the ocean.

Ariel cocked her head while she stared at her friend. "At least think about giving him a chance? Please?"

"Okay." Leigh nodded. "I'll think it over."

Jeremy shielded his eyes as he stared down the beach. Two women caught his eyes, including the small dog, racing in and out of the water about a hundred yards out. One was pregnant but still rocked a black bikini under a sheer poncho. *Is that...?* He squinted harder but nearly fell off his deck.

He could always go check them out. But given Leigh's behavior toward him, he hesitated. Maybe it was just time to give up—just concentrate on hammering out a custody agreement with their child and call it a day.

All of Roy's suggestions that sounded like begging and pleading weren't going to work for him. He lowered his hands and inhaled a deep breath. She wanted him to leave her alone.

So he was going to do just that.

Chapter 31

Leigh rose with the sun, but she was far from being cheerful. In fact, if she was being honest with herself she was downright depressed. Her memories of splashing around in the moonlight had been replaced with images of Jeremy's angry face and hurt reaction two days before. She had promised Ariel that she'd think more about taking a chance with Jeremy.

Once upon a time, she thought she knew what she wanted and how to get it. But once she put her plan in motion, she discovered that there were several potholes in the road.

Dolly started barking the moment her foot hit the floor. "C'mon, girl. Let's get you something to eat."

Today she was going to sit out on the deck and actually get started writing again. After a four-month self-imposed hiatus she thought her brain would be teeming with ideas. However, after an hour, she still stared at a blank page on her laptop.

"Maybe we should just take a walk along the beach?" she said, glancing down at the dog. But Dolly had long ago stopped paying attention to her and had gotten down to the business of chasing her tail. It was an adorable sight and it put a smile on her face, as she absently rubbed her belly.

Boy or girl?

She really didn't care. Her mother was right. As long as it had ten fingers and ten toes, she'd be happy. But before she knew it she found herself daydreaming about all the various traits her child might inherit. Would she have Jeremy's intense dark eyes? How about his adorable dimples? Would she be tall like him? She wondered what rich complexion her child would inherit. Would it be his milk-chocolate skin color? Or her cinnamon brown? Or somewhere in between? By the time she had finished painting a picture in her mind, she was smiling so hard her face hurt.

"I can't wait to meet you—and teach you so many things." Jeremy's image surfaced. "I also can't wait for you to meet your father. I think you're going to like him," she said. "I know it's odd for me to be making such predictions, but I have a feeling that your father is going to adore you. Spoil you. Don't ask me how I know these things, I just do."

He would do those things for you, as well, the voice in the back of her head insisted.

Her eyes swam in a vat of tears because just as she was sure of Jeremy King being an excellent father, she was sure that he could be so much more than that.

So why are you pushing him away?

"Because I'm scared," she answered herself, and then opened her eyes as the morning breeze swept her tears away.

Jeremy decided that it would be best for him to get to know his new beachfront community. Sure, he knew the beach well, but Malibu also had a host of treasures tucked along the Pacific Coast Highway. One place he'd heard of many times was an Italian restaurant called Giovanni.

He doubted that the place would be as good as his brother's place in Vegas, but he'd give it a shot. The moment he walked into the place, he knew that he'd found the restaurant where he'd be eating a lot of lunches and dinners. Today he chose to eat outside where he could look out onto the beautiful scenic view of the deep blue ocean and an even bluer sky.

Leigh had cravings.

And since she'd been staying at her girlfriend's summer place this past week, she'd been craving Italian food nearly every day. Giovanni was such a short drive from the house that she usually didn't bother grabbing Dolly when she made her way to the famous restaurant.

"Ah, Ms. Matthews," the hostess greeted, smiling the moment she walked through the door.

A warm flush burned Leigh's cheeks. She hoped that the staff wasn't beginning to think of her as a little piggy. Four months pregnant was a little soon to be saying that she was eating for two.

"Would you like to be seated or will you be ordering take-out again?"

"It'll be…" Leigh's gaze swept over the room, and

suddenly spied the large figure sitting and watching the waves on the back deck. Her pulse quickened and that flush had now blanketed her body.

"Ms. Matthews?"

"Actually, I, uh—see my party out on the deck," she informed the hostess.

"Oh, okay." The woman brightened. "Enjoy your meal."

"Thanks." Leigh swallowed hard and put one foot in front of the other. Despite her entire body doing the whole quivering-and-tingling thing, she was slowly transforming into that daring and determined woman she was on the first night she laid eyes on Jeremy King.

When she stepped out onto the deck and approached the bar, it was just sheer luck that the gentleman that was sitting next to Jeremy paid his tab and strolled off. For a few seconds, she lingered back and asked herself one last time if she truly wanted to do this.

Yes!

The answer came back so fast and forcefully that her lips curled up into a smile as she approached.

Please let him look at me the same way.

"Is anyone sitting here?"

Jeremy glanced to his side. "No." And then over his shoulder, "It's all yo..." He blinked.

"Thanks," she said, ignoring his shock and making herself comfortable. "Bartender, I'll just have some club soda. Thanks."

Jeremy slowly pulled out of his shock. "What are you doing here?" His gaze raced up and down her body.

Leigh looked over at him and hoped that she wouldn't be ensnared in his eyes. "Actually..." She leaned toward him and hoped that he would get what she was doing. "I'm here on a blind date."

His brows leaped to his hairline. "Is that right?"

"I know. I know. They can turn into some real horror stories. But I have a good feeling about this one."

Jeremy started to respond, paused and then turned his entire body toward her. Finally, that glowing warmth returned to his eyes and he looked at her the way a man does when he loves a woman. "You know, it's kind of funny that you say you're on a blind date."

Leigh smiled. "Oh? Why?"

"I happen to be on a blind date myself."

Her eyes lit up as she thrust out her hand. "You don't say? Well, I'm Leigh Matthews, and you are...?"

Jeremy's sexy lips exploded with a smile. "Well, Ms. Matthews, you happen to be looking at your date. The name is Jeremy King. I'm pleased to meet you..."

Then There Was One

Chapter 32

"So she got her new beginning?" Dr. Turner said, smiling.

Quentin nodded. "Yep. Jeremy said that they talked for hours at that restaurant until the employees had to tell him that it was time to lock the doors. Then they went for a long walk on the beach, where they talked until the sun came up. They both said that it all passed by in the blink of an eye. But I think that the best part was when he finally walked her back to her friend's house and tried to put the moves on her, and she told him that she didn't sleep with guys on the first date."

Dr. Turner laughed.

"Oh, you like *that* joke. Well, believe it or not, Jeremy still managed to get her in front of the preacher before his son arrived. It seemed like as soon as Leigh gave herself permission to take the risk, she was like a daredevil. Hell, she's knocked up again now."

Dr. Turner smiled, and then shook her head. "I still find it fascinating that you possess such wisdom and keen insight when comes to other people's love lives. But when it comes to your own, you're willing to put blinders on. It's all so fascinating."

"Oh, I see my problems just fine. It's just that I don't know what the hell to do with them."

"So you ignore them and hope that they go away?"

"Well, it worked for a while. I just didn't know that eventually I'd crack up," he joked.

Dr. Turner braided her fingers together.

"Oh, how fast the worm has turned," Q said, shaking his head.

"So how do you feel now that your little boys' club is no more?"

Quentin sucked in a deep breath before he gave her an honest answer. "Disappointed, but what are you going to do?"

"That was going to be my next question. What *are* you going to do? You're the sole owner of three successful gentlemen's clubs. That's got to keep you pretty busy."

"It does." He nodded. "That's the one good thing about it. I'm constantly flying around."

"And how often do you get home?"

"Which home?"

"Your real home," she said. "Where your mom and dad live, where your brothers live? Don't you miss them at all?"

"Of course I do. But you're not asking the right question."

"Which is?"

"Do they miss me?" He met and held her gaze. "I

have a phone just like they do. Planes fly to where I live just as they fly to where they are. Frankly, I think they're all happy to be rid of me."

"Oh, I doubt that."

"Why?"

"Unless you're about to tell me that you're on the FBI's Most Wanted list for some heinous crime, what would make them feel that way?"

"Well, I'm no angel. I can tell you that."

"There are some things, Quentin, I don't need to be told."

"Sassy." He grinned. "I like sassy women."

"You like women period," Dr. Turner amended.

"There is that."

Dr. Turner grinned. "I have to tell you that I really like your cousins. Each of their stories was different and they certainly married different women. Do you think there's a chance that there's a woman out there for you?"

"Oh, there are plenty of women out there that I enjoy. Some—a few times a week."

"How do you think you're ever going to find or understand love if you're too busy running away from it?"

"Maybe I like to play hard to get?"

"Or maybe you don't have any idea how to have a real, intimate relationship? Maybe your fascination with not just your cousin, but your brothers as well, is that you envy their ability to take their masks off and be vulnerable."

"A *real* intimate relationship? Where'd you get that? Out of a textbook?"

"How about you try to answer the question?"

"Of course I know how to have an intimate relationship. I have them all the time."

"There you go again. How come all roads lead to sex with you?"

"I never had any complaints."

"Do you stick around long enough to hear them?"

He rolled his head away in a huff. "I do believe my time is up." He pushed himself up onto his feet.

Dr. Turner shook her head as she climbed to her feet. "You always leave just when things are getting interesting."

"Is that your professional way of saying that you'll miss me?"

A smile eased back across her lips. "Have a good day, Mr. Hinton."

"Good day."

They performed their usual ritual as she walked him to the door. "Next time, I expect us to talk about your relationships," she told him. "All of them—girlfriends, crushes, hook-ups and even your short trip down the aisle."

"Are you sure about that? I have stories that will…"

Julianne Turner pressed a silencing finger to his lips. "Don't."

Quentin smiled behind her finger. "Scaredy-cat."

They shook hands as her next client stood up in the waiting room. *Nice hands.* "Tell Reggie I said to watch his back." He winked and then watched a burst of color paint her cheeks.

Walking out of the Peachtree Towers, Q actually had an extra pep in his step. He smiled at all the ladies and snuck in a couple of double takes at their passing rear views. As he approached his black Mercedes, he slid on his favorite sunglasses. Once he was behind the wheel, he felt the urge to call Sterling. This time, he waited until the urge passed and started the car.

A few minutes later, he was whipping through the streets of Atlanta, rather enjoying having his car back all to himself. No ghosts, spirits or mirages of his sister-in-law. "I can't believe it. She's gone." Shaking his head and laughing, he reached to turn on the radio. He couldn't have pulled his gaze from the road more than two seconds, but when he glanced back up, he was speeding straight toward a woman, screaming in the middle of the road in what looked like…a wedding dress?

Quentin closed his eyes and slammed both of his feet on the brakes. He could feel the back of his car fishtail and even smell the burning rubber. Then all at once, everything stopped.

Since he could clearly hear his heart hammering in his chest, he felt safe to conclude that he wasn't dead.

"ARE YOU CRAZY? YOU COULD HAVE KILLED ME!"

Quentin's head whipped around just as the woman ripped off the billowing veil swirling around her face, and recognition slammed into them.

"YOU!"

* * * * *

REQUEST YOUR FREE BOOKS!

2 FREE NOVELS
PLUS 2 FREE GIFTS!

KIMANI ROMANCE™

Love's ultimate destination!

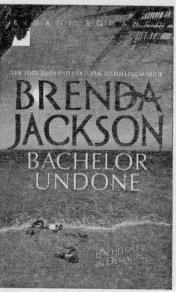